RESIST

RESIST

sarah crossan

GREENWILLOW BOOKS
An Imprint of HarperCollins*Publishers*

Resist

Copyright © 2013 by Sarah Crossan

www.epicreads.com

The text of this book is set in 12-point Fournier.
Book design by Paul Zakris

Crossan, Sarah.
Resist / by Sarah Crossan.
"Greenwillow Books."
pages cm
Sequel to: Breathe.
Summary: Alina, Quinn, and Bea, now outlaws and outcasts, make their way to the last enclave of the Resistance but once there, they discover they can count on no one but each other and may, in fact, have to betray those they considered allies.
ISBN 978-0-06-211872-1 (hardback)
[1. Science fiction. 2. Survival—Fiction. 3. Adventure and adventurers—Fiction. 4. Insurgency—Fiction. 5. Environmental degradation—Fiction.] I. Title.
PZ7.C88277Res 2013 [Fic]—dc23 2013011914
13 14 15 16 17 LP/RRDH 10 9 8 7 6 5 4 3 2 1
First Edition

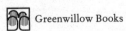 Greenwillow Books

To Aoife
With love
Always

PART I
THE JOURNEY

1
ALIПA

We didn't think sailing to Sequoia would be easy, but we hoped for better luck than freezing rain and winds. The slightest miscalculation and we'll end up at the bottom of the river.

"Help me!" I shout, throwing my weight into my heels and tipping backward to keep the rigging from slipping out of control. The rain hits us horizontally, and makes ice of the deck. The boat creaks and lurches forward. The sails flap wildly as my cousin, Silas, stumbles toward me and grabs the cable. Almost effortlessly he pulls it taut, and I quickly tie a stopper knot to keep the sail from ballooning out and capsizing us. "That should do it," I say, my voice thinned by the storm.

Silas pulls up the hood on his coat. He hasn't said much

since we set sail. No one has. What is there to say now that The Grove's a ruin—now that everything the Resistance ever fought for has been destroyed?

At least the storm keeps us too busy to wallow in memories: the screams and blood; the tanks; soldiers rushing at us with guns; our friends lying dead. And the trees, our whole forest, shriveling while we watched.

I can still taste the toxic foam in my throat.

I follow Silas to the cabin where our tiny group of survivors is taking shelter from the squall. My hands burn from the cold. I rub them together, then tuck them inside my coat and under my armpits.

"We did everything you said," I tell Bruce. I never thought I'd be so grateful to have a drifter on our side, but whatever harm the old man caused on behalf of the Ministry all those years ago, doesn't matter now. Without him, we wouldn't have known how to get the boat going, let alone save it from the storm.

"You young'uns did good," he says, scratching his gray beard and keeping his eyes on the view out the filthy window, where the outline of city buildings on the shoreline is barely distinguishable through the haze of spray and rain.

The boat dips and the wheel rips out of Bruce's gnarled hands. My stomach reels. I adjust the valve on the airtank buckled to my belt, and the tank hisses as more air is released into the tubing. I inhale deeply through my nose. As Silas steadies the wheel with Bruce, I squat next to Maude. The old woman has a blanket wrapped around her like a shroud; only her head and one scrawny arm are exposed. "Did you manage to collect all the airtanks from the deck?" I ask. Without air, we may as well jump into the river—finish ourselves off quickly.

"You think I'm some kinda nitwit? I put 'em over there." She points to the corner of the cabin where the tanks are untidily piled. We have ten, and there are seven of us. How many days of oxygen is that? How many hours?

A sob comes from the opposite corner. My fellow Resistance members, Dorian and Song, are bending over Holly, one of The Grove's gardeners. I don't know her well, but I'm glad for everyone who survived.

I grab an airtank and go to them, keeping my stride wide to stay balanced. Holly is shivering so fiercely her teeth are clacking together. Although she lived at The Grove with Song and Dorian, and learned to survive on low levels of oxygen, her breath is quick and shallow. "She's hyperventilating. She needs this," I say, holding out the airtank.

Dorian stands up and runs his hand through his hair. "She won't take one."

I try to put a hand to her forehead. She swipes me away, scratching my hand with her nails.

"She's gone loopy," Maude crows, rubbing a hard scab on her elbow.

Keeping his hands on the wheel, Bruce peers at Holly from under his thick eyebrows with an expression that tells me he's seen this kind of thing before. I'm sure he has. The Switch sent people mad as the oxygen levels plummeted and everyone slowly suffocated. And he and Maude lived through it. But maybe this is worse. What's happening now feels like the end. "She'll be okay," he says quietly. Maude tuts, but she doesn't contradict him; she isn't that heartless.

Holly mutters something. "What is it, Holls?" Song asks. He doesn't touch her. Instead he presses his own slender brown hands to his heart like he wants to feel what she feels. His eyes are watery and filled with aching. Is it possible they're an item? Romantic relationships between Resistance members were always forbidden, but maybe that rule was ignored more than I knew. Silas was with Inger, after all.

"Air," Holly moans. Song reaches for an airtank, but Holly shakes her head. She turns to the cabin door. "Fresh air," she says, as though there's such a thing.

Dorian sighs. "We're sailing through a storm." The boat pitches backward in answer to his warning. At the wheel, Bruce and Silas grunt and struggle to keep us upright.

"Let's wait until it passes," Song says gently.

Holly gazes at her boots, which are flecked in hardened black foam. "I want to go out and feel the air." She bites her bottom lip and picks invisible lint from her pants. "Then maybe we can go back to The Grove and take showers to warm ourselves up."

I envy Holly's retreat. If I could pull away from reality a little bit, what we've seen might not hurt so much. "I'll take her out for a minute," I say. "Might clear her head."

Holly stands, pulling her hood over her short, frizzy brown hair. Her nose and ears are already red from the cold. "Where's Petra?" Holly asks.

I take her hand and lead her to the cabin door. "She's back at The Grove taking care of the trees," I say. It's not untrue. Our leader clung fiercely to a doomed tree as we ran. Petra couldn't leave behind her life's work. And she paid the ultimate price.

And then my throat tightens as I remember Jazz scampering up a tree to be with her. Jazz was only a child. She didn't deserve to die. No one did. "Alina?" Dorian says. He's behind me.

"We'll just be a few minutes," I say, and force the door open against the wind.

Holly and I turn our backs on the lashing rain and head for the bow. I let go of her hand and she clings to the rimed railing, leaning forward and smiling. She allows the biting surf to spray her face and water to trickle down her neck. The boat rocks against a heavy wave, and I grab the railing with my ungloved hands, but Holly lets go. Maybe it was a mistake bringing her outside. "Let's go back in," I say.

Holly squints into the bleary distance, and her bottom lip quivers. "I knew we'd lose the war," she says. Over the roiling of the waves and wind, it sounds like a whisper.

I don't tell her we haven't lost because it would be a lie. We're no better than drifters now, refugees heading for Sequoia and hoping they'll take us in. All we've been left with are our lives, and I'm not sure that's enough anymore. As though reading my mind, Holly steps on the bottom rung of the railing, and hoists herself onto the other side, so she's suspended over the prow like a living figurehead. I throw my arms around her.

"Holly, what are you doing? Get your ass back on the deck."

The boat dips forward, and she begins to cry. "Let me *go*."

My feet slip. "Help!" I scream.

Within moments, most of the others are on us and Song is helping me drag her back over the railing. Once she's safely lying flat on the deck, he shakes her. "What the hell's wrong with you? How dare you do that? How dare you!" He rests his head on Holly's stomach and sobs. Holly strokes Song's tight curls and gazes at the clouds.

"We'll carry her inside," Dorian says. He glares at me through the driving rain.

"How was I to know what she was planning?" I say.

Dorian shakes his head and puts his hand under Holly's arms.

Although the rain is still drubbing the boat, the wind has settled, making sailing smoother. Dorian, Holly, and Song doze in their corner. Bruce and Maude are whispering and caressing each other's wrinkly hands. Silas is at the wheel. I go to him and stare out at the river through the cracked window of the cabin. Dilapidated buildings along the embankment have spilled into the river after decades of neglect. "You should have let her jump." His voice is low.

"Are you serious?" A lump swells in my throat. Are our chances of survival that slim?

"Dorian claims to know where Sequoia is, but when I showed him the map, he was pretty vague. As far as I can work out, we've a search radius of around ten miles."

"We'll find it. We've done harder things, Silas."

"I'm not sure we have. How long do you think our oxygen's going to last?" he asks. I glance across at the stack of airtanks and then at Maude and Bruce wheezing in their facemasks. Maude looks up at me and, for no particular reason, scowls. Despite what we've been through together, we still aren't friends.

"We have a few days," I say.

"If that." Silas keeps his eyes on the burnt sun.

"Do you have a better idea?" I ask. I'm not being argumentative; I really hope he's thought of something.

He shakes his head. "Sequoia's our only shot at not being drifters. If we find it, we can resume planting and make contact with the pod, with my mom and dad." He stops and looks at me. His eyes are red-rimmed, though whether it's from the foam the Ministry's army used to destroy The Grove, tiredness, or despair, I can't tell.

I take Silas's arm. "Harriet and Gideon are fine," I say. Even if a civil war *has* broken out in the pod, my aunt and uncle are too smart to be dead.

A blast of wind pitches the boat toward the bank and Silas pulls the wheel sharply to the left. I'm thrown off balance and fall onto my face. A thick, metallic taste fills my mouth.

"Sorry," Silas says. "You all right?"

"Fine," I say. I lift my facemask and wipe away the blood with my sleeve. Under the circumstances, it would be childish to complain about a split lip.

Maude starts up. "Stop!"

I am about to snarl at the old woman, tell her Silas is doing the best he can to keep the boat steady, and turn just in time to see Holly sneaking out the cabin door. I dash after her. "Holly, no!"

She is already at the bow, climbing over the railing. By the time I reach her, she's hanging over the water, jostling from side to side with the current. And she is smiling. Silas's words rebound in my head—*You should have let her jump.* But I can't. She isn't in her right mind.

"You'll feel better tomorrow, Holly." I hold tight to one of her arms. Ice chips from the freezing river nick my face.

"Nothing will be different tomorrow," she says. She turns briefly and catches my eye. "Everything's gone."

"We have to hope," I say.

Holly laughs mirthlessly. "I'm all out of hope," she says, and lets go. The railing bites into my chest as I'm wrenched forward. I hang over the railing, gripping Holly's arm, but she's heavy and my hands slide to her wrist. A violent spray from the keel drenches her. She gazes up at me with a look of perfect serenity. My fingers burn. "You're hurting me," she says. And then it happens: her wet skin slips from my grasp.

Holly hits the water and is devoured. And all I can do is watch.

Heavy footsteps pound the deck. "Holly!" Song cries. He leans over the railing and searches the waves breaking against the hull.

But Holly is gone.

I turn away.

Everyone but Bruce is on deck, staring at me.

"I couldn't hold her," I say.

"Holly?" Song howls.

Dorian puts an arm around Song, and pulls him back from the railing.

"We'll dock for the night," Silas says. "Now everyone, back inside."

Silently, we file into the cabin. I slide onto the floor. One of Holly's brown boots is lying next to the pile of airtanks, the laces loose and frayed.

I will not feel guilty. I couldn't hold her. It was her decision to die. I close my eyes and press my knuckles against the lids.

I no longer feel cold. I feel nothing.

"Poor girl lost the fight," Bruce says to no one in particular.

And I am left to wonder: What are we fighting for, anyway?

2
BEA

Sometimes I wished I believed in God, like people did before The Switch. Knowing there was a grand plan and that someone you loved wasn't gone forever must have given them a lot of comfort. But even if my parents are in a better place, God couldn't reverse time and bring them back and that's what I want: the chance to hug my parents, to smell my mother and father again.

When I pined for Quinn, I thought I knew what people meant when they talked about having broken hearts. I didn't know a thing. Now, my insides are all eaten up. My heart pumps what little oxygen I have around my body, but the breath doesn't make me whole.

Even though it's covered in slush and lumps of ice, Quinn, Jazz, and I are following an old railway line from The Grove into the center of the city. From there we'll track the river west. I have the old map Gideon gave me before I slid out of the pod, and Jazz has fingered a place on it she thinks is Sequoia. We have to trust she's right because we don't have another choice.

Quinn puts an arm around my waist and squeezes me. "Maybe we should rest," he says. He must hear me wheezing through my facemask, but this isn't a safe place to stop. The temperature is dropping with the sun, so we need shelter, but the graffiti-covered buildings around us look like they're about to topple. I shake my head and without asking me, he turns the valve on my airtank to allow more oxygen into my mask.

But there's no knowing how long it'll take to get to Sequoia. When he looks away, I turn it back to fifteen percent.

"A tunnel!" Jazz chirrups, pointing at an underpass a few hundred feet ahead. She bounces away, kicking up the slush with her feet as she goes.

"Be careful!" I call out. I pull the map from my coat pocket and unfold it for what must be the hundredth time. "There should be a train station after the tunnel. Saint Pancras," I tell Quinn. He takes our moment alone together to hold me. Without meaning to, I stiffen.

He steps back. "You all right?"

"I wish we'd found more people alive," I say, diverting his question. I don't want him to worry, and there's nothing he can do to sweep away the cinders of grief anyway.

"We're going to get through this," he says. I nod, pull the beret Old Watson gave me over my forehead, and smile weakly.

"Stop smooching and *hurry up!*" Jazz insists. She's already way ahead. She pulls her facemask down over her chin—having grown up at The Grove and spent her life training her body to subsist on low levels of oxygen, she doesn't need to wear it all the time. She spins in circles, opening her mouth to the sky. Her spirally red hair, singed at the ends, blazes like fire against the snowy backdrop. You'd never know she was the one survivor we found in the rubble that was once her home.

Quinn takes my wrist and forces me to look at him. "Against the odds, we got out alive and found each other."

"I just wish . . ." I think of my parents' motionless bodies, their blood spreading across the stage as the fighting broke out. I was all they ever had and they worked every day of their lives just to pay the air tax, so I could breathe. Thank goodness I have Quinn ... but I want them, too.

"Do you think Maude made it?" I ask.

"That scrappy lunatic? *Of course.* Jazz said as much, didn't she?"

I am about to say that Jazz can't know for sure that anyone made it when there's a shrill scream followed by a thud.
We spin toward the sound. "Jazz?"

She's gone.

In a second, Quinn is off. I trail after him, unable to keep
up. He halts on the tracks and desperately glances around.
"Jazz!" he calls. "She was *right here*," he says, as I catch up.
We stand and listen.

Silence.

We zigzag back and forth over the track, stopping when
we reach a barbed wire fence on one side with old bits of
plastic bags caught in it, and a procession of rusting train
carriages on the other. Then we inch toward the tunnel, calling Jazz's name into the dusk. After everything awful that's
happened, I brace myself for the worst.

I pick a red hair from my coat, and it floats to the ground.
"Let's split up. We'll find her quicker," I say.

"And lose each other? No way." He takes my hand and
we peer into the tunnel without going inside. The light at the
end is a semicircle of gray.

"Do you have a flashlight?" I whisper, so my words
won't rebound.

"I don't have anything." He sighs, and I touch his hair
with my gloved hand.

"You have me," I tell him. "And we're going to find Jazz."

I peer into the tunnel. "But there's no way she's in here. She wasn't that far from us. Let's go back."

He puts a finger to his ear. "What was that?" he says. I stay as still as I can, but all I can hear is my own breath and the faint ticking of the airtanks.

Quinn turns and charges along the tracks.

"Careful!" I tell him, following and almost tripping. Quinn stumbles and circles his arms wide at his sides to steady himself. As I get to him, I see what he almost fell into: an opening.

The manhole is protected by a heavy, circular metal plate, which is tilted slightly. Quinn clutches one side of it, while I take the other. On the count of three, we haul the leaden covering away from the hole and it lands with a clang. And there she is, several feet below. "I've been calling and calling," Jazz groans.

"We didn't hear you. But we're here now," I say. I sit and swing my legs over the manhole.

"Are you kidding?" Quinn says, grabbing me.

"It isn't far to jump," I say. He snorts. I shrug him off and feel my eyes harden, but I don't know why; he's just trying to protect me.

"*I'll* go," he says. He sits, then uses his arms to lower himself slowly into the hole, careful to avoid landing on Jazz. He adjusts her facemask, so she can breathe easier.

"I'll lift her and you pull her."

Jazz's bruised face appears through the opening. I sit in the snow, take her under the arms, and lean back, using my full weight to drag her out. She whimpers the whole time.

"Now me!" Quinn calls. I stroke Jazz's forehead, leave her lying on the frosty ground, and bend over the hole. Quinn raises his arms toward me. I strain against his weight, but he's so much heavier than Jazz he doesn't budge when I try to lift him.

My temples throb. "I'm not strong enough," I mutter, crumpling at the edge of the hole. I hate having to admit this, even to Quinn. "I'm going to find something for you to stand on." I might be weak, but I'm not stupid.

I rush toward the decomposing train to my right. When I step aboard, the floor buckles under me. I hold on to a rusting fire extinguisher attached to the wall, then creep inside. Most of the seats have been ripped out of place or knifed open, their frothy green innards spilling onto the floor. Only two seats are intact. I shut my eyes, but it's too late; I've already seen the parched bones, one set significantly larger than the other. And on the floor next to them are two skulls: a large one and a small one. And a knife.

They probably took their own lives: one slice to the throat is all it would have taken, and I learned in history class that people resorted to worse during The Switch, when they were gasping for air and starving to boot. But who were they? A parent and child, perhaps? No one will ever know. Two lives wiped from the face of history as though they meant nothing—like so many before and after them.

Quinn calls my name. I need to focus.

I reach for a seat, mildewed and broken, and tow it from the train, my arms burning.

I force the seat down the manhole, and it lands with a *whump*. Quinn puts it on its side and, wobbling, uses it as a stool. After two attempts he pulls his chin and elbows aboveground before finally crawling out. He lies on the ground and breathes heavily. "I need to start doing more push-ups," he says, and I can't help smiling.

But beside us, Jazz's whimpers have turned into sobs.

Her corduroys are ripped open below the knee. "You have to be quiet, Jazz," I say. We can't know who's lurking. The whole area could be crawling with drifters. Or the army could be out hunting for me already.

I pull at the flap of Jazz's pants, then turn away so I won't be sick. She isn't just bleeding: a deep, jagged gash runs all the way up her leg to the knee and a piece of bone is sticking out.

Quinn appears at my side. He stares at the wound, his jaw slack. I untie my scarf and tightly bind Jazz's leg. She bites on her fist. "It hurts . . . so . . . much," she says.

"What are we going to do?" I ask.

"We'll get her to the station and then. . ." He trails off. "Do you have the strength to carry her?"

"I have to."

"And we can't stop, even if she screams," he says.

"I won't scream," Jazz says through tears. But she does scream. And scream and scream and scream.

By the time we've carried Jazz through the pitch-black tunnel, and all the way into St. Pancras station, she's unconscious. And I'm barely able to walk myself. Our oxygen is never going to last all the way to Sequoia if we keep exerting ourselves like this.

We set her down beneath a marble clock and slump next to her. She doesn't stir. I slide my hand into her coat and place it against her chest. I relax when I feel the heartbeat.

"It's bad," Quinn says. I can't speak through my panting, so I sit catching my breath and gaze at the station's vaulted glass ceiling. Stars speckle the night sky. It's beautiful.

Quinn bends toward me. "We'll make it through this, you know," he says. He's trying to be positive. But Jazz's leg will get infected, and then what? We leave her here to rot and move on?

"She'll die, and then we will," I say.

He shakes me. "Why are you talking like that?"

I push him away. "Because in case you hadn't noticed, everyone dies, Quinn."

"*We're alive.*" He removes his facemask, then pulls mine from my face so he can kiss me quickly on the lips. A few weeks ago, I wanted nothing more than to know Quinn loved me. When he kissed me for the first time, it was like an elixir—but today, his lips don't revive me. "You have to be strong," he says firmly, sliding both facemasks back into place.

And he's right. Mom and Dad wouldn't have wanted me to give up. They would have wanted me to fight, like they did in the end. Even if the fighting kills us.

3
RONAN

I've been a prisoner in my own home for two days, and I
don't know how much more of it I can take. When we got
back from the battle at The Grove, Jude Caffrey bundled me
into a buggy with armed stewards and sent me home instead
of letting me help contain the riots. He said it was for my
own protection, but never bothered to say what I need to
be protected from, and anyway, I hardly think the stewards
commissioned to protect me could fend off an attacker better
than I could.

The only reason I haven't given them the slip is because
I don't want to leave my sister alone. Niamh was hysterical when I got home. She'd been in her bedroom with Todd
something-or-other when the stewards barged in. They
frog-marched them to the basement where they kept them

until I got back. And when I did, she asked me about a thousand questions: Where had I been? What was happening? When could we leave? But I couldn't answer her. The mission to The Grove was classified. And even if I could have answered, I didn't want to talk about it. I went straight to my room and ripped off my uniform and dirty boots, throwing them against the wall. We'd been told we'd be fighting terrorists. Well, that was the biggest crock of crap I've ever heard in my life.

Neither my nor Niamh's pads have worked since then, either. The screen's nothing but static. Every so often raking shots are fired outside or a voice booms through a megaphone. And strangely, no one seems to know where my father is. I'm not his biggest fan, but I am beginning to feel uneasy.

"You married?" Niamh asks the steward on duty guarding us from the perils of our own kitchen. She twists a piece of hair around her finger until the tip is bluish. Todd is elsewhere.

"Give it a rest, Niamh," I say. The guy must be forty and Niamh's only flirting because she's bored.

"Just making chitchat, Ronan. You might want to try it some time," she says, lifting herself up onto a bar stool and leaning forward against the stone island, her head resting on her hands.

I go to the window. The stewards surrounding the house look like a human fence, and beyond them the street is deserted. "How much longer is this going to last?" I ask.

"Please step away from the window," the steward warns. He's shorter than me and thin as a whip. But I do as he says and take a jug of juice and a handful of strawberries from the fridge.

"Want something?" I ask. Normally our housekeeper, Wendy, would see to visitors, but she's been banished to her annex, and Niamh and I have been feeding ourselves for the first time in our lives.

"No," the steward says curtly, then tilts his head in the direction of the hall. "Wait here," he whispers for what must be the twentieth time today. He slides along the kitchen wall until he's out of sight. I pour a glass of juice.

"Those dirty subs do nothing but cause trouble. I hope Daddy's dealing with them," Niamh says. She pauses. "Do you think Daddy's all right?" She has an arm outstretched, admiring her polished nails. She's pretending she isn't worried, too.

"He can take care of himself." I don't know anyone who'd dare cross my father—I certainly wouldn't. But it *is* strange that he hasn't called, when we're on lockdown.

Niamh takes her pad from a drawer in the kitchen island.

"Why won't this thing work?" She bangs it on the stone top. "Hell!"

The steward reappears at the kitchen door followed by Jude Caffrey, who pulls off his facemask, unbuckles the tank from his belt, and dumps everything onto the floor. The steward spins around and stands with his back to us. "Ronan. Niamh," Jude says. He's wearing the same soiled clothes I last saw him in, and his knuckles are grazed. He hasn't shaved in a long time.

"Why are *you* here?" Niamh asks rudely.

"Take a seat," I say, and tap a stool.

When he comes into the kitchen, I see Todd is standing behind him. Todd rests against the arched doorframe with his T-shirt in his hand. His chest is bare and his hair is standing up like he's been wrestling. "Is it over?" he asks.

"The pod's been pumped with halothane gas," Jude says, sitting on the stool. He addresses me as though Todd hasn't even come into the room. Todd squints and steps further into the kitchen. He's waiting to be acknowledged. Or at the very least noticed.

"And what does that mean?" I ask.

"If you go outside without a tank, you'll black out," Jude says matter-of-factly. But I'm not stupid; he knows that isn't the question I'm asking.

My mouth goes dry. "Jude, is this a coup?" I ask. "Where's my father?"

"You haven't seen any coverage of the press conference on the screen?" he asks, his tone reproachful.

"The screens have been tampered with," Niamh snaps. No one but Cain Knavery's daughter could get away with speaking like this to the general of the pod's army.

He arches an eyebrow. "You, leave us," he tells Todd, who's finally found his way into his T-shirt.

"So, I'll get an airtank from the basement, yeah?" Todd says. Everyone, including Niamh, ignores him.

Jude closes his eyes and massages the lids. "Go help your boyfriend, Niamh," he says.

"*Excuse* me?" Her jaw drops and she takes several moments to be deeply offended. "You're in *my* house."

"Please, Niamh. Let me speak to Jude." I dip my head to one side, and she stomps out of the room after Todd.

Jude stands up, slides his hands into his pockets, and rocks back and forth, side to side, in his dirty boots. The creamy marble floor is covered in muck he's carried through the house. "It's important you're safe. We'll keep snipers on the roof for another couple of days, and I strongly advise you to stay indoors," Jude says. He is broad and tall, but he looks unusually tired and defeated.

"Do you think I need a babysitter?" I ask.

"I don't doubt you're able to take care of yourself. It's a precaution, that's all." I've been training under Jude Caffrey with the Special Forces since I was thirteen and he knows I could take down an assailant with two fingers. And I did— just days ago at The Grove.

Jude moves to the sink, turns on the tap, and puts his neck under the running water. He shakes his head and stands up straight, the water running into his shirt collar. Then he pushes his thinning hair out of his face with wet hands and clasps them behind his back. He's stalling, I realize, and my gut aches. What is he so reluctant to tell me?

"The pod's gone mad. You know the auxiliaries have rebelled," he says.

"They have every reason to," I snap. I've never questioned what the Ministry stands for, but that was before seeing the trees at The Grove, before *destroying* them at Jude's command.

He looks like he's about to say something, then changes his mind. I take a short breath. "Where's my father?"

He pinches the bridge of his nose, and I brace myself against the wall because it's obvious why Jude's so nervous. My ears ring. "Your father's dead, Ronan," he says.

I wince at the words. My muscles tense. "What?" I say. I've heard him; I need time to take it in, that's all.

"I'm sorry," he says.

"Yes," I say. I stay on my feet, which is more than I managed when Wendy told me my mother was gone. All I could do back then was moan into the kitchen floor. Today I retain my balance. And my composure.

But I'm so damn thirsty. My mouth is dryer than ever. I return to the fridge, get the jug and drink straight from its lip, juice spilling across my mouth and all over my shirt. Jude takes the jug from me. His jacket is missing a button. A loose thread hangs where it should be. I focus hard on it. I have to focus on something. Maybe the button was ripped off at The Grove.

"You're in shock. Sit down," he says. He's probably right. And if I'm feeling like this, how will Niamh take it?

She doesn't know, and I'll be the one to tell her. The air seems to have thinned. I pull at my collar.

Jude leads me to the kitchen table, where he lowers me into a chair. "Breathe slowly," he says. I push him away. I don't want his hands on me.

"I knew something like this must have happened," I admit. I take large gulps of air as the words *dead* and *forever* spin in my head. I wasn't my father's favorite, and we weren't friends. Still, I didn't want this.

"At the press conference, Quinn started a—well, your father was mobbed and attacked, but it was a heart attack that killed him. By the time the medics arrived, it was too late."

"What should I do?" I ask. I need him to tell me what life looks like now—what comes next.

But Jude's an army man; he thinks I'm asking how we catch the perpetrators. "Well, you know we've been chasing the Resistance inside and outside the pod. We've nearly got them all rounded up. You can help with that."

"Me? No . . . I want nothing more to do with the Special Forces."

He squints. "Let's talk about this tomorrow."

"I don't want to talk about it tomorrow. I want out. Those people weren't terrorists. They were *gardeners*, Jude. And most of them were my age." I've tried not to think about those we killed, but it comes back to me now: the faces of boys and girls, only a handful of them wearing bullet-proof vests, not one of them holding an automatic weapon. They had rifles and shotguns. It wasn't a war at all—it was a massacre.

"Those people are responsible for your father's death."

He knows the only reason I joined the Special Forces was for my father's approval. But strangely, now he's dead, I couldn't care less if he rolls in his grave. I have no interest in working for the Ministry and spending my life subjugating people for no good reason.

"No. The Ministry's lies are responsible for that riot, and I won't be a part of that anymore."

"You don't really have a choice. Do you know how much your training cost?"

"I'll pay back whatever it cost. We have money."

Jude sighs. "None of us have money, Ronan. This house, the buggy, your housekeeper, dammit, even your air supply . . . who do you think pays for it all?"

"But my father had shares in Breathe. A pension."

"Perhaps," he says. "But Special Forces soldiers don't quit. You're one of the Ministry's most dangerous weapons. They aren't going to let you loose. Who's to say you won't defect?"

"But *you* can cut me loose."

He smiles. "If only that were true. I'm as much a slave to them as anyone."

"I'll refuse to fight," I say. They can't *make* me.

"Get real. What do you think they'll do to you . . . and to your sister? Have you forgotten what happened to Adele Rice?"

"She was killed by—" I stop and stare at Jude, who nods slowly. It was all over the news: Adele Rice, Special Forces elite, went missing and was suspected dead after a mission to The Outlands. The Ministry blamed the "terrorists." Were *any* of the supposed terrorist attacks true?

My stomach tightens and bitterness against my father, the Ministry, and Jude Caffrey surges. I swallow hard and have a desperate urge to go up into my studio and throw paint. Why didn't I stay up there years ago and do what I love instead of trying to be the soldier-son my father wanted?

"The ministers have invited you and your sister to the chamber next week. They'd like to pay their respects," he says. He stands, puts on his coat, and retrieves his airtank from the floor.

"Right," I say.

"It's protocol," he says flatly. "And again, I'm sorry, but my advice, if you want to stay safe, is to stay useful. The Special Forces is a prestigious group and we'll need you to clean up the mess in the pod. If I were you, I wouldn't give up on us just yet." He turns to the door as Todd and Niamh stroll into the kitchen. Niamh's red lipstick is smeared across Todd's neck and white T-shirt. I grip the edge of the table to stop myself from jumping up and knocking him out.

"I'm taking this." Todd holds up an airtank. Niamh comes into the kitchen and flops into a seat beside me. "Listen, Niamh, I'll see you at school, yeah?"

Niamh chews on a thumbnail. "Okay," she replies, and smiles.

"Should I wait for you to call me, or should I—"

"Just get out," I say.

"Huh?"

"Leave," I bite out.

"Why are you being such a jerk?" Niamh asks.

"I'm going anyway. No worries," Todd murmurs, and steps out of the room.

"I'm telling Dad," Niamh says. We're both practically adults, yet when I look at her, I see my baby sister—the six-year-old who ten years ago, wearing a yellow knit dress, was told her mother was dead and clung to me for weeks. She would've clung to my father if he hadn't spent every day either in his room with a bottle or at the Ministry. He was never the same again and committed himself completely to work.

I sit back down and gaze at Niamh, who is glaring at me. How can I be the one to tell her our father is never coming back? Why should I be the one to destroy her world?

"Please tell me what's going on," she says.

Jude looks at me seriously. "I'll go and let you two talk," he says.

Niamh frowns. "Talk about what?"

4
QUINN

While Bea and Jazz get some kip, I scout the station for drifters, climbing the escalator to the upper concourse—a glass
atrium bursting with light. The sky is this amazingly bright
blue, and if you didn't know any better you'd think it was a
summer morning.

At the end of the concourse, where the light is bright-
est, is a jumble of discarded solar respirators. Hell, even the
drifters have legged it.

I stoop over one of the solar respirators, a metal box that
looks like a rusty mini-fridge, and turn it on. It sputters to
life, then hums loudly. I pull my facemask from my nose and
mouth to test the one attached to the respirator. The air coming from it is humid, but I can breathe all right. A tightness I
didn't even know I had in my chest relaxes; at least we aren't

going to suffocate anytime soon. With Bea I've tried to be more positive than I feel, but that's only because she needs me to be strong. She's lost way more than I have, and she hasn't given up. Not completely, anyway.

I refit my facemask and pull my father's long coat more tightly around me.

Maybe he thought that saving my life made him a model father or something, but it doesn't. Anyone would have done the same, or more. And if he could see me now, he'd know that sending me into The Outlands to fend for myself wasn't far from a death sentence anyway.

Who am I kidding? Of course he knew that.

But at least I can walk, which is more than I can say about Jazz, and if we don't do something soon, we'll have to watch her die because there's no way we can treat her leg ourselves. If only we'd managed to make it to Sequoia unharmed.

I slump on the floor and nudge a solar respirator with my foot. Maybe I should go there alone and bring back help. Bea could take care of Jazz in the meantime. They have air and water. And this station is as good as it gets for shelter out here.

It's probably the worst idea I've ever had, but when I hear Jazz call out, I figure I don't have any other option.

5
BEA

I wake up on the cold station floor, and Quinn is missing.

"Petra," Jazz mutters, and tries to sit up. She lets out a screech, crumpling back onto the tiled floor. I slide closer and elevate her leg using Quinn's backpack. This should help stop the bleeding. Then I take her head in my lap. "I thought it was only a nightmare," she says. She begins to cry, and I can tell from her eyes that it has nothing to do with the pain in her leg.

After a few minutes, a noise echoes through the station. "Quinn?"

"Coming!" And he's with us again. "I heard a scream," he says, and lowers a rusting, dented solar respirator onto the floor.

"It was me," Jazz admits.

He pushes his hair away from his eyes and crouches next to her. "How bad is it?" he asks. Cautiously, he presses his hand to her forehead.

"I'm fine," she says, and leans away from him. Her eyelids flutter as she courts unconsciousness again.

Quinn turns to me. "I found a ton of those respirators. This place must have been swarming with drifters. But there's no one here now. You'll be fine."

He smiles, but it looks forced. "What are you talking about?" I swallow hard.

"Hear me out, Bea."

"No," I say.

"We can't carry her across the country."

"You're leaving?"

"One of us has to get help, and I won't let you go out there alone." I don't want to be without him. Not again. Not ever. I try to speak, but the words get trapped in my throat, and I cough. He pats me on the back. "Give me the map and let me go," he says.

"Where? *Where* will you go, Quinn?" My voice is a squeal.

"I'll find Sequoia. How hard can it be to locate a building big enough to house a whole movement? Someone will be able to help, and I'll be back. Alina will be there." He lowers his voice. "Jazz doesn't stand a chance if we all stay here."

"There has to be another way." Now I do cry as the weight of what's happened and what will happen crashes down on me. I want to be stronger, I just don't know how.

He wraps his arms around me, holding me up as much as embracing me. "I'll be back. I promise," he says.

My parents made a promise like this, and it was the last time I ever saw them. I let him hold me. But I don't believe him.

"They work. I checked," Quinn says, unloading another respirator, and pressing his hand against the solar panel bathed in light from above. He turns a knob on the top, nudges it with his foot, and we listen to the old thing grind to life. "And they're mobile, so you can carry them . . . if you have to." I nod even though the respirators are enormous; I'd never even be able to lift one. "But you should stay here, so I'll know where to find you," he says.

Beside me, Jazz mewls and turns over in her sleep.

"What day is it?" I ask. I want to feel grounded to something reliable, predictable. And unless I know when he left, how will I know when to expect him back? When to stop waiting?

Quinn blinks and calculates using his fingers. "Monday," he says. "Or Tuesday. Let's say Monday. Look, every time the sun comes up, throw something in there." He points at a tarnished water fountain attached to the wall.

"And when should I stop counting?"

"Bea." He sighs. "I'll be back."

"Don't go," Jazz says, waking up. She winces with pain. "Can't you give me a piggyback? I'm light. I'm really light."

She's already sweating a fever, though she's shivering. "You need to conserve your energy," I tell her.

Quinn buttons up his coat. "Tell me this is for the best," he says. "Please tell me I'm doing the right thing." I don't answer but follow him outside into the derelict city. The sunshine has melted some of the snow. The air is still frigid. I tuck my chin into my chest.

"Your air won't last long," I say.

"Stop it," he says.

"*You* stop it."

"Bea . . ." He takes my wrist, lifts his mask, and pushing back my sleeve, kisses it. I close my eyes, and he takes off my glove and kisses the palm of my hand. Eventually he has to put his facemask back in place, so he wraps me up in his arms. I rest my chin on his shoulder. "I can't read you," he says.

"I can't read myself anymore." I take a deep breath and push my hair away from my face. "If Jazz dies, and you don't come back, I'll head for Sequoia," I say.

He looks up at the rows of broken clerestory windows

set into the red brick of the station and nods. "Give me two weeks. You can survive here for two weeks."

"Yes," I say, but we both know Jazz won't make it that long.

We stand for a few moments longer, holding hands and looking at our boots in the sludge.

"Why did it take me forever to see you?" he asks. He puts his hands around the back of my neck and pulls my head toward him so that our foreheads touch. "I love you. You know that, don't you?"

I nod, but I don't tell him that I love him, too. Maybe he'll be back, maybe he won't; my love won't change what happens.

6
RONAN

Niamh is admiring herself in my bedroom mirror. She's dressed in my father's black mourning robe, and it should look weird, but Wendy's taken it in so it fits, and Niamh wears it as though it were made especially for her. Usually I'd make a snarky comment, but I just watch her. "What do you think?" she asks.

I climb out of bed, pulling on the pants I left draped on the chair next to it. "I think I'd appreciate some privacy."

"You should be up. I don't know how you can sleep." Today the ministers will pay their respects in the chamber. But that probably isn't what Niamh means; ever since she found out our father died, she has spent all night in his bedroom, sobbing into the pillows. I let her grieve—someone should.

"You feeling better?" I ask.

"No, Ronan," Niamh says. "Our dad is dead. I feel like crap."

I stand behind her. My eyes in the mirror have dark circles beneath them. I look older than I did a week ago, which shouldn't really surprise me.

I pull a sweater over my head and push my hair away from my eyes. Wendy bustles into the room with a tray.

"Morning," she says.

"Hey," I say. Niamh doesn't bother looking at her. Wendy sidesteps Niamh, balancing the tray on her hip, and as she brushes past me, I have a feeling she wants to give me a hug. Wendy brought us up after our mother died and was the closest thing I had to a parent. But my father didn't want her trying to replace my mother, so she stopped cuddling us. Maybe my father threatened her, and I was too shy to admit that a hug now and then would have been all right.

Wendy puts the tray on the dresser. "Toast and tea," she tells me. "Have it while it's hot." On her way out, she stops in front of Niamh. "You look lovely."

Niamh shrugs. "I know," she says, though Wendy is already out of the room. "And it would be nice if you made some effort too, Ronan."

"Give me a minute's peace, and I will," I say.

"Well, we leave in ten minutes, so hurry up." She blows me a theatrical kiss and sweeps out of the room.

Niamh and I make our way up the marble pathway to the senate. The whole area's been cordoned off and stewards are lining the streets to prevent anything from kicking off, though the pod's been pretty quiet since everyone was anesthetized. No one's interested in challenging the Ministry now—not when consciousness depends on compliance. I turn to Niamh, about to reassure her, but she has her head up and eyes fixed on the entrance. She doesn't look one bit afraid. So why am I?

The antique wooden doors to the senate swing inward and a group of stewards bows. A dimly lit lobby ends in a broad, winding staircase. "Ms. Knavery. Mr. Knavery," the stewards mutter, each one bending lower than the last.

We're led up the stairs, down a pink-tiled hallway, and into a sealed cavity between the outer door and the Chamber of Governance. Our fingerprints and faces are scanned, and we're given swabs so we can provide saliva samples. It takes a few minutes for the screen to come to life: *Niamh Jean Knavery, Ronan Giles Knavery —Authorized.*

The Chamber is a golden walled amphitheater with tiered seats set around a central platform. Down in the well of the gallery is a row of solemn officials perched in high-backed chairs. The room goes quiet as we shuffle along an empty row at the back. Anyone wearing a hat takes it off, and a few people stand. I recognize most of the ministers from dinners and parties my father dragged us to. Back then they were all smiles—not today. And the stoniest face of all is Lance Vine, the new pod minister, though why he looks so grim is hard to tell.

Jude Caffrey is one of the ministers sitting on stage. He catches my eye and nods. I nod back. It's good to have a familiar face I know to focus on, should I need it.

Vine approaches the lectern and clears his throat into the microphone. When he's satisfied everyone's listening, he begins. "Welcome," he says. For such a thin man, his voice is surprisingly deep, and any ministers still standing or murmuring quickly shut up. "I stand before you today as your newly appointed pod minister. Yet this position comes at a price. Today we honor the memory of Cain Knavery and, as a mark of respect, offer a moment's silence in the presence of his children. Thank you for coming. We are deeply sorry for your loss." Niamh sits up straighter. I bite the insides of my cheeks. I've no interest in being eyeballed and even less in being pitied. Vine lowers his head. The ministers mirror him.

And the silence is under way: time to think about my father. How many nights he came home steaming drunk, needing to be placated to stop him from smashing up the kitchen. Or the times he had to be carried to bed. Or the day he chased me up the stairs with a belt for daring to contradict him. A tear trickles down Niamh's cheek. What does she remember that I don't?

"Thank you, ministers," Vine says. "And now to today's agenda. Item one is pod security."

"Is that it?" Niamh hisses. "Our dead father gets one minute?"

I shrug, and Vine is continuing. "We must restore order. Our authority must not be challenged again." He bangs his fist against the lectern, and the chamber booms with the noise of it. The ministers applaud. "We have reports of RATS escaping via the trash chutes during the riots, and of new terrorist cells in The Outlands. We must not allow the grass to grow under our feet." He simpers. This is a joke, and the handful of ministers who get it titter. "We will deploy the army to finish the job."

The chamber goes silent, and I freeze. I can't go out there and kill innocent people. I won't.

Jude jumps up. "May I address the chamber?" he asks. Vine nods and steps away from the lectern as Jude approaches it. "The army was severely damaged during the last campaign. We lost too many soldiers, and depleted our fuel supply for the zips. I can't vote for an immediate deployment of troops." The ministers shift in their seats.

"So we let them get away with it?" someone calls out.

"We let the RATS escape?" another voice adds.

"We need to find another way," Jude says, and seems to stare at me. "We could send scouts on a reconnaissance mission. Young people the RATS would trust. I could have the junior Special Forces ready in days."

Niamh prickles up. "Does he mean *you?*"

Jude keeps his mouth straight and his hands clamped to the lectern. I should have known better than to expect any compassion from him—a man who sent his own son into The Outlands to die. How could he do that? I know by now that Quinn was the one who started the riot in the pod—but even *I* didn't want him dead, not when all he did was tell the truth.

The chamber is heavy with silence and all eyes rest on me. Some ministers look troubled, but most are beaming, delighted by the scheme. Jude's expression is impenetrable.

"Tell them you'll do it, Ronan. For Daddy. Those bastards are responsible for this." Niamh tugs on her black mourning robe. I take her hand and squeeze it.

But I won't advocate for this mission. Besides, I hardly think that what I say matters. They'll send us whether I agree to it or not. Niamh pulls her hand out of mine and does start to cry.

"And in the meantime, you'll recruit and train a new

army?" someone asks. "If this is a reconnaissance mission, we have to be ready to attack once they're found."

"Of course," Jude says. "I'll begin recruiting today." Is he smiling? I want to tear onto the stage and throttle him.

"Thank you, General," Vine says, and moves on to item two on the agenda.

Because item one has been resolved: I am going into The Outlands again, whether I like it or not.

7
ALINA

Silas lowers the anchor for the final time. He wipes his brow with his forearm and ties the roping in place. The deck moans as it collides with the jetty. We've come as far as we can in the boat: the river winds west, and it's time to head north.

Song unbolts the gate in the railing, slides a narrow gangplank between the boat and landing, and steps ashore. "Mind your step," he says. His eyes are dull.

We haven't talked about The Grove, and with Holly gone, we have something else to blot from our memories. Not that we can.

"You're sure it's north?" Silas asks Dorian.

Dorian nods. "Not far now. A couple of days at most." It doesn't sound like much, but we left The Grove over a week ago. We're freezing and hungry and our air is dwindling quicker than we thought.

"Make sure we've got all the airtanks and weapons," Silas says. He stands with his hands on his hips, his chin raised. He's good at this—appearing unbreakable. And that's what we need now: someone to pretend everything will be okay.

Maude steps up to the gangplank and holds the rail. She coughs loudly. "Haven't you got anything warm to put on?" I ask her. A persistent drizzle has replaced the pouring rain.

"What do you care?" she asks, elbowing me out of the way. She totters down the gangplank, then pulls an old, damp blanket around her like a cape.

"You don't look too toasty yourself. Stick that on, love," Bruce says to me, holding out his coat.

"I'm fine," I tell him, even though I'm so cold I can no longer feel my toes or the tips of my fingers. He shrugs and puts on the coat himself.

I follow Maude down the gangplank and onto the jetty where the solidity of the land makes me wobble.

"I wish we could hide it," Dorian says, looking up at the towering masts of the boat.

Silas tuts. "Let's get a move on. Everyone stay close," he says.

We march along the jetty and onto the riverbank. "It looks the same everywhere," Song says. We've left behind the city's high-rises and cathedral spires that seem to pierce the clouds, but all along the riverbank is the usual desolation: tumbledown buildings, smashed-up cars, warped roads, and toppled lampposts. Bones are scattered among the debris; animal or human, it's hard to tell. In the distance are folds of hoary, barren fields.

I used to think that if I traveled far enough and walked quickly enough, I'd find a cluster of untouched trees. It was a fantasy, and a childish one; beyond the city's devastation is more devastation. It just happens to be of the rural variety.

"What if they won't let us in?" Bruce wonders aloud.

"Do you have a better idea?" Silas snaps. His mood has been increasingly prickly.

"Take it easy." I place a hand on Silas's arm. He flinches and kicks the wheel of a rotten baby stroller, which spins and squeaks. Then he storms ahead, carrying a bag of guns, a full backpack of supplies, and several airtanks. Part of me wishes we could talk about what's happened. Everything we've seen. But it's too soon, and Silas isn't one for talking anyway.

"People who go to Sequoia never come back," Song says, turning to me, his voice as gentle as ash.

"Petra didn't want defectors. If you went to Sequoia, you had to go for good. You had to choose a team," Dorian reminds him.

Song bites his bottom lip and I stop to look at the sky. The sun is up, but thick, white clouds make it impossible to locate. I sigh and try to wiggle my toes. I still can't feel them.

"Hurry up," Maude says, pushing me from behind. "I'm freezing my berries off 'ere!" Bruce smiles and links her arm through his.

"They'll let us in because we're all on the same team," I say loudly, so Silas can hear. "We all want the trees back. We all want to breathe again." He doesn't turn around or stop walking. Maybe he doesn't hear me, but I don't think that's it.

"You're a drifter now. No better than me," Maude says. She laughs. No one else does. And a thread of fear trickles through me.

We rest only once, at dusk, when we find a stranded bus along a stretch of open road, frozen scrub poking through the cracks in the tarmac. We climb aboard, the vehicle creaking under our weight, and I choose a spot at the back where I throw off my backpack. Then I check the gauge on my airtank. A little over a quarter tank of oxygen remaining. Maybe I should ask Silas for the particulars on our air supply as he's the one carrying the spare tanks, but if we don't have enough air, I'd rather not know.

I'm too tired to care that the bus seat is stippled black with mold. If it kills me, it kills me. I lie down and curl up, my airtank between my legs.

Maude has chosen a row behind me and hacks until she spits up.

I close my eyes and wait for sleep to creep toward me. Maude is restless. She bangs the back of my seat. "Oi, you," she croaks. I sit up. Everyone else is already lying down, only their feet poking off the edges of their seats visible. "You reckon Bea's okay?" she asks, frowning.

"I know as much as you do." General Caffrey only retreated from The Grove because fighting broke out in the pod. I wish I could be certain Bea was nowhere near it. Or Quinn. Is it possible that their return and the civil war were completely unrelated?

"You lied," Maude grumbles. "I only rounded up all them drifters to help yous fight 'cuz I thought Bea would be in trouble if I didn't. That were a dirty trick." She points a finger at me, the nail broken and black.

"Technically, Petra lied to you," I say. Then I add, "Bea's tougher than she looks."

"She's ain't the sort you meet everyday, tha's for certain. A real doll." She studies the cracked window.

This is the closest we've ever come to a real conversation. "Get some sleep, Maude," I say, using what I think is a kind voice.

Maude glares at me anyway. "You ain't my boss, missy. I'll do what I bloody well like."

"Well, I'm going to rest." I turn away and curl up into the seat again. After a minute I hear Maude lie down, too.

I listen to the others snoring and try to picture something calming to help me sleep, but all I can see is Holly's face as she let go of the railings. And then Abel's face is next to her in the water. They are both being swallowed by waves. This wasn't how it happened for him, of course; the Ministry murdered him. Probably turned him out of the pod without an airtank.

It's been days since I thought about Abel, but now all the guilt and shame about his death steal back in: how he was only on that mission in the pod because I wanted to spend time with him; how I was too stubborn to abandon it even though he begged me to. He probably lied to me about who he was, but it doesn't change the fact that I cared about him. And because I did, he's dead.

I tuck my knees up under my chin. I feel so cold. Colder than ever before.

8
RONAN

I'm leaving the pod in less than an hour and I haven't even packed. Instead, I'm in my studio smearing thick black and white swaths of paint across a board. It doesn't look like much—just a choked monochromatic muddle.

I thought that coming up here would help me figure out how I was going to get out of this bullshit mission, but all I have to show for the mulling it over are the paintings—no solution at all.

I'm not scared of The Outlands: We're all being kitted out with enough food, air, and medical supplies to last a month, and no half-starved drifter would be a match for me. But to hell with gathering information on so-called terrorists for the Ministry and Jude Caffrey, just so they can cut down innocent people. And I'd refuse to go if it wasn't putting Niamh at risk—I'm all she has left.

I go to the sink and wash the brushes. Then I take one last look at the painting, what will probably turn into a devastated soccer stadium, and lock the studio door.

Once I'm ready to go, I meet Niamh by the front door. "When will you be back? I'm worried," she says. I can't remember the last time she's said anything remotely affectionate, and it makes me gulp.

"When I kill the bad guys, I suppose," I lie. I'm not killing anyone.

Anyone else.

I'm going to get out there and find somewhere to hunker down long enough that it seems like I tried, even though I'll return empty-handed. If I do happen to find anyone, I'll warn them.

"You will be back though," Niamh says.

"Don't be silly," I say, and heave my bulging backpack up over my shoulders.

"Be careful, you big asshole," Niamh says. She leans in and kisses me awkwardly on the cheek. Her lips are dry.

I laugh. "You be careful," I reply, and without doing anything else that might trigger more emotion in either of us, head for the waiting buggy.

• • •

Jude Caffrey is standing next to the press secretary at the border. He raises his hand. I pretend I don't see him and make my way to the gates where the rest of my unit is waiting. I have no intention of buddying up with him when he's spent his life lying and embroiling his soldiers in the Ministry's lies.

Robyn, the youngest member of the Special Forces, smiles as I approach. "Sorry about your dad," she says.

"Thanks." I pause. "We've all been rounded up, huh?"

"Everyone." She stands back, so I can see the others. Mary, Rick, Nina, and Johnny all turn my way and wave. I raise a hand in greeting. "First time a junior unit's been sent out alone. We heard you offered us up," Robyn says. She pulls her thick ponytail tight.

"What? No." I sound more defensive than I mean to.

"Are we even ready to go out again?" Robyn asks. She looks at me askance, and I think what she means is, *do we want to?* None of us had expected the trees at The Grove. And it's changed everything. For some of us, at least.

Rick comes forward. He's eighteen but looks thirty. "Nice one, dude. I was bored to death at home. Kept saying we were ready to get out there again. I'm pumped to be doing this. *Pumped!*"

"I didn't suggest it," I say. Rick is a thug. He's always been a thug.

"General Caffrey said you did." Mary is pointing at Jude.

"We're pleased," Nina says.

"Better than spending the next year in the gymnasium," Johnny adds.

Their excitement is palpable. I turn to Robyn, who bites her bottom lip. The others might be pleased, but she isn't. And neither am I.

Jude steps forward and without any kind of pep talk, hands each of us a small pouch and launches into directives. "You've been issued new pads with long-range tracking devices for two-way communication. In case of a malfunction, you've also been given walkie-talkies. Primitive but functional. Make contact at least once a day, so we know you're alive."

"Alive?" Rick scoffs. "I don't think you need to worry. A bunch of tree-hugging hippies won't be a match for us." He punches his own abdomen in a gesture of stabbing someone in the gut.

What's wrong with him? Hasn't he killed enough people? "Oh, shut your mouth for once, Rick," I say.

Robyn gasps, and Rick scowls as he throws a punch at me. I grab his fist and twist his arm behind his back and up toward his neck. He groans. "All right, all right, let go," he says, and I release him, pushing him away from me, as the others look on speechless. I've never turned on anyone before. But I should've shut Rick up a long time ago.

Jude shakes his head. "Lucky we aren't sending you out together." He pauses. "If we did, you'd just be at each other's throats. Besides, you'd be searching forever, so each of you is being sent in a different direction. As soon as you find something suspicious, make contact. We need a location. Once we have that, the army and zips can get out there and do some damage. Hopefully we'll be back up and running by then."

"Have we permission to kill?" Rick asks. He gives me a sideways glance.

Jude pulls at the sleeves of his military jacket. "Your job is to find the RATS. Radio in for further instructions."

Robyn scratches the tip of her nose. "How long have we got?"

"As long as you can last," Jude says, and makes to leave as the press secretary rushes over, her heels clacking against the ground.

"Can we have a picture of Ronan at the border?" she calls. "Pod Minister Vine thought it'd be good PR if Cain Knavery's son made a statement. The press are going back to work in a few days and they'll lead with this."

"Sure," I say, and the press secretary opens her pad, snaps a picture, then smiles, waiting to record me. "After all the destruction we've brought about so far, I'd say that this mission is . . ."

"Write whatever you think," Jude says, suddenly standing between me and the press secretary and cutting me off. He puts his arm over my shoulder and pulls me away. "Enough time wasting," he says. I look back at the press secretary, who's still smiling despite not getting her interview, which is probably because the story's already been written.

The border is guarded by armed stewards, who stand aside for us, and we walk unobstructed through the gates and down the glass tunnel. We attach airtanks to our belts and slip facemasks over our mouths and noses. It feels different from the other times we've marched outside. Before, I was excited to save the pod. But the best way to do that now is to go out there and do nothing.

We push through the revolving doors at the end of the tunnel and into The Outlands. Six robust buggies, their engines running, are waiting.

"I guess this is it," Robyn says. She wrings her hands. The others mumble agreement and adjust their airtanks.

"We'll drive you out about thirty miles," Jude says. "Far enough to save some time, not so far they'll hear you coming. Good luck." And that's it. Mary, Rick, Nina, Johnny, and Robyn each pick a buggy and climb in.

I look up at the pod. I could leave now and never return. Disappear by choice. Jude's made it clear that the Ministry won't release me, and if I try to resist, they'll have me killed.

But if anyone could survive in The Outlands, I could.

The question is, do I want to? In training we met our fair share of drifters driven so crazy by loneliness they didn't know what planet they were on. One old guy was so hungry he tried to eat his own arm. And what about Niamh? I can't leave her to fend for herself. Who knows what they'd do to her?

"Get a move on," Jude says. He throws my backpack into the only vehicle without a driver.

"What are you doing?"

"I'm driving you," he says. "We need to talk."

We don't talk. We drive in silence for a long time over the rutty terrain, and I watch the wipers swish back and forth across the greasy window.

Eventually Jude brings the buggy to a halt and cuts the engine. He sits with his hands on his knees staring ahead for several minutes. I don't try to ease the tension. If he has something to say, he should say it.

"You know by now that Quinn was the one who almost brought the pod to its knees?" He turns to me.

"If you mean that he's also responsible for the death of my father, then yes, I know," I say. Our eyes lock. He waits for me to detonate. But I'm not really angry with Quinn. How could I be now I've seen what the Ministry was up to?

If anything, I'm angry with myself for being so stupidly naive for so long and never standing up to my own father like Quinn did.

I wait for him to say more. "Quinn's alive," he says. He rests his forehead on the wheel and sighs, and for the first time in a week, I don't despise him.

"Go on."

"I did the wrong thing sending him out here alone, and I didn't want the army or zips sent out because if they find him, they'll kill him. You, on the other hand . . ."

"You think I'll *help* him."

"You want out of the Special Forces, and I can give you that."

"You said you couldn't."

Jude rubs his chin. "Everyone has his price, and I know the right people. I can get you and Quinn new identities— biometrics, the lot. It's been done before. But it would mean becoming auxiliaries. It's a high price. I can't offer you any better."

I gaze at the fogged windshield. I've been to Zone Three twice in my entire life. All I remember were the dirty faces of the children and the darkness. It was so gloomy. Is that what I want?

"There was a tracking device in the coat Quinn was wearing, and this is the last place the signal came from before the battery died." He points outside. "All you have to do is find him and keep him safe. Then I'll bring you both back to the pod with me. An auxiliary life won't be much for either of you. But you'll be alive."

"So the others are on a wild goose chase?"

"They're being driven far from here," he says. "They won't find anyone besides drifters unless there really is another cell somewhere. But finding another cell is about as likely as finding another pod." We've been told since we were kids that there are other pods. Another lie. Another damn lie.

"I'll think about it," I say. I pull up the collar on my coat and tighten the belt.

Jude offers me a handgun. I take it and push it into the band of my trousers, then throw the semiautomatic I'm holding onto the back seat. I don't want a gun like that. I won't need it. "All I'm asking is that you do the right thing," he says.

"I suppose that's what you'd do," I say snidely.

"Me? I wouldn't even know what the right thing was."

Jude leans across my lap and pushes open the passenger door. I climb out, lugging my backpack behind me and throw it to the ground. The road we're on is warped and covered in plastic traffic cones, and the rest of the area is nothing but mounds of sad gray rubble and half-standing buildings with one or two walls fighting to stay alive.

"Do this one thing and you'll never have to compromise your principles again," Jude says. "You'll be done with all the lies and killing."

And without waiting for my answer, he shuts the door, revs the engine, and is gone.

9
BEA

I kneel next to Jazz and place the back of my hand against her forehead. She's still burning with a fever. The scarf I bound her leg with is sopping wet. I unpeel it and examine the wound. The skin around the gash is yellowing and the smell is gut wrenching. She's losing so much blood, she'll bleed to death before long, and if that doesn't happen, she'll die of the festering infection.

"Please stop the pain," she begs in a voice so controlled and desperate, all I want to do is hold her and have her suffering seep its way into me.

I look at the escalator and wonder whether there could be a pharmacy up on the concourse. "I'll be back," I say, jumping up with my backpack. I could clean her wound and help stop the bleeding, but only if I can find what I need.

"Please don't go," she whimpers. "Bea!"

"Two minutes," I assure her, clambering up the escalator.

I pause on the sun-drenched upper concourse, taking in the row of stores on either side: their glass doors and windows are smashed in, the stock looted, and the signage covered in graffiti.

A store selling nothing but tights and socks has moldy merchandise strewn across the floor, and an electronics store is littered with broken screens and leaking batteries. And as I should have guessed, the pharmacy has been hit worst of all—tubes, bottles, cans, and loose pills of every size and color are scattered across the floor. I pick my way through the mess and go behind the counter. I use my toe to root around on the floor for anything intact, but the sedatives, painkillers, and antibiotics have already been eaten up by drifters. I do spot a travel-size sewing kit and a small bottle of methylated spirit, which I stuff into my backpack.

I leave the pharmacy and step into a store with faded pictures of exotic foods and drinks in its window. Maybe alcohol will be enough to kill her pain.

I scour every shelf, throwing aside bruised tins and empty cans. Then I lie on the floor to check that nothing has rolled out of sight. Defeat seizes me, and then, as I'm about to return to Jazz, I spot a door with a crooked STAFF ONLY sign hanging from it. When I push, it squeaks but swings opens.

Moldy cardboard boxes are piled high like children's giant building blocks, and most are empty, but eventually I find six untouched bottles. I pull one out and try to unscrew it, but it's been sealed with a strange type of lid hidden down inside the bottleneck. I have no time to figure out how it works, so I smash the bottle's neck against a filing cabinet. The alcoholic stench sends me reeling. I pour a little of the liquid into my hand, sniff, and let the tip of my tongue taste it. Definitely drinkable, but unlike any alcohol I've tasted before. It's thick and red and bitter. I look at the label—*Malbec*. I stuff the bottles into my backpack, and a scream echoes through the station.

"Jazz?" I fly from the store.

Jazz is writhing in half-sleep. I pull a bottle from my bag and smash it open, take Jazz in the crook of my arm, and pull the mask from her mouth. "Here," I say, awkwardly filling my cupped palm with the red alcohol and holding it to her lips.

She sips from my hand. "Ugh," she says. "What is it?"

"Medicine." She continues to drink, and when she's drowsy, I lower her onto the floor and reattach the mask. The alcohol calms her down, so I can look at her leg again. It's bad. So bad, I'm not sure that what I'm doing is a good idea. But I have to try something.

She stirs. "Bite on this," I tell her. I push a piece of thick cloth under her facemask and slide it between her teeth. I arrange everything I've collected on the tiled floor, then run a long piece of thread through the eye of the needle and pour the methylated spirit over it. Then I use the spirit to clean her wound. She squeals, but I quickly tie her hands and legs together with scarves so she won't try to stop me.

"It's okay," I say. She lets out a groan muffled by the cloth in her mouth. "Stay calm," I add, this time to myself because my nerves and nausea won't help anyone.

I sit on her chest, bite the insides of my cheeks, and use the tips of my fingers to jam the jutting bone back in place, pulling the skin over it. She bellows and writhes and finally passes out.

I pinch her skin, sticky with blood, and slowly, with trembling fingers, pierce it with the needle and pull the cotton through. Jazz thrashes, as she floats in and out of consciousness, but I keep a knee on her chest, congealed blood seeping through my fingers as I pinch and sew back and forth, back and forth, until the stitches are halfway up her shin, the bone is hidden, and the wound closed.

I pull away her facemask and remove the cloth from her mouth. She's still breathing. Gently.

"I'm sorry," I whisper, because I may have made things worse.

Now, all I can do is wait—for someone to save us, or for Jazz to die.

10
ALINA

We've been walking for the best part of two days. My feet have blisters and my muscles are tight and burning. Even Song and Dorian are exhausted and have started wearing airtanks.

"That *has* to be it," Dorian says.

We're in the middle of nowhere, standing on the dip in a cracked road surrounded by miles of flat fields dotted with old brick houses and long-dead tree stumps. Silas unfolds the map, looks at it, and juts his chin toward a set of ornate iron gates, rusting but still standing at the end of the road. "There?" he asks.

"We've been circling in on the area all morning. This is the only place we haven't checked," Dorian says.

"We can't waste any more air on maybes," I mutter. I feel

momentarily lightheaded and allow a little more oxygen into my facemask.

"We'll see," Silas says, stuffing the map into his coat and leading us down the road, his gun hanging at his side.

As we move closer I make out a lane beyond the gates. I press my face between the railings. "The lane bends. We've no way of knowing what's down there," I say.

"Then let's check it out," Dorian says. He waves Song forward and together they ease open the gates. Silas doesn't stop them, and neither do I. But it seems strange that there's no lock.

"Hope they've got the kettle on," Maude says. "I could do with a cuppa."

The lane is overgrown with weeds and peppered in old bicycles and broken glass bottles, but on either side is a low, sturdy brick wall that looks newly built. Silas has taken the lead again, and I stick close to him.

Suddenly a disembodied voice punctures the silence. "Stop! The lane is protected with mines. One more inch and you'll lose a leg." Silas's right foot is suspended in the air. He tilts his weight into his left heel and steps back.

"We come as friends!" he calls out.

"Resistance," Dorian says.

"Friends don't need weapons. Throw down your guns," the voice calls out. We look at Silas for direction. "Put the guns down or we'll open fire!" the voice booms. Silas places his gun gently on the ground behind him and we all do the same. Instinctively I put my hands up.

And then we are surrounded. Each of the twenty or so soldiers who appear are wearing balaclavas, but, crucially, no airtanks. They leap onto the wall and aim their rifles at us.

A beefy soldier in a tight tank top, arms covered with black tattoos, all thorns and barbed wire, lowers his gun. "Who's in charge?" he wants to know.

Silas is, of course, but he doesn't step forward, not when any one of us might disagree.

"I'm the leader here. Kneel before me, minion," Maude says, and cackles. I shoot her a warning look; somehow I don't think this guy is going to find her entertaining.

"*He* is," Dorian says. He points at Silas. I can't tell if he's being cowardly or magnanimous.

"Yeah?" The tattooed leader jumps down from the wall. He doesn't seem to notice the cold. The others, dressed in green fatigues, stay where they are, still aiming for our heads. "Well, you're trespassing."

"We're from The Grove. We're fellow Resistance," Silas says.

The man laughs. "Resistance and gasping for air?" Dorian pulls off his mask and leaves it hanging around his neck. I elbow Song, who quickly follows Dorian's lead. "So what? Some of you can breathe. Maybe Petra's methods have improved, but you're wrong about us. We aren't Resistance. We want nothing to do with you people." He peels back his balaclava, stuffs it into his back pocket, and crosses his muscled arms in front of his chest. He is handsome, despite a dark scar down one side of his face. But he knows it: he looks at me and cocks his head to one side. I swallow hard and wait for him to look away.

"The Grove's gone," Silas says.

"You're lying," he says.

"It was destroyed by the Ministry. We have nowhere else to go," Silas says, and a mild feeling of shame rises in me as I realize how weak we must seem.

"This isn't a refugee camp. There were hundreds of you at The Grove. We haven't the space. I suggest you turn around and tell Petra the answer is no."

Silas drops his head. Dorian and Song exchange a look. Maude and Bruce shrivel into themselves. I step forward, and the man doesn't warn me to stop. He raises one eyebrow. "We aren't envoys. Petra's dead, her people are dead, and the trees are gone. We're all that's left." I feel the others watching me. Was I wrong to say what happened out loud?

The man is silent. He puts a finger to his ear and nods. "The landmines have been deactivated," he says. He has an earpiece in—he isn't the leader at all. The other soldiers, all carrying guns, jump down from the walls and surround us, retrieving our weapons from the ground.

"Get your manky hands off my gear!" Maude screeches, but the soldier taking her gun rams her in the ribs with it. She lets out a yelp.

Silas's eyes widen. "Tell your goons to behave properly," he says.

But the man smirks. "And why would I do that?" He looks at my airtank and then into my eyes, the only part of my face not covered with the mask, and I can tell he's unimpressed by my need for it.

"We aren't useless. We're all well trained," Song says. "I'm a biochemist. I can help create a storage system for oxygen."

"You only need one skill here," the man says. He steps forward and pulls my mask away from my face. Silas only has to flinch and a soldier cocks his rifle to stop him from intervening. The man holds me by the chin and pulls me closer. I hold his stare, refusing to be intimidated, and he smiles and replaces my mask, gently pulling the straps tight at the back of my head. I take a long, deep breath from my dwindling air supply.

"Let's go and find out what Vanya wants to do with you," the man says.

Dorian is the first to follow, but the rest of us hang back, exchanging glances.

"Did we come to the right place?" I ask under my breath.

"We came to the only place left," Silas reminds me.

We round a bend in the lane and a wall appears. Although the bricks are old, the wall itself isn't mossy or crumbling or threatening to collapse. It looks newly constructed, the cement cleanly holding the bricks together and the wall itself topped with broken pieces of multicolored broken glass to prevent anyone scrambling over the top. At each corner of the wall is a camera tracing our movements as we file under an archway protected by steel doors and a batch of armed guards. "Coming through," the tattooed man says, and the guards heave open the screeching doors.

Inside I expect to see an old prison or school or hospital, but Sequoia is none of these things: it is a giant white palace, virtually unspoiled, and sandwiched between two gleaming conservatories. A dry fountain adorned with flying copper angels sits before it, and swirling here and there are orderly pebbled pathways and edgings. Most of the Palladian windows in the palace still have glass in them, and those that don't are covered in plywood painted over in white, so they blend in with the building. It looks nothing like the heaps of rubble in the city, and for a moment I am transported to what it must have been like before the Switch. Despite this, I don't feel like smiling. Something's missing.

I elbow Silas. "No trees," I say. A burning rises in my throat. I cough and hold on to him to stop myself from collapsing.

"Dorian, your tank," Silas calls out, holding me up. My empty airtank is unbuckled from my belt and replaced with another. Within seconds, I'm alive again. I blink at Silas. "Why didn't you say you were low?" he chides. I shrug, and he rolls his eyes.

Most of the soldiers are smirking, standing waiting for us between two undamaged colonnades. "Come on," Silas says.

We're ushered up stone steps, through a pair of wooden doors into a cavernous foyer, and whisked up several flights of stairs decorated with faded, gold-framed oil portraits. Although the exterior of the building is virtually undamaged, inside is cold, with damp patches shining like fresh bruises on the ceiling.

When we reach the top floor, the tattooed man flips open a box attached to the wall and pulls out a retractable mask. He presses it to his face and inhales. He sees me watching. "We've installed oxyboxes all over the compound. Pure oxygen," he says. "Saves on pumping into each room."

"What about those who can't breathe on a limited supply?" I ask, my hands fingering my airtank.

"We've not many like that here," he says, and passes the mask to another soldier.

The hallway is long and lined with doors. Above each,

is a sign: *Meditation Room 6 – Yoga Room 10 – Testing 1 – Testing 2 – Dispensary – Propagation.* I tug on Silas's coat and point. He nods. Although we haven't seen their trees, rooms like this imply that what they do is not all that different to what we did at The Grove. We might be safe here.

The man waves away the soldiers still accompanying us when we get to a set of doors at the end of the hallway. Then he frowns. "Try not to piss her off," he says.

The room is lit by natural light filtering through vast casement windows, and in front of them, stretched out on a scuffed, velvet daybed, is a slim woman with short hair that looks like she's haphazardly cut it herself. She's wearing a plain black shirt and wide-legged pants.

She looks up from a retro pad she's reading and lazily rolls onto her side. "Maks," she says, greeting the tattooed man. She stretches her arms to the ceiling, then slowly stands. "What a medley of mortals."

Maks laughs. "Understatement," he says.

The woman, Vanya, stops in front of Silas. "Hi," she says, drawing her finger down his face. He looks away. "Do tell me you don't need this thing," she says, tipping her nails against his airtank. Her hands are lined, though her face is smooth and clear.

"They do," Maks says. He's standing behind me and places a hand on my shoulder. "We almost lost this one a few minutes ago." I wriggle but his hand remains where it is.

"Well, we don't use tanks here," she says. "We're close to needing nothing whatsoever."

"*I* don't use one," Dorian says. His face is awash with pride, and if he were standing closer, I'd kick him. We all had our roles within the Resistance. Silas's and mine were in the pod. It isn't our fault we need so much supplemental air.

"I been suckin' in fake air for fifty years, and no one's gonna make me give it up now. I am what I am, and I ain't ashamed of it," Maude pipes up.

Vanya's nostrils flare. "Drifters?"

"Actually, I'm a catwalk model," Maude says. She wiggles her hips.

"And what are we meant to do with them?" Vanya speaks to Maks through clenched teeth. He removes his hand from my shoulder, and I relax enough to check the gauge on the airtank and adjust the levels.

"They'd make excellent benefactors," Maks says. I have no idea what this means, no one does, but we don't ask. Instead we listen.

Vanya sniffs and looks at me from top to bottom like I'm something about to be sold. Rather than fighting it, I stand tall and clench my jaw to prove how strong I am. I must be desperate.

"We want to join you. Help you," Silas says.

She puts her hand on his chest. "That sounds lovely," she says. Maks snickers. Silas blushes. He looks everywhere but at Vanya. "But once you join, I won't let you leave," Vanya says. Her hand rests on his chest, but she looks at each of us in turn to make sure we understand that she is addressing all of us. She might be teasing Silas, but beneath the flirting is serious distrust. And I hadn't expected anything less. Petra would never have welcomed newcomers without first threatening to kill them. When you live in fear of your world being destroyed, you have to be merciless.

"We're happy to stay," Dorian says.

Vanya smiles and steps away from Silas. "I'll have Maks escort you to one of our cabins as a temporary measure. Tomorrow we'll get to know each other a bit better."

"Of course," Dorian says. Silas squints at him. His bootlicking is beyond irritating—it's dangerously close to disloyalty.

"But tell me: Did anyone else survive at The Grove?"

My stomach hardens. The room is silent. We shake our heads and look to the floor. Holly survived, but no one will mention her.

"We *told* 'em to leave," Maude says. "We warned 'em. No one can say as we didn't." This is true, though it doesn't make us feel any better, and I want to tell Maude to keep quiet.

"You're *sure* no one else made it out?" Vanya asks.

"The whole place fell in on itself and was foaming the last time we saw it. We waited as long as we could," Silas says.

"I'm sure you did," Vanya says. She turns her back on us.

"This way," Maks says, and we are led out and along the hallway. Maks marches ahead, leaving a gap between him and us.

"At least they're letting us stay," I say.

Within seconds, Song is between Silas and me. "Do you know who that was?" he whispers.

"Shh," Dorian says. He points at Maks.

"Who?" I whisper.

"Vanya is Petra's sister."

"Her sister?" I say. I didn't know she had one.

"Vanya made wild threats, then disappeared. Walked into The Outlands and never came back. We weren't even allowed to mention her name."

"What are you lot whispering about?" Maks asks. He stops and waits for us to catch up.

"I was admiring your tush, sweetheart," Maude says. She winks at Maks. And we all laugh far too loudly, trying to cover up our doubt and panic. Why didn't Vanya mention it? And why did she flee The Grove in the first place?

11
QUINN

I stand beneath a rotten awning to get out of the rain for a minute and pull out the map. From the look of it, Sequoia is more than one hundred miles from St. Pancras, and I've walked less than half that. It's only been a handful of days, and I'm already completely knackered. *And* I've used far too much oxygen. Jazz said I should follow the river as far as Henley, then take the old roads, which is easier said than done. In their search for The Grove, the Ministry has had their way with the whole bloody city, and the route along the river is blocked every few miles by fresh mounds of rubble.

What was I thinking? Bea's got no one except me, and I just up and leave her. Now I'm alone, and Bea's practically alone, and I've no way of knowing when we'll see each other again.

The awning creaks under the weight of the water collecting in one corner, and I quickly step into the rain to avoid getting dumped on. The road's narrow, dark, and most of the buildings have been demolished. In the dust are the marks of tank treads. I kick a sneaker lying in the road, pull up the collar on my coat, and move on.

I round a bend and where the road should continue is a massive stack of rotting cars and trucks. I've no choice but to climb, using the car windows and wing mirrors as footholds. I slip and slide on the wet vehicles and when I reach the top, I'm relieved to see that the way ahead is clear and the river is in sight.

And then something moves.

Not one thing—two.

Two people.

They stop abruptly and look in my direction. I claw my way down the other side, catching my hand on a piece of jagged metal as I duck out of sight. The gash isn't wide, but it's deep. I wipe it on my trousers, and with nothing on me to use to clean it, I lift my facemask and spit onto the wound. It stings like hellfire. I curl my hand into a fist to stop myself from shouting. "Shit," I say aloud.

I turn left toward the river, then scoot along it. As I get to a break in the embankment, flanked on either side by what must have once been stone lions, I stop. Steps lead to a jetty and tied to the jetty is a rowboat. It isn't big, and isn't new, but it's floating.

I don't wait around. I sprint down the steps.

The boat is tied up with a frayed piece of rope, the oars are in the hull, and other stuff is scattered on the floor: a flask and an airtank, a sleeping bag, a pair of socks, a gun.

Further along the bankside an identical boat has been tied up. So if they see me, they'll have a way to follow, and there could be a gun in that boat, too. Either way, I need to protect myself. I jump into the boat, and it rocks and bangs against the jetty, water lapping the sides. I sit down to stop myself from getting tipped into the river, grab the handgun, and stuff it into my coat. I open my backpack and shove the sleeping bag into it.

And I freeze because I hear footsteps. And then I see a girl, her head bobbing above the wall along the embankment.

She darts down the steps, and when she sees me, she turns and shouts, "By my boat!" As she reaches the bottom step, she trips and lands in a heap at the foot of them.

I untie the rope tethering the boat to the dock. "No!" the girl pleads. "Wait!" She's hunched over holding her belly. She pushes her hair out of her eyes and struggles to stand up. I begin to row. It's harder than it looks; the current on the river is strong. "I need the airtank," she says. She's already wearing one, so I keep rowing. Is she mad? Who wouldn't need it?

"Please," she sobs. She yanks open her coat. Her belly is round. She's no more than sixteen, with large, glassy eyes. Her coat's soaked through and her hair is stuck to her cheeks. I can't steal from a pregnant girl. I'm not that low.

"You're with someone," I say. She nods and glances over her shoulder. I don't know whether or not I can trust her, but I stop rowing, and the current drags me back to land. I throw her the rope and, straining, she pulls the boat into dock.

"Thank you," she says as a tall guy about my age appears at the top of the steps. He's not wearing an airtank and is panting desperately. I throw the tank in the boat to him as he approaches. He catches it, puts the mask to his face and inhales a few times. His bottom lip is swollen, and he has two black eyes. He looks like the kind of person Silas might team up with.

"Get out of the boat," he says.

I don't take any chances: I put my hand inside my coat, resting it on the gun. "Are you Resistance?" I ask.

"Get out of the boat," he repeats. I reach for a post, keeping one hand on the gun, and pull myself onto the jetty.

"I'm heading west," I say.

"Where are you going? You don't look like a drifter. And you don't look like Resistance either," the girl says. She probably means I look pampered.

"I'm heading to a place called Sequoia," I say.

The girl stares, and without waiting to find out more, the boy reaches into his jacket and pulls out a handgun. I don't know what to do, so I grab the gun from my own coat and point it at the girl, which is a stupid thing to do. I'm obviously not going to shoot her. "No need for any of this," I say.

"Who *are* you?" he snarls.

"Quinn," I say. "I've left my girlfriend alone in the city with a dying child. I need to find a doctor."

"How do you know about Sequoia?"

"Someone from The Grove told me about it," I say.

"Are we going to kill each other?" the girl says, and stands between us.

"Get out of the way, Jo," the boy snaps. I think he might really kill me, if he had to.

"We're going to Sequoia, too. You can come with us." She turns to the boy and gestures for him to lower his gun, but he doesn't. "He should come with us," she repeats.

"Your purple tattoo," the boy says. "You're Premium scum."

I touch my earlobe. "I was," I say, and put the gun into my coat pocket. "They think I'm dead."

"Yeah?" he says. "They think I'm dead, too." Jo steps aside as he finally puts his gun away and begrudgingly holds out his hand. "I'm Abel," he says.

PART II
THE CHOICE

12
ALINA

A hard knock on the cabin door wakes me. I roll off the bunk and open it.

"Sleep well?" Maks says. He looks at my bare feet and allows his eyes to travel the length of my body. If anyone else did this, I'd throw a punch. But Maks is huge. And we're guests.

"I slept fine." I cross my arms over my chest, and stare right back at him.

He looks behind me at the others. "Vanya's ordered breakfast. She wants you to join her. No need to bring the golden oldies. Can you remember the way to her suite?"

"Yes," I say, even though everything about yesterday is a blur. Maks leaves, and I quickly shut the door to keep out the cold.

"What a meathead," Silas says, sitting up in his bunk and stretching.

And soon everyone's up. Dorian and Song spend a few minutes each on the oxyboxes while Silas and I lower the density of oxygen in our tanks.

"Why ain't *we* wanted?" Maude complains. "You're gonna get back 'ere and find us boiling in a pot. I hope you like the taste of bunions."

"She probably doesn't trust drifters," I say. "She griped about it yesterday. But you're with us, and we'll let her know that. Don't worry." Maude cuts her eyes at me. Bea's the one she trusted because Bea's the one who saved her. But if she knew me, she'd know she can trust me, too, now we're on the same side—I'd never betray a comrade.

We follow a pebbled path from the cabin to the back of the main house. A guard talks into a radio then waves us through, and once inside, we let Silas lead us along darkened hallways and up a flight of stairs until he stops and points. "I'm pretty sure it's those doors," he says, and is about to speak again when a muffled scream roots us to the spot.

The hairs rise on my arms. "What was that?" I say.

"Upstairs," Song whispers.

"Shh, just listen." I hope that what comes next is a laugh,

or better yet, nothing at all. But another scream rings out—louder and longer.

"We have to see where it's coming from," Silas says.

"We can't go snooping wherever we want," Dorian says.

"You think we should ignore it?" Silas steps up to him.

I put a hand on each of their arms; we can't come apart now. "It might be nothing," I tell Silas. "But we should check just in case," I say, turning to Dorian.

They both nod, and we all follow the scream up another set of stairs. At the top I gently try a few unyielding doorknobs until I find one that gives. Behind is a narrow staircase. "I'll keep watch down here," Dorian says.

At the top, we step into a tapering hallway, dark apart from a sliver of light at the end. We tiptoe toward it, and there's another scream. When we reach the door, we pause.

"Do we want to know?" Song whispers. Of course I don't want to know. I want Sequoia to be a haven. A home. But I grasp the handle and turn it slowly.

A guttural scream greets us. And a sweating girl sitting up in bed wearing a white gown. When she sees us, she pushes her hair from her eyes and leans forward, squinting as though she isn't sure how real we are. She is wearing a facemask and breathes out short, sharp breaths. On the other side of the room, a man has his back to us. He didn't hear us come in, and the girl doesn't alert him. The room is clean and bright, empty apart from her bed and a counter top.

The girl rolls onto her side, grasps her stomach, and grunts.

"Count the time between the contractions," the man says calmly, never turning around.

"Give me something for the pain," she begs, and that's when we take off. Without firmly shutting the door, we careen down the hallway and almost land in a heap at the bottom of the stairs.

"Well?" Dorian says.

Silas examines the ground. He looks like he might faint. And the girl in labor screams again.

When we finally reach Vanya's room, she looks at the clock on the mantelpiece. "We don't encourage sleeping in," she says, her voice husky. Maks is sitting in a pink armchair. He is looking only at me. I stand straight.

"We got lost," Silas says.

"Well, you're here now." Vanya gestures toward a table piled with food, and we sit and eat. There isn't the variety there was at The Grove—no fruit or bread—but there are plenty of synthetic dishes and a variety of cooked potatoes. I spoon a heap of what looks like singed twigs and bark into my mouth. It's salty with plenty of crunch.

Vanya smiles. "You like? That's something we're particularly proud of," she says.

"Protein," Maks adds.

"We found a few scurrying around in the kitchen and now we have thousands and thousands," Vanya says. "We farm them in a cabin near to yours . . . cockroaches." I cough and almost choke. I have never eaten a living creature before. I should be disgusted, but I can't help rolling the bug around in my mouth in amazement, and trying to conjure up an image of what the creature would look like alive. Does it have eight legs? Wings?

"They survived?" Song says. He picks up a cockroach between his fingers and chews on it.

"*We* survived," Vanya says. She is at the head of the table and Maks is at the opposite end, next to me. His foot presses against mine, and my muscles tighten. "Was the cabin comfortable?" Vanya asks. We nod. "And when you got lost, I presume you got to see a few things."

"Not much," Silas says. "But I hope we can help here, or at the very least learn to fit in."

"I think you'll be a wonderful addition," Vanya says, and touches Silas's face. When she sits back, she puts a finger into her mouth like she can taste him.

Silas's neck flushes, but he doesn't object to Vanya's flirting, just like he never objected to Petra's temper and violence.

At The Grove, we all learned how to defer to a leader.

"Why do you need that?" Vanya asks, pointing at my airtank. Now I'm the one whose face burns. Even though it isn't my fault, I'm ashamed for needing so much air. I look into my plate. "Silas and I lived in the pod and smuggled out plant clippings. They still pump at thirty-five percent, so we need a bit longer to adjust," I say.

Vanya sips a glass of water and eyes me mistrustfully. But I'm eyeing her, too. Where are the trees? And why has no one mentioned there's a girl here giving birth as we speak? Isn't it something to celebrate? I have a horrible feeling there's more to Sequoia than Vanya wants us to know. "And what percentage are you at now?" she asks.

"Twelve," Silas says.

I look at my gauge, which is at fourteen percent. "Twelve," I say.

Vanya tuts. "Reduce it to ten. If you feel dizzy, use the oxyboxes. You've seen them?"

"How do they work?" Song asks.

"We didn't have them at The Grove, you see," Dorian adds.

"I'm fully aware of what you had and didn't have at The Grove," Vanya says, and sits back in her chair. "Don't pretend you don't recognize me, Dorian, because I recognize you. You were infatuated with Petra back then—thought she was some kind of deity. And all she was doing was making love to trees. Pathetic."

Anger burns in me. Growing trees wasn't some hobby; it was the key to freedom—to survival. I am about to tell Vanya as much, when I sense Silas's eyes on me. He shakes his head so slightly you'd have to be watching for a sign to even notice. I keep my mouth shut.

Dorian sets down his knife and fork and wipes his hands on his pants. "We thought you died, Vanya," he says.

"Do I look dead?" she purrs.

"No."

"So, tell me, was Petra still prohibiting relationships?" Silas nods. "What a drag!" Vanya raises her glass in the air and laughs. "How will the human race endure if we do that?" She is chuckling, her mouth a wide grin, but there's something quite serious in her tone.

"Why did you leave us?" Song asks.

"It's complicated. Families always are," she says. "And I'd tell you everything except I have no guarantee you're not here as spies. There's a chance The Grove is still standing and my sister has sent you here to steal my people. Or maybe you're here to kill me."

If only, I think.

Silas lowers his head. "I assure you, The Grove is gone," he says slowly.

"Well, I'd like to check. Can you do that for me, Maks?"

Maks pours himself a drink and waves it at us, almost spilling it. "And what will we do with them in the meantime?"

Vanya rubs her temples as though overcome by tiredness. "Start by giving them iron, immunity pills, and a boost of rockets."

"Rockets?" Song asks.

"Oh, Petra would never have approved. Rockets will increase the number of red blood cells and reduce your need for so much oxygen," Vanya explains.

"EPOs," Song says.

Silas glances at me for less than a second, but it is long enough for Maks to notice. "They aren't optional," he says.

Vanya stands up and steps away from the table. "Okay, take them to the clinic for testing," she says, her back to us.

"What are the tests for?" Silas asks.

"Membership tests," Maks says. He grins, but it is shallow. He stands up. "Ready?" he asks.

We aren't, but it isn't a question.

13
BEA

Three pebbles, a bottle cap, a metal badge, and a hair clip. Each makes a hollow clink as I drop it back into the fountain. Six things, but I'm sure we've been here longer than six days. Did I forget to count off a day? Did I sleep through a couple?

All Jazz wants to do is doze, and she's stopped eating.

I return to her side, where I kneel and touch her forehead. She's burning up worse than ever, and I've no way to keep her temperature down apart from pressing cold clothes against her skin. I can't bear to examine her leg. Last time I checked it was swelling. If the infection gets into her bloodstream, there'll be nothing I can do. How long does that take to happen? A week? Longer? Or has it already happened?

Her lips part. "Is Quinn back?" she asks.

I stroke her cheek with the back of my fingers and keep my voice sunny. "Quinn's always late, but he'll be here. You concentrate on resting." She stares up at me and twists her mouth—she's a child, not a fool. "Can I do anything for you?" I ask.

"Some of that medicine," she says, and points to the bottle of alcohol I've been using to sedate her.

"I have this," I say, and break off a piece of a nutrition bar, which I try to press between her lips. She shakes her head, so I reach for the bottle. She takes a mouthful and grimaces. It doesn't taste nice, but it's keeping her calm.

I look across at the fountain. If I missed a few days, maybe we'll be rescued soon.

Please God or Earth, or whatever else is out there, let us be rescued soon.

Please.

14
QUINN

After sleeping for a few restless hours, we get up with the dawn and head for Sequoia. Jo and I row one boat while Abel rows the other. We're fighting against the current and the wind and after only an hour my arms burn like hell, not to mention the hand I cut on the stack of cars yesterday. My pants are soaked from the rain and slosh of river water coming into the boat, and I'm barely resisting the temptation to ask how much farther we have to go, when Abel calls out, "Over there!" He points to a dock and Jo waves to show she's heard.

Abel ties up his own boat then pulls us in. Jo steps ashore first and arches her back and groans. "I'm so sore," she says.

"Thought I was the only one flagging," I say, climbing out of the boat.

"The wind's too strong. It'll be easier to walk," Abel says.

The city is shrinking and fewer of the buildings here have been bombed by the Ministry's rampage over the past few weeks.

"I remember where we are," Jo says. Her face clearly betrays the fact that we're nowhere near Sequoia, and I'm no closer to getting help for Jazz and Bea.

Abel jumps back into his boat and throws his supplies onto the dock.

"Why are you both so far from home?" It's the first thing I've asked, and considering the questions whirring in my head, it's a pretty timid one.

"I was on a mission," Abel admits matter-of-factly. "A spy. Didn't turn out quite as planned."

"You were spying on the pod?" I ask.

"The Resistance, but I was in the pod. I was hoping to get into The Grove, but got caught and almost beaten to death by the Ministry." He touches his bruised face and glances at the tattoo on my earlobe without changing his expression. "If it hadn't been for the rioting I probably would've died. The place was chaos, so some big shot threw me out a back door expecting I'd suffocate." He looks at Jo, and she smiles. It feels good to know that at least one person benefitted from the rioting, and I have an urge to tell him I was responsible. But too many other people died because of what I did, so I keep quiet.

"I ran away from Sequoia," Jo says without being asked. "I was looking for The Grove and so was Abel once he got out. We met there. In the ruins. I'd heard about what Petra was trying to do. I'm sorry she's gone." I don't tell her that Petra was a mad bitch.

"So Sequoia's the next best thing," I say.

"It's a thing," Jo says, her voice flat.

Abel steps onto the dock again, opens a compartment in his backpack, and takes out a protein bar that he breaks into pieces and shares with us.

"Did you leave because of . . ." I point at her stomach. She looks down at herself.

"Sort of."

"Shall we go?" Abel says.

We move along the dock, up a short road, and find ourselves surrounded by hundreds of rusting cars positioned in perfect rows and columns. We weave our way through until we come out onto another, wider road, clear but for the odd fallen lamppost or overturned truck. Abel picks up his speed. Jo and I follow slowly.

"Is Abel the baby's father?" I ask, when I'm sure he can't hear.

"Abel? No." She inhales deeply. "The father's in Sequoia. He's kind of vile."

"A lot of dads are," I say.

Jo comes to an abrupt halt and seizes my arm. "It isn't a joke. If you cross Maks, he'll kill you."

She releases me and walks on, linking arms with Abel. I watch, feeling a bit jealous that they have each other.

I miss Bea.

15
RONAN

The road is slush, strewn with cement blocks, sheets of broken glass, and misshapen metal poles. I would take pictures to use in a piece, but it isn't exactly the time or place to be worrying about art.

When Jude drove off, I took a moment to enjoy the solitude. I've never been alone before. Not truly. And I liked it: the feeling of space and freedom and sky. In the pod you're never far from other people—a breath away. But those feelings are already wearing thin, and it's only been a day. The reality is that The Outlands isn't a haven for peace—it's a graveyard. There's nothing but human bones and the remnants of death everywhere: rotting mattresses, chipped teapots, dried-up pens, and shriveled tree stumps.

The idea of hiding out here forever is foolish. How would

I breathe once my airtanks ran out? What would I eat? Who would I talk to? I'd go mad or be dead within a couple of months.

So I'm searching for Quinn because the only option left is to take Jude up on his offer—find his son and become an auxiliary.

It'll be better than death.

It has to be better than death.

Doesn't it?

16
ALINA

The nurse I've been sent to see is so tall and thin she looks like she's been stretched. Even her nose is unusually long. She hands me a cup of water and three tablets: one white cylinder and two tiny red eggs. "Take these," she orders.

"What are they?"

"Mandatory, that's what they are," she says.

I swig some water, pretending to swallow the tablets but hiding them under my tongue, and as the nurse turns, I spit them into my hand and stuff them into my pocket.

"Up here," she says. I climb onto a table and lie down. She ties a rubber band around my arm and hands me a ball. "Squeeze this." She taps the inside of my elbow a few times, and before I can react to what's happening, sticks me with a needle. I jump but bite away the urge to squawk. "Stop wriggling," she snaps as she unties the rubber band and fills a vial with blood.

Once she's got five vials, she spins around, her rubber-soled shoes squeaking against the floor, and stores my blood in a rack in the fridge. Then she reaches into a cupboard and pulls out a tiny bottle of clear liquid.

"Time for your rocket." She shakes the bottle, presses a syringe into the lid, and lifts the needle to the light, tapping it a few times with her finger. She studies a droplet of clear liquid rolling into the tip. We've been told this shot contains EPO, which will increase our number of red blood cells and drive down our need for oxygen. That's the opposite effect from the vaccinations we were required to take in the pod, but I don't care. I don't want to be injected with anything. Not here. Not anywhere.

I consider resisting, and the nurse, sensing it, looks at me over the rim of her spectacles. "Problem?" She dabs my arm with alcohol. I close my eyes, and she jabs me with the needle.

I think we're finished, and lift myself onto my elbows, but I'm wrong. The nurse smiles and tosses me a rough blanket. "Take off your pants and underwear and put this over your lap. I'll be back in a minute." She closes the door and is gone. I look down at the blanket and then at a string of unfamiliar metal implements lying on the counter. I stand up and pace the tiny lab.

The idea of someone examining me down below is humiliating in more ways than one. Not only am I terrified to let the nurse look at me and insert things into me or scratch things away, but my hair smells like someone's been sick into it, and when I took off my boots last night, my feet stank—I can't even imagine what the rest of me smells like.

I'm not a crier, but for the first time in a very long time, my eyes prickle. I rub at them roughly and when this doesn't work, I slap myself sharply across the face. It stings, which is what I need. "Get a grip, Alina," I say aloud.

I kick my boots into the corner of the room and stare down at my baggy, damp socks, which I leave on, climbing out of my pants and underwear and throwing them next to the boots. As the door opens, I jump up onto the table, covering my legs with the blanket.

The nurse quickly grabs a facemask from the counter, which she slips over her mouth and nose. It isn't attached to any airtank; it's to protect me from germs, though she's probably wearing it to protect herself.

She sits on a stool and releases a set of stirrups hidden in the table up and out. "Put your feet in these and lie on your back."

"What's this for?" I ask. "I mean, the blood sample will tell you everything you need to know. I'm not carrying a disease if that's what you think. I lived in the pod, you know."

We have regular health checks there. I'm clean."

The nurse grimaces. "I'd hardly say you're clean. Lie down."

I stay sitting. "What's it *for?*"

She tuts. "Shall I get Vanya to come in and explain? Maks?"

I shake my head. What if they decided to stay and watch over the exam? No.

I lie back. "Shift your butt to the end of the table," the nurse says, jabbing something against my tummy, rolling it back and forth while she stares at a screen. She lifts the blanket and yanks my knees apart. "You're going to feel some pressure," she says, but it isn't pressure—it's pain, like I'm been sliced open. I clutch the sides of the table and hum. *You're okay*, I tell myself. *This is not going to kill you.*

After a few moments, she switches off the screen, pulls the blanket over my legs, and lowers the stirrups. "Get up now."

I stagger as I stand, using the blanket like a kind of skirt, and lean against the counter, my head between my arms. It's a peculiar feeling, this weakness, and I don't like it.

"When did your cycle begin?" She unpeels the rubber gloves from her hands and tosses them in the trash can. I'm tempted to lie, because it's none of her damn business, but

I don't know what these tests are for, or what the consequences of the results will be. So I tell the truth. "Nine days ago," I say.

She nods. "And how many days did it last?"

"Six," I say.

She records the dates on an ancient-looking pad and opens the door. "Go to Room 28. Down the hall, take your first left, and it's the fourth door on the right." She yawns, revealing a mouth of missing teeth. "Do you want a napkin for the blood?"

"Get lost," I say, slamming the lab door, and hurtling down the hall and away.

As I turn left, I almost collide with Maks. He towers over me, his arms crossed over his chest to accentuate the size of his biceps. "Done with your medical?"

My face reddens. "Yes."

He presses his lips together into a taut smile and tucks a loose strand of my hair behind my ear. I flinch, then hate myself for being so easily discomforted by him.

"Well, that's the worst test over with. Well done for making it through." I can't tell if he's being sarcastic. He rubs my chin, smiles, and marches away. From behind I can see he has a pistol tucked into the waistband of his trousers, and I don't like it.

We have surrendered our weapons.

I peer through the round window of Room 28. Silas, Dorian, and Song are sitting at desks. I slink inside and they all turn around. "What are we doing in here?" I ask.

"A written exam of some kind," Silas says.

"Well, it's better than getting another medical," Dorian says impassively.

"I'm nervous we're being recorded," Silas says.

Song rises and examines the walls, baseboards, and each desk. "Hard to tell," he says.

"You okay?" Silas asks.

I wring my hands. "I'm fine."

"Did you do everything they asked?" Silas says.

"Yes. Except swallow the tablets." I pat my pocket and stare at the floor. "Anyway, what happened to you?"

Silas, Dorian, and Song look at one another. "I don't know what they do here, but it isn't what we were doing at The Grove," Silas says. Song is still checking under each chair and fiddles with the electrical sockets and oxybox. "They wanted *samples*," Silas continues. My mouth drops open. He doesn't have to say any more. After the physical exam I was given, it wouldn't take a genius to guess what kinds of samples he means.

"How could we do it?" Song says. "Not on demand."

"I did it," Dorian admits, unabashed.

"What?" Silas says.

"We said we'd cooperate, so I was cooperating." He scratches his nose.

"*Cooperating?*" Silas clenches his jaw, working hard to control his temper. He roughly scratches his head.

"Where are we meant to go if we get chucked out? Petra threw everyone in a cell for a few weeks. Is this that much different?" he says.

"The nurse gave me a pretty thorough exam," I murmur. I can't look at any of the boys.

Silas groans. "Oh, Alina," he says.

"It must be for some sort of genetic testing," I say.

Song shakes his head. "You can work out genetics using blood samples, and they've got plenty of those."

"Then what is it they want?" I ask.

Song inhales deeply through his nose. "I think"—he pauses—"I think they're checking to see how fertile we are."

17
BEA

After going back up to the pharmacy and rummaging on the floor for almost an hour, I find some ancient painkillers, and although I have no idea whether or not they're working, I shovel them into Jazz every six hours. Even in her sleep, she moans softly.

"Am I going to die?" she mewls, waking at last.

"Of course you aren't, silly," I say, which is probably a lie. Even if Quinn finds his way to Sequoia, he has to get back here and by then it'll have been weeks since Jazz's fall.

And what scares me most is that as each day passes, my hope wanes a little more, when hope is the only thing I have to hold on to.

There was nothing I could do for my parents just as there's nothing I can do for Jazz. I try not to remember their bodies lying limp on the makeshift platform, blood blooming beneath them while the crowd stormed the stage. All I could do was watch on Old Watson's screen, so far away from where I was needed. At least I'm here for Jazz. And I have to be strong for her and wait until the worst happens . . . or a miracle.

I cradle Jazz's head in my lap and hum a doleful tune; I can't remember any happy ones. It's to calm her, but it's for me, too, because if I don't hum, I'll cry, and Jazz shouldn't have to see that.

"Are you sleepy?" she asks, peering up at me. I pull her head tight into my body—all the pain she's in and she's worried about me. "I'll be quiet so you can rest," she says, and clenches her jaw.

"I don't need to sleep," I tell her, one hand stroking her freckly face, the other hand clutching the knife. But my eyes sting from fatigue. My shoulders droop. My head feels so heavy. "Maybe I'll try to get a few minutes," I say.

"Bea!" Jazz's urgent whisper wakes me from a murky dream, which I forget as soon as I open my eyes.

"Are you okay?" I ask.

"I tried to move. I shouldn't have. It still hurts." She is sitting up and shivering. Her little hands are frozen.

"It's okay. Relax now," I tell her. I fumble for the pills. I was foolish to spend my life studying politics and philosophy, thinking *that* was the way to a better life, when I should have been learning how to survive in the real world. If only Alina were here. She'd know what to do, and Jazz might have a fighting chance.

Jazz nudges me and squeals. A yellow discharge is seeping from her wound. I bend down to get a better look. "No, Bea! Look!" I follow the line of her finger down her leg to her feet, across the tiled floor of the station to the other end, where a pair of boots appears.

A boy.

I rub my eyes in case I'm still in a dream. Then I grab the knife and jump up, slicing the air with it.

How much more am I meant to endure? When am I allowed to surrender? If it weren't for Jazz, I might drop the knife and do just that. As it is, I swing the knife again. "Get out of here."

"Let's talk," the boy says. "All I want to do is talk to you." Calmly, he unburdens himself of his backpack and holds his hands in the air. One hand is holding a gun.

Jazz screams in terror.

And so do I.

18
ALINA

As soon as we're done with the tests and back in the cabin, Maude hitches up her skirts. Her knees are bleeding and her hands are caked in mud. "What's your answer to this, smarty pants?"

"What happened?" I ask.

"What do you mean, what happened? Where were you all day?" Maude kicks me in the shin, and Bruce pulls her away before I retaliate. I don't want to fight anyway; I have a raging headache.

"It ain't her fault, Maddie," Bruce says. Maude removes her boots, hurling them at the wall and barely missing Silas.

"Didn't they test you?" Silas asks, rubbing his temples. We've spent the last four hours cooped up in that dingy room answering math, science, and logic questions as well as filling in surveys about our skills and hobbies. None of us are feeling very peppy.

Bruce sits on his bunk and rubs his dirty, bare feet. "Just after yous lot left, we was given gardening gloves and told to dig," he says.

"No medical testing?" Dorian asks.

"Of course not. Not if I'm right about what they want to know," Song says. I want him to be wrong about the fertility screening, but none of us can think of another explanation for the intimate medical exams.

"What do they wanna know? What's going on?" Maude squawks. "I don't wanna be no servant. The drifter life ain't easy, but at least we was free."

Maks throws open the door to the cabin without knocking. With the light at his back, only his bulky silhouette is clear. "Dinner," he says, stepping inside.

"They're exhausted," I say, indicating Maude and Bruce. "Why were they put to work? They should be meditating and training to breathe on lower levels of oxygen. Are you trying to kill them?"

Maks narrows his eyes. "If we wanted to kill them, we'd have them digging their own graves, not vegetable patches." Silas tugs on my sweater, warning me not to answer back because that's exactly what I'm about to do. Maks nods triumphantly and leaves.

"We should think about finding somewhere else to live," Silas says.

"You think she'll just let us walk out the way we came in? Petra wouldn't have."

Song takes a lungful of air from the oxybox. "And it's pretty well fortified here. They've used the old rubble and brick to build new structures. It's solid." He raps his knuckles against the wall of the cabin to demonstrate how sturdy it is.

"You know what's weird?" Bruce says. "No forest. We walked all round this compound today, probably five acres, and nothing."

"Not a single tree?" I ask. It doesn't make sense. "You probably missed them."

"Really? Oak trees and alders and whatnot? Yeah, cuz they're a cinch to hide," Maude says.

"Maybe they know trees will lead the Ministry here," Dorian says, buttoning up his jacket.

"Then where's the air coming from?" Song asks.

"Greenhouse," Maude says. "Big thing behind the annex. Some little trees in there, all right. Apples and pears and the like. But they got veggies mostly. And tomato vines."

"That won't be enough to make a difference," I say. The whole point in raging against the Ministry is to restore the earth to what it had been. Trees are a symbol of that, and also the only plants big enough to set people free. It might take us a millennium, but we have to start somewhere.

"I suggest we go to dinner and discuss this later," Dorian says. "They'll be waiting."

We all nod in agreement. It's best not to raise any suspicion just yet.

The red brick annex is newly built using old materials. We file in along with everyone else and choose seats around a long table as far from the stage at the front as possible. The tables are empty apart from cups and water jugs, but as we sit down, servers appear from swinging doors holding platters of food over their heads. No one joins us at first. They file into the hall in pairs and seem to take their places in predetermined seats. I'm about to stand up in case we're sitting where we shouldn't when a young man with long, curly hair sits next to me, and some girls join him.

"You found the loners' table then," the man says, and laughs. "I'm Terry." He holds out his hand. "You can take off the masks. They pump a little air in here so we can eat comfortably."

"Alina." I pull off my mask and take his hand.

Opposite sits a girl with thin eyebrows and icy blue eyes who introduces herself as Wren. A black scarf is tightly wound around her head, covering up her hair. "We've never had a whole group join us before. Always individuals. The rumor is The Grove's been destroyed. Is that true? You think others will follow you here?" she asks.

Maude reaches across the table and snatches a hunk of cake from a platter. Terry politely fills everyone's cup with water.

"I doubt it," Silas says. "They're all dead."

"Oh," Wren says, emptying her cup in one long gulp and reaching forward so Terry can refill it. "The Ministry wants us all dead, don't they? As I see it, our best bet is to finish them off first." Wren holds my gaze for a moment. Terry and the others at the table nod, and I do, too. If there were a way to get rid of the Ministry, I'd love to hear about it.

The dining hall falls to a hush, and as Vanya and Maks enter, everyone stands. Vanya takes her place at the center of a table on the stage and Maks sits by her side. He catches my eye across the room and winks. I pretend I haven't seen and focus on Vanya. "Here's to life!" she shouts. Everyone cheers as the remaining platters are distributed.

"We have to give thanks," Song says. He hasn't touched anything on his plate. Instead he's looking around, slightly horrified, as everyone tucks into the food on the platters.

"Just eat," Silas says.

"I'm not going twice in one day without giving thanks . . . or remembering," Song says.

"What's he mean?" Wren asks, giving me a prime view of the food she's chewing.

He means we have to remember where our food came from, but I don't think that's what's really worrying him. "We haven't forgotten Holly, you know." I place a hand on his arm and rub it gently. No one did this for me when Abel disappeared, and I wish they had; just a pat to tell me I wasn't alone.

"Song's right," Silas adds, softening. "We should keep our traditions alive."

"We thank the earth," Song says. I put down my knife and fork and Silas and Dorian do the same. Maude and Bruce are oblivious. Terry and Wren watch silently. "We thank the water. We thank the plants and trees—the roots, leaves, fruits, and flowers. We give thanks to one another. We give thanks to the spirits of all those who have died. We offer our devotion in the earth's name. We salute you." I hold my palms together in front of my heart and bow my head.

"So it is," we say.

"Is that voodoo or something?" Wren laughs.

"We acknowledge that nature has more power than we do," Dorian explains.

Terry wipes his mouth with the back of his hand. "But it's humanity at the center," he says. "Well, not humanity. Us. You."

"Do you know your pairings yet?" Wren asks. She licks her lips.

"Pairings?" I ask. I almost don't want to know.

"Wren!" Terry snaps, and as he does, a commotion at the top table has Vanya waving and shouting. "Troopers to the gates!" No one moves.

Maks leaps from the stage. "Troopers!" he bellows. "Weapons!" He dashes past our table and slams through the doors. Around fifty others scramble to their feet and gallop after him.

"What's happening?" Silas asks, jumping up.

"We must have more visitors," Terry says.

19

RONAN

I take slow steps through the station toward the girl wielding the knife and the hissing child, and try to examine their faces in the waning light.

I recognize Bea Whitcraft right away, even with her mask on. I don't know her personally, but I've seen her picture, and the word WANTED, flash up on the screen about a hundred times a day since the press conference.

They didn't show any video footage, of course. I had to ask the press secretary to send me that as a favor. I had to know how it happened, and what I saw was my father shoot Bea's parents in cold blood. So now they're saying she's a terrorist, though she looks more like a drifter.

On the floor are empty bottles and bloodstained rags.

"Can I help you?"

Bea swings the knife. "What do you want?"

"Who cares? Stab him," the child mutters. Her pallor is frightening, and she doesn't seem able to move from the floor. One leg of her pants is torn open, and blood has dried on the tiles around her. She's crying, and there are tear tracks down Bea's face, too.

"I won't hurt you," I tell them. "I heard noises, that's all. I came to look." Niamh complained about what she called Quinn's stupid attachment to Bea, which could mean that if I've found her, he's close by.

I stash the gun in my pocket and inch closer. Bea winces at each step, and when I'm near enough to touch her, she stiffens. "Get back," she says. She holds the knife inches from my face. Her eyes are wide with fear, exhaustion, or madness—maybe all three.

"The girl is very sick," I say. Gently, I push Bea's hand and the knife away from my face. But she swings it back toward me and presses the tip so hard against my neck, she nicks the skin. I'm not expecting it and jump back, wiping the blood. She holds her arm out farther and straighter. "I told you to *stay away*," she says.

I could easily wrench the knife from her, but if there's a chance she knows where Quinn is, I have to gain her trust. So instead, I step way back and pull a flashlight from my backpack, which I shine at the child's leg. It's red and swollen, the skin taut, and a long gash is yellow. My stomach lurches. Bea looks at me steadily.

"How long has she been like this?"

"I don't know. A week?" she says, her chin trembling. The child hasn't long left, not without real medical attention.

"I see," I say. I consider lying, but I have no reason to. "I can get her help. I'm Ronan Knavery."

She looks at my earlobe, then holds the knife up again. Her expression is hard. "Your father killed my parents," she spits. I can't deny this because I watched it again and again on the video footage, so I nod. But if she hates me just because of what my father did, there's no knowing how she'd react if she knew I was personally responsible for so much destruction at The Grove. The number of people and trees I cut down doesn't bear thinking about.

We watch each other, neither of us speaking, until she sniffs. "You look like your father," she says. People have told me this before, as a compliment, but she's insulting me. She clenches her jaw.

"I know," I say. "But I'm not him. And I'm really sorry for what happened to you." I speak quietly, gently, hoping she'll trust the sincerity in my tone.

"So I suppose you're here to bring me back and see me hanged."

"No. I'm looking for someone else."

Her features give nothing away. "We're all that's left."

I hold my breath. "From what?" I ask, when I know what she's going to say.

"From The Grove. A safe place that your father razed to the ground."

When we left The Grove, it was collapsing, but I'm sure I saw survivors fleeing. Did I imagine it to make myself feel better? Did we kill them *all*? The people *and* the trees?

And Quinn? Where is he?

Bea is studying me.

"Actually, *Quinn's* father was in charge of that mission," I say, watching for a reaction.

"Quinn?" the child murmurs through semiconsciousness, and Bea quickly hushes her.

So the child knows him, which could mean he's been here. And maybe he'll be back, although I can't be sure Jazz didn't meet him at The Grove when the Resistance supposedly captured them.

I root in my backpack and pull out a strip of penicillin, pressing one through the foil and holding out my hand. "Antibiotics." She looks at the pill in my palm, suspicious. "If I wanted to hurt her, I'd have used the gun," I say. "Now put away the knife . . . Please."

Still holding the knife, Bea reaches out with her other hand for the pill. I consider wrestling the knife off her.

I don't. I drop the pill into the pit of her palm and step away. She eases the girl into a sitting position and presses it between the child's lips, forcing her to sip some water from a flask. The child manages to take the pill before her eyes roll back in her head—she can't fight her fatigue.

We were warned about terrorists in training, and back then my mind filled with images of stocky, square-jawed youths wielding guns and throwing grenades. I didn't picture anything as pitiable as this: a child being eased into death by a hollow-cheeked girl fighting for her own breath on a dirty, solar-powered respirator.

"I can radio the pod," I say. I doubt Jude would help, but she's a child, and I should try. It's the least I can do after what I did to her home. Were her parents at The Grove? Were they killed?

"Touch any kind of radio and I'll cut you," Bea says.

I hold my hands in the air. "I understand," I say.

She erupts, jumping up and pushing me. "How dare you? You don't understand a thing!"

I stare at her and lean away. "My father died in the riots, too," I say.

"It's not the same thing. My parents were good. Your father was . . . he was . . ."

"He was an asshole," I say, and she blinks. I pause. I don't want to say something untrue. "But I *wish* I loved him more."

Her eyes well with tears. "When people leave, you always wish you'd loved them more." She wipes her eyes and sniffs. And then she is sobbing and pressing her face against her arm to stifle the noise.

I've never been able to cry like this. My mother spent long days in bed, coughing and moaning, until one morning she was gone and the noise was replaced by silence. I cried only once—quietly and alone in my room. Why didn't I honor her by mourning?

I delve back into my pack and pull out the radio. Bea looks up. "No," she says, starting toward me again.

"If she doesn't get to a hospital, you'll be digging a grave."

"They'll kill her."

"She's dying anyway."

Bea chews on her lips.

I stand up and walk away.

"Where are you going?" she asks.

"She could wake up and cry out while I'm making contact. I want them to think I've found the person I'm meant to be hunting."

Bea doesn't argue or ask any questions. "Her name is Jazz," she says.

The rumble of the buggy's engine can be heard when it's still miles away. Bea pries each finger on Jazz's hand from its grip on her arm. "You'll be okay," she says, almost like she believes it. She kisses Jazz lightly on the forehead, and stands up to gather her things. "What will you tell them?" she asks me.

"I found her alone and scared." Jazz nods to show she'll corroborate the lie. "Now find somewhere to hide and only come out when you hear the buggy leave," I say.

Bea turns to Jazz. "You're not as much of a brat as I thought you'd be," she tells her, and laughs.

"Bye," Jazz says. She chokes back her tears. And Bea doesn't let herself cry either. She nods and moves away.

I watch her leave, then take Jazz out to the roadside where we sit shivering under the winking stars and sliver of a sickle moon. Her wounded leg is so bloated, I doubt they'll be able to save it. Hopefully they'll save her.

"Can you imagine what it must have been like to live out here before The Switch? So much space." I am talking to myself more than to Jazz, who shuts her eyes. I hold her tighter. "People used to travel across the whole world. No one stayed in his own country. Now even Outlanders don't get very far. We're all trapped. Trapped in the pod or on this big island. Is there a difference?" Jazz reaches out, takes my thumb in her cold hand, and closes her eyes as the buggy trundles out of the shadows, its bright lights, like giant eyes, blinding.

I stand holding Jazz in my arms. The buggy slows and

stops. Jude steps out and stands in front of the vehicle.

"Who's that? And where's Quinn?" Jude growls. He is wearing loose-fitting trousers and an old sweater rather than his uniform and looks like a very ordinary man. A dad.

"I haven't seen him." He wouldn't have thought a RAT was worth the journey, so I lied when I radioed in: I told him I'd found Quinn.

"Then why the hell . . ." He stops, steps forward, and peers at Jazz. He sweeps her hair away from her face. "What am I meant to do with her?"

"She needs a doctor."

"This wasn't part of the deal." He wheels around.

"I'm close to finding Quinn. And I want to take you up on your offer. I'll become an auxiliary if it means I don't have to kill any more innocent people."

Jude turns. "They weren't all innocent," he says, looking at Jazz, who he almost killed. "And anyway, why should I believe you?"

"I only lied about Quinn to help her. And I doubt I'll find anyone else who needs saving," I say, thinking of Bea.

He opens his arms. "Hand her over," he says coolly, and without flinching, studies her leg.

"Is Niamh okay?" I ask.

"She's still angry. Your sister has a good deal of your father in her," he says. "You, though . . . you didn't catch it."

"Nope, and Quinn didn't catch much of you either," I say, in case he thinks that this spell of conscience and unexpected concern for his own son makes him some sort of hero. Jude stares, and Jazz squirms.

I step out of the glare of the headlights and into the shadows. "The drifters are vicious. Watch out for them," Jude says on his way back to the buggy.

Carefully, he places Jazz in the rear seat and climbs behind the wheel. He reverses roughly over the rubble, and is off.

I return to the station. "Bea!" I call out. Within minutes she appears. She's shivering. My heart lightens. I was worried she would have run off, and I don't think I want to be alone out here.

"Do you think she'll live?" she asks.

"She has a chance," I say.

The top buttons of her coat and shirt are open, exposing pointy collarbones and pale skin. I go to her, and she holds out her hand. "Thank you," she says. I take her hand and shake it, and finally one corner of her mouth curls into a faint smile.

"I am glad you found us," she says.

"Me, too," I say.

20
ALINA

Vanya orders us to finish eating our dinners—the troopers have everything under control. "But what if it's the Ministry? They nuked The Grove. They could do the same here," I say. Is it possible that the chatter in the room is masking the sound of zips and tank treads?

"I'm sure it's nothing Maks can't handle," Terry says. He takes a spoonful of white powder from a bowl and sprinkles it over his steaming dessert, then pushes the platter toward my plate, but I'm too nervous to eat. Is nowhere safe? I'm exhausted, and I don't want to run anymore; I want to stay in Sequoia and have it be home. Is that too much to ask?

I rub my face vigorously, to wake myself from pointless daydreaming, when the room stirs. Vanya stands and Terry climbs up onto the bench to get a better look. Then he hoots and dashes toward a growing crowd.

All at once, the hall is a volcano of cheers.

"Can't I eat my grub in peace?" Maude complains, disinterestedly chomping.

"Come up on stage!" Vanya calls. The crowd edges forward and the first person to appear on the platform is Maks. He's holding his pistol in one hand, a balaclava in the other. Vanya puts her hand to his chest.

A girl climbs up onto the stage after him, and when she turns to the side, it's clear she's at least six months pregnant. Yet she's no older than fifteen. Her hair is lank and her clothes torn. She is still wearing a facemask, which Vanya rips off and throws aside.

"Jo!" someone at our table shouts.

"Welcome back!" Vanya says, and everyone claps. "And someone new. Welcome to you also." Another figure, taller, mounts the stage. But it can't be. I glance at Silas who, without even looking at me, nods. "Who are you?" Vanya asks.

"Quinn," he says aloud. Everything around me goes fuzzy. Why is he here? And where's Bea?

"And one more," Vanya says, pulling the last visitor onto the stage. Is it Bea? I close my eyes. I can't look.

I reach for the table as the room erupts in a round of riotous cheering.

"Open your damn eyes," Silas says, shaking me. "He's

alive." And when I see what he sees, I gasp.

Bea is missing, but Abel stands on stage. Abel is alive. He scans the room and our eyes meet. His mouth drops open. I hold up my hand in a half-wave and he shakes his head in disbelief. His face has the mottled yellow-and-purple look of someone who's been beaten up, but he's here. The Ministry didn't kill him after all.

"I can't believe it. He's goddamn, bloody-well alive," Silas says through his teeth.

"Yes," I say. I'm smiling. For the first time in a long time, I'm happy, and I don't care how ridiculous I seem.

And then I realize Maks is following Abel's gaze. He looks at Abel, then at me. Abel and me. And although every one else in the room is cheering, Maks is frowning.

He is not very happy with Abel's homecoming at all.

Without saying so, Silas and I decide to keep what we know about Abel to ourselves. Dorian, who I'd mentioned Abel to back at The Grove, doesn't remember the connection. "At least he's alive," I whisper when we're back in the cabin. Silas splashes his face with cold water.

"You say it like it's a good thing," he throws back. He's right: we already knew Abel wasn't Resistance and that he duped us, but we still don't know why. "And you shouldn't get your hopes up," he adds.

"What do you mean?" I say.

"Just because he went missing and has turned up doesn't mean he's here because of you. You're not to let your guard down again, Alina."

I nod, embarrassed, and Silas pats me on the back awkwardly, lies down in his bunk, and pulls a blanket over himself. But Maude's frantic. "If *Quinn's* here, then where's Bea?" she wants to know.

"I promise we'll find out in the morning," I tell her, and reluctantly, she goes to bed.

My mind is racing; I can't sleep. Not until I know what Abel's up to, why Quinn's here, or where Bea is. I lie awake listening to Maude and Bruce snore in unison. Dorian is in the bunk next to me. He turns over, mutters something, and restlessly kicks and coughs. Silas and Song are silent.

I throw my legs over the side of my bunk. The stone floor is biting cold. I put on my socks, my pants, and within seconds, I'm dressed and out the door.

The cabins, outbuildings, and main house are dark, but no sooner have I stepped onto the graveled pathway than a floodlight illuminates the area.

A girl carrying a gun confronts me. She doesn't point the weapon, just blocks my way. "Where are you going?" she asks. She steps closer. "Oh, you're one of the new ones. Someone should've told you that you're supposed to stay in at night."

"I didn't know," I say, trying to sound dense.

"Well, you do now," she says.

"Where are Abel and Quinn?" I ask.

She glances at the main house. "Abel's probably in his old room. I don't know Quinn," she says, and gestures at my cabin with her gun.

I walk back slowly, and when she heads in the opposite direction, I sprint toward the main house and slam my body against it. The floodlights go out, and I am in darkness.

I skirt along the edge of the house feeling for a way in, but every door is locked. I turn a corner and the guard is there, sitting on a bench reading an old paper book by flashlight. She looks up briefly, waves the light this way and that, then returns to her reading. Another guard appears from a door behind her.

"That time already?" she says, slipping the book into her jacket and stretching.

"You can do my shift if you like," the other one says. They laugh. "Any probs?"

"Pretty quiet. I found one of the newbies wandering around, but she went back to bed."

"Which one?"

"The one Maks has his eye on. I wouldn't like to be her."

"Really? Oh, I would." They laugh again and saunter toward the annex chatting. They activate the floodlight and the whole area is awash in light. I watch them go and try not to think about what it means that I've caught Maks's notice.

The door the guard came through is open, and the guards are less than fifty feet away and making their way back. I hurry across the courtyard and almost break my neck tumbling through the open door and down a couple of uneven steps.

I scramble to my feet and scamper along a hallway to another door. It opens with a warning creak. I duck as I go through. Beyond it is a wider hallway with a series of doors on either side, and I creep along, examining the signs above them: *Dispensary—Research Lab 4—Research Lab 5—Screening—Library.* I scurry up a flight of stairs and find several doors with no signs. Surely these are the bedrooms.

I kneel and press my ear against the keyhole waiting for the sound of movement or a recognizable voice. The house remains wrapped in silence. I check the next door. Nothing. So I keep going, trying each door and waiting a few moments before moving on. By the time I've reached the end of the hallway, I've tried twenty doors. I stand with my back against the wall, feeling suddenly foolish. How did I think I'd find anyone?

I pick my way back down the hallway when I hear glass shattering. I stand rigid, waiting for an alarm to ring, then think better of it and sprint down the hallway and away. I round a corner and before I can stop, I yelp and clatter into someone running in the opposite direction. We both end up on the floor, but I jump up first and hold my fists ready. The person looks up and repositions his facemask.

"Quinn?"

"Alina?"

I pull him to his feet. "What are you doing in Sequoia?"

"Looking for you," he whispers. He looks like he's about to hug me, but changes his mind. "Jazz had a bad fall. We have to go and help her."

"Jazz?" I can't believe it. The Grove was falling in on itself when we left it, and Jazz had climbed into the trees covered in toxic foam.

"Yes," he says hurriedly. Someone coughs in a room near us, and Quinn gestures with his hand for me to follow him. We tiptoe down the hallway and slink into a room.

He points to the floor where shards of glass glisten. "Be careful. I knocked the stool over and the water glass went flying." The curtains have been drawn and the moon is barely illuminating the room through the clouds. A bed is tucked into the corner and next to it a stool is lying on its side. The window is wide open and a raking breeze makes the curtains flap and smack against the wall.

"What's going on?" I point at the open window.

"I was searching for a way out. Thought I'd be less likely

to be seen this way. Turns out I might die, though." I follow him to the window. We look over the ledge. The room is three floors above a stone path. "We have to leave," he says. He looks like he hasn't slept or eaten in a long time, nothing like the person I met in the vaccination line weeks ago. How can so much have changed so quickly? It hardly seems possible.

"Where's Bea?"

"She's keeping Jazz safe. Is Silas here? Do you think he'd come with us? We'll need him."

My throat relaxes. "I knew Bea would make it," I say.

"Well, she'll be a goner if we don't get to her soon. So will Jazz." He looks out the window like he's considering jumping. I lead him to the bed, where I make him sit and tell me everything, from the moment he left The Grove until he arrived in Sequoia. He speaks quickly, skipping important details, so I have to keep making him go back and explain more.

"So can we go now?" he says finally.

"Maybe Vanya will help," I say.

He scratches his head. "I tried to tell her earlier and she just smiled. There's something rotten behind that smile, Alina. After the way Petra treated me, I'm not taking any chances."

I try to reassure him. "We'll speak to her again tomorrow."

"What is this place? I haven't seen one tree," he says. A few weeks ago he never would have noticed. If Quinn can change, maybe anyone can.

"We aren't sure what's going on, but the pod's looking like an option," I say, and laugh.

Quinn stares at me. "Is that a joke?" he asks.

I shake my head, because actually, it isn't. "I promise we'll convince Vanya to do something," I repeat.

"What about *Bea*?"

"Does she have air and water?" I ask.

"Yes," he says, "but—"

"It's just one night," I tell him, even though one night is all it would take for everything to turn into a catastrophe.

I go to the door. "How did you meet Abel?" I ask, turning the handle.

"By chance. Do you know him?"

"Kind of. Is he the baby's father?"

"Jo said he wasn't. Why?" A wave of relief rushes over me, followed by shame for even caring when there are so many other, more important things to worry about.

The lights are still out in the main house. I inch along the hallway and as I am about to descend a level, there's a scuffling.

"You're hurting me," a voice says. Cautiously, I lean over the banister and make out the tops of two heads. It's Maks and Jo. She's trying to break free of his grip. "Vanya put me in another room. Why can't you leave me alone?"

"You humiliated me," he snarls. Jo shrinks into herself.

"Please let me sleep on my own, Maks," she says.

"And how can I be sure you won't have run off by morning? You think I'm gonna let you out of my sight again? You're coming with me."

"I'm not your property," she says, wrenching her arm from him and backing away. She's barefoot and wearing only a light, white nightshirt.

Without another word, Maks smacks Jo hard across the face. She crumples into a heavy heap. "You're carrying something that belongs to Vanya and that means you belong to Sequoia and to me. You think I don't know why you ran away?" She looks up at him and before I can duck, sees me. But she doesn't give me away; she holds out her hands and lets Maks help her to her feet.

"I'm sorry," she says. She puts her free hand to his chest and then, standing on her tiptoes, kisses his lips. "I've been so scared. Are the trials working? Are the babies okay?"

"He doesn't want you, you know," he says, pinching her chin between his thumb and forefinger. "It's me or no one, Jo."

He takes her arm and leads her away, but not before Jo manages to flash me a warning look. Like she has to.

When I open the back door, I can't see any guard—just an empty chair with a mug next to it on the ground. I creep into the night and scamper back to the cabin.

"Where the hell were you?" Silas asks as I climb back into bed in my clothes. Maude and Bruce are still snoring. Song is lying like a corpse, his mouth open. Dorian has his back to me.

"Quinn says Bea and Jazz are in trouble," I say.

"Jazz is alive?" Silas asks.

"She was—days ago," I say.

21
BEA

Ronan and I are sitting in cracked green leather chairs
under layers of blankets, scarves, and coats on the balcony
of what was once a restaurant in the station. The sunrise is
obstructed by decrepit buildings. Ronan shows me a blurred
photograph on his pad. "Don't you want a clear image?"
I say. I fiddle with the gauge on my airtank. It would be
wiser to keep myself plugged into the solar respirator and
save the air, but it was too big to fit through the narrow balcony doors.

"I just want the color. I'll mix it when I get back." He
pauses. "Can I have one of you?"

"What for?"

"So I can ping it through to the Ministry and pick up my
reward. Your capture is very valuable." He laughs, but that

there could be a fraction of truth in what he's said makes me turn away. Not before he's managed to take a picture of me.

"Delete it!" I try to snatch the pad.

"No," he says.

"What if someone sees it and recognizes me?"

"It's as smudged as the other one. And anyway, no one's interested in the photos artists take." He studies the picture and then looks at the real me. "Why are you out here, Bea?" he asks.

"Because your father wanted my head on a plate," I remind him.

"But why did you join the Resistance in the first place? Are things really so bad in the pod for auxiliaries?" he asks. Can Premiums be so self-involved they completely fail to notice how ninety-five percent of us live?

"Have you ever even been to Zone Three?"

"A couple of times," he says sheepishly.

"If I could have changed things from inside, I would have," I tell him.

He is silent for a long time, looking through the few pictures he's just taken. "There has to be a way to make things fair. Nothing's impossible," he says finally.

"*You* can try working on things in the pod. I'm never going back. Anyway, I'm waiting for someone." I still haven't mentioned Quinn. As far as the Ministry knows, he's dead, and no one should think otherwise.

Ronan gazes into the distance, then closes his eyes. His eyelids twitch and the lashes flicker as sleep comes for him. And then he opens one eye and peers at me. "Are you going to get some rest or just watch me?"

My cheeks get hot. "Out here? It's below zero."

He reaches down and pulls a lightweight blanket from his backpack, which he throws at me. "Try that," he says. I pull it over my chin and tuck my feet under my butt. "Better?" he asks. I nod and close my eyes.

I wake to find Ronan shaking me. "Bea, wake up," he whispers. "Bea." I yawn.

"How long did I sleep?"

"Never mind that. Move!" he says.

"What's happening?" I try to stand and stretch but he takes hold of my thighs, so I can't.

"They'll see you!" he says.

I slide off the chair and onto the balcony floor. "Is it the Ministry?"

Ronan shakes his head. "I have no idea who they are. They must have spotted us."

I suddenly feel less cold. My aching limbs lighten. It must be Quinn and Alina and Sequoia come to save me. "At last, they're here!" I say, trying to get a glimpse of the road.

"I'm pretty sure you don't know these people," he says. "This way." Reluctantly I slither through the balcony doors behind him and into the restaurant, which is strewn with dozens of chairs like the ones outside. "Stay low," he says, remaining hunched. We go to a window.

"Do you know *them*?" he asks. It isn't easy to see through the grimy window. I rub the glass with my sleeve and put my face to it. Three bearded men dressed in rags are inspecting the station. Each is armed: one with a broken pitchfork, one with a baseball bat, and another with a thick metal pole. And they have bulky solar respirators on their backs. "Drifters," Ronan says. He pulls out his gun and loads it with a handful of bullets.

"What are you *doing*? They aren't monsters." Certainly not Maude, and not those who Jazz said helped defend The Grove. I grab for Ronan's gun, but he pushes me away so hard I fall, landing on my arm and twisting it. I groan, but he doesn't apologize or try to help me up.

"Shh," he says, finding a broken windowpane and taking aim.

"Give them a chance," I say. I crawl to the window. The men skirt the station, all the time peering up.

"They look like they're on their way to a lynching. Don't be naïve, Bea." The condescension in his voice makes me well up with anger.

"You've been out of the pod two seconds and think you

know everything. Watch and learn."

"Where are you going? Come back. *Come back*."

I march out of the restaurant, down the staircase, and outside, where I stand by the exit.

I'm about to speak to the men when the one carrying the baseball bat turns his back on the station and shouts. "Oi, Brent, you sure it was this building? I can't hear nothing." He shuffles away and leans against a van on the other side of the road.

"Chill your boots, Earl. There's definitely meat in there. I heard it squalling last night," Brent says, using his metal pole as a kind of walking stick.

"Yeah, well if there ain't, maybe I'll just eat *you*."

Brent jabs Earl in the stomach with his pole and cackles. Even from a distance I can see his black teeth.

Earl quickly recovers, and when he does, he bashes Brent's knees with his baseball bat. "Watch it, or next time I'll use your head for batting practice." This doesn't seem like bravado; I'm sure they'd happily kill one another.

I've made a mistake.

I back away from the road and through the station doors, but when I spin around the third man, the one with the pitchfork, is standing staring at me. "Well, well, well. Look at the treat we've got here," he says, and rubs his belly.

I dip to the side as the man swings for me. Luckily

he's half-starved and carrying a solar respirator and isn't fast enough. I hurtle up the stairs and into the restaurant. "Ronan! Ronan?" I call.

But he's disappeared.

"Get back here, you stupid cow," one of the men hollers. The others hoot.

I jump over broken chairs and overturned tables, smashed plates and glasses, and when I get to the kitchen door, push on it. I expect it to swing open, but it doesn't budge. Something's blocking it on the other side. I scan the restaurant. There's no other hiding place or way out unless I dive off the balcony. I find a broken bottle and hold it by the neck as the men saunter in, their eyes gleaming.

Earl swings his baseball bat, and they all grin. He comes closer and I try dodging him, but he's quicker than the man with the pitchfork. He leaps at me and knocks me to the ground. Earl pulls me up straight using my hair. His face is flecked with scars and his thinning hair is greasy and matted. "Annoying," he says, "but comely. What do you think, Getty?"

The man with the pitchfork throws down his weapon and steps up. "She'll do," he says. He unbuttons my coat and ogles me.

Brent shuffles forward. "Dibs on her airtank," he says, loosening it from its belt.

"Leave that 'til we're finished," Getty says, shoving him.

I try to thrash free, but when I do, Earl, who's standing behind me, pulls my hair harder. "Settle down," he croaks.

It's obvious what these savages are planning, and I can't endure it. Anything but this. Anything.

I whimper, wishing I'd let Ronan shoot them. Where is he now? And where's Quinn?

Getty holds my face next to his, and licks my cheek. Even through the mask I can smell his rotten breath. I cry out, and they laugh. "Please don't," I say, looking into his eyes, but he's too far gone to see my humanity.

He throws off his heavily stained jacket and scrapes his finger along my collarbone. "I'm first," he says. And I decide, in that moment, that I will shut down and think of Quinn and my parents and Maude and anything else that is not this, is not now.

"Ready?" Earl asks.

I shut my eyes. "Quinn!" I shout. "Quinn!"

But he doesn't hear me.

No one does.

22
QUINN

I dream about Bea and wake up in a sweat, my mind whirring with images of her body on the tracks of an old railway line being pecked at by hungry drifters, their mouths like beaks. She was calling my name over and over even though she was already dead. It was horrible.

I'm stuffing things into my backpack, ready to find Alina, when Vanya barges into my room. "How did you sleep?"

"I had nightmares," I say, still feeling the effects of the dream.

"It's always hard to sleep in a strange bed," she says with this weirdo smile on her face. She flutters by me and throws open the curtains. "A glorious day!"

"Not for my friends, it isn't. They need help before it's too late." I move to the door. "Do you have a buggy?"

"A buggy? Of course we have a buggy, Quinn. This isn't The Grove." She sits on the end of the bed and pats the spot next to her. I stay where I am.

"A child's bleeding to death," I say quickly, pointing out the window.

"Sounds serious." She shifts her weight on the bed and the springs creak. The more composed she is, the more my limbs jitter. If she isn't interested in helping, then what does she want?

"Is there a doctor or nurse? All I need is a buggy and medic . . . *please*." I'm not used to begging anyone for anything, but I'd gladly get on my knees and lick her shoes if it meant she'd help. In fact, I'd do absolutely anything.

"No one's leaving here," she says, and grins like this is some kind of joke instead of a person's life we're talking about.

"I won't let my friends die!" I shout.

She rises and comes to the door, where she stands ridiculously close to me and speaks slowly and quietly. "This is not a hotel, Quinn. You can't pop in and then leave when you've showered and had a good meal and long rest. Abel should have explained that to you. I've arranged for you to complete some tests this afternoon. If you want to live here, I suggest you comply with our requests. I'm more than a little irritated by all the disruptions."

"I'm not hanging around here while they're out there. What kind of crazy woman are you?" I seize her arm and, like a wild drifter, she spins around and punches me on the ear. She's stronger than she looks.

"*Never* lay your hands on me," she snarls.

I push past her and out the door into the hallway. "Going somewhere?" Maks says.

Vanya cracks her knuckles and a vein in her neck pulses. "Take him to the lockup. Give him a few calmers and administer the physical tests," she says. And with that, she turns away.

"You're worse than Petra," I say.

Vanya spins around. "I take that as a compliment," she says.

"So that's it? Jazz is going to die?" I push Maks off and step away from him. He's beefy, but I'm fast. If I make a run for it, I might get away.

"Jazz?" Vanya says slowly.

"Yes. She's just a child."

"Well, that changes everything. Come with me."

I'm wasting precious time sitting in what can only be described as Vanya's boudoir while Maks is sent on an errand. Vanya isn't cool and creepy anymore, she's flustered. She keeps firing questions at me: "Who is this Bea? How old is the child? Where was she born? Who are her parents? How did she end up at The Grove?" I don't have any answers—and the less I give her, the more Vanya frets.

Eventually Maks drags Alina and Dorian into the room. "What's going on?" Alina asks.

"You said everyone from The Grove died. You lied." Vanya says.

"The place was decimated," Dorian says. He looks at Maks who, denied the opportunity to beat me up, may have his sights set on him.

"Quinn tells me there are more survivors," Vanya says.

"How would *he* know?" Dorian spits. "His father was the one who destroyed The Grove. What's he doing here, anyway?"

Alina elbows Dorian in the gut. Maks smirks. "We can trust Quinn," she says. "If he claims there were survivors, then there were. We didn't know."

Vanya goes to the oxybox on the wall and takes a lungful of air. "So people were in there when you ran for it?"

"We tried to get Petra out," Dorian says. "She refused. She climbed a tree and wouldn't come down. We have no idea what happened to the others because we were all stationed at different locations. But Petra—she was determined to die." Dorian is rambling and making himself breathless.

"Quinn found a child," Vanya says. "Who could that be?"

Alina and I have already gone through this, but Alina pretends she's working it out. "Jazz was the only kid at The Grove," she says pointedly. "We tried to save her, but she wouldn't leave Petra behind."

Vanya taps her chin and studies me. "I don't like this," she says.

"Help me find them," I say.

Vanya turns to Maks. "Get the zip ready."

"A zip? Thank you." I sigh.

"I'm not doing it for you," Vanya says. "I'm doing it for my daughter." She marches into the adjoining bathroom, leaving all of us gawking after her.

Maks is standing with one hand on Dorian's shoulder, the other on Alina's. He pushes them aside and takes after Vanya. "Jazz is your daughter?" he asks.

"Yes," Vanya calls from the bathroom. "Now go and find her."

23
RONAN

By the time I make it through the back exit of the station and around the front, hoping to take the drifters by surprise, they've vanished. And so has Bea. She'll have run, and I hope she has the sense to go back into the station as it's the only building not on the brink of collapse. "Bea!" I yell, hopping over fissures in the road and hurtling back through the doors.

I hear them braying before I see them. "Get on with it, Brent, don't be a sissy. If you're not in the mood, let me have a go." I finger my gun and climb the stairs. When I peer through the glass in the restaurant door, they have Bea trapped by the balcony, prodding her like a cold dinner. "Don't," she peeps. "I'll give you anything you want."

"We know you will." They hoot. Bea sobs. She's no

longer wearing her shirt. She is trembling in her bra and pants.

I slink into the restaurant, planning to be on top of them before they notice, but in my haste I don't look where I'm stepping and glass breaks under my foot. The men spin around. And they don't waste a second. Two of them dive toward me and only hesitate when I raise my gun, ready to shoot.

"Careful, hombre," one says.

"Let's talk about this," the other suggests.

"Down on the ground," I say. They snicker like this is the silliest thing they've ever heard.

"Shoot them," Bea says, her voice eerily calm. The man still holding her smacks her. Bea's knees buckle, and I fire.

One man falls without a sound. I fire again to be sure he'll never get up and the others grab their weapons. The one holding Bea presses the pitchfork to her throat.

"Try that with me, you little bastard, and I'll rip her open," he barks. "Now hand your gun to Earl." The drifter with the baseball bat eases toward me.

"Stay where you are," I say.

"Don't give him the gun. We'll both be finished if you do," Bea says. "*Shoot* him."

"Can't you shut her up?" Earl says, turning. The guy with the pitchfork knocks the side of Bea's head with the heel of his hand.

I close one eye, focus on the forehead of the man hold-ing Bea, and pull the trigger. I am driven back only a frac-tion. The drifter crumples to the ground and as he does, Bea seizes the pitchfork from him and rushes at the last man. He turns, but it's too late: the last thing he sees before he dies is Bea thrusting the prongs of the pitchfork into his chest.

She lets go of the weapon, watches him slide to the ground, and collapses. The delicately ridged track of her spine is clear through her chalky skin.

Her shirt and sweater have been trampled into the carpet, and when I shake them, glass and dirt cling to the fibers like a razor-edged reminder of what's happened.

I throw them aside, remove my coat, and pull my own sweater over my head.

A sob comes from deep inside her belly as I touch her gently on the back. She covers her chest with her arms. "Here," I say, and turn away.

"I should have listened to you," she says. "I was trying to be strong. Now I'm a killer."

I turn back around and crouch beside her. "It was him or you."

"I thought you'd left. I thought I was alone." She can't say any more. She's crying too hard.

"I'd never have left you," I say. I watch her and breathe in the deathly silence of the station. My gun is still warm. I fasten the safety catch. The men I killed are sprawled across the carpet. Perhaps I should feel a shred of remorse, but I don't.

All I care about now is getting back to the pod. And I'm going to have to convince Jude to find a way to help Bea instead of Quinn.

Because she shouldn't have to live out here.

No one should.

24
BEA

Ronan leads me to one of the green chairs, turning it to face the windows, so I don't have to look at the drifters. He opens up a compartment in his backpack filled to the brim with protein and nutrition bars and hands me one. I pull away my mouthpiece and take a small bite, which is all I can stomach. "You have to keep up your strength," he says.

He's watching me for signs I'll break down, but I wish he wouldn't. Every time I catch his eye I see the pity and horror of what might have been. And I'm ashamed. It was my own fault. I wanted to prove to myself how strong I'd become. And I wanted to prove to Ronan that everything he knew about drifters was untrue. Except it wasn't.

"What are you even doing in The Outlands, Ronan?

Isn't there a servant at home waiting to run you a hot bath and cook you a meal?"

"Yes," he says. "But I told you, I'm looking for someone." He pauses. "For Quinn Caffrey. His father sent me. Do you know where he is?"

I want to trust him, and after what he's just done for me, I probably should, but if Mr. Caffrey's the one looking for Quinn, it must mean trouble. "I haven't seen Quinn since the pod."

Ronan studies me. He knows it's a lie. "Well, I have to find him," he says. "Will you help me?"

"I wish I could."

"I'm a member of the Special Forces, Bea. I was at The Grove. I know what the Ministry did because I was there fighting for them."

I sit up, pull off the sweater he gave me using one hand to keep my facemask in place, and fling it at him. How could he have destroyed all those trees? And killed so many people?

He doesn't have the face of an enemy, but that's what he is—he's his father's son. "You. Make. Me. Sick," I say, and head back into the restaurant, where the three dead men are still bleeding into the carpet.

Ronan runs after me and forces me to look at him. "I didn't know what we were doing until it was too late. I know the Ministry is full of crap. I want out, and Jude said he'd help. If I find Quinn for him, he'll change my identity and I can leave the Special Forces. He'll do it for Quinn, too. . . . And you, I'm sure." But he doesn't sound so sure. No Premium father would want his son involved with the likes of me.

I scratch Jazz's dried blood from my hands. "I don't want to go back," I say simply. "And how could *you,* after you've seen what's possible?"

"I'll become an auxiliary. I'll be like you." He says this like it's the most magnanimous gesture in the world. It's all I can do to put my hands behind my back to stop myself from punching his puffed-out chest.

"Do you know what it's like to be an auxiliary? Do you like running or dancing or kissing or anything remotely normal? Because once you become *like me,* every breath will cost you. You think that's a life I want to go back to or one I'd want for Quinn? Leaving the Special Forces and living in Zone Three isn't going to solve anything. You'll be in hiding, that's all. A coward in hiding." I stop. I've been shouting, and my throat hurts. I didn't hit Ronan, but from his guilty expression, I might as well have.

"I don't want to hurt people anymore," he whispers, looking at the floor.

"So fight to make things better."

Now it's his turn to be angry. "And how will I do that?

The Resistance worked for years to steal cuttings and build a new world. I'm one person. It's not like I could overthrow the government."

Maybe I'm being hard on him, but that's because it's only people in his privileged position who can change things. "What if we *could* overthrow the government?" I ask.

He stomps on a glass bottle and it smashes into a hundred pieces. "How?" he asks.

I don't know yet. But at least I know that he's willing. And if he is, we'll find a way.

2 5
QUINN

Sequoia's zip looks like it was dragged kicking and scream-
ing from a swamp. The paint's peeled away and the blades
are covered in rust. I'm not sure it's even going to make it
off the ground let alone into the city and back again, and I'd
refuse to get in if I had another choice. Maks sees my expression and slaps the side of the zip. "Found this beauty at an
old RAF barracks," he says.

I climb into the back next to some dude whose nails are
bitten to the quick and the skin around them raw and peel-
ing. When he sees me looking, he curls his hands around his
rifle to hide them.

Maks sits next to the pilot. "Here," he says, and throws
two pairs of enormous earphones into the back. "We're
ready," he says, his voice crackling through them.

The zip comes to life, the blades rotating so hard I'm rocked from side to side. The pilot sniffs and speaks: "Sequoia control. Takeoff direction: zero seven. Flight plan: eight hundred feet. Ready for immediate departure."

"Sequoia station. Copy that. Clear to takeoff," I hear.

"Roger that." The pilot pulls back the steering column, and the zip lifts away from the tarmac. It creaks like hundreds of unoiled door hinges, and I grip the seat, scared witless that the whole thing's going to come to pieces in the air.

The pilot pushes the column forward and the zip's nose tilts forward with more creaking and groaning. But soon we're high above the ground looking down at a land dotted with gray and black mounds of rubble and impassable, ruptured roads. I've never seen anything like it before and I want to take it all in, but I'm too worried about Jazz and Bea to enjoy the scenery. I hope we aren't too late.

We lurch to the left, and I hold on to the door handle to stop myself from sliding along the seat. We careen over a wide river and sunken dock.

"Bit of wind. Nothing to worry about," the pilot says, righting the aircraft.

Maks swivels in his seat to look at me. "You scared?" he says. I shake my head—*no*. He raises his eyebrows. "Maybe you should be: I wouldn't want to be you, if Vanya's kid's croaked it." He laughs at the idea and turns away.

I look out at the fields again and think about Jazz. She already had an infection when I left. By now there's every chance it's killed her, and if it has, Bea and I won't have anything to sweeten Vanya's fury.

How will Bea be coping with the loneliness? Will she have stayed in the station? "How long until we get there?" I ask, but my earphones aren't miked, so no one hears me over the noise of the blades.

All I can do is wait.

26
BEA

Ronan and I have been pacing for an hour. Out onto the balcony and back inside, brainstorming ways to take the Ministry down. But every idea we hit on is full of holes. After everything that's happened, we need a watertight plan.

"It's useless," he says at last, falling into a chair on the balcony. "If there was a way, someone would have thought of it by now."

I don't agree. Just because no one's managed something in the past, doesn't mean the future's lost. I'd be no good at hand-to-hand combat or shooting guns, but I'm smart. And I'll figure this out.

"You told me that the army's numbers were down since The Grove." I sit next to him and focus hard on a window with its glass knocked out.

He shakes his head. "Not enough to weaken the pod's defenses. And anyway, Jude's recruiting more."

A fork has found its way outside. I pick it up and fling it across the street, where it disappears through the broken window. Ronan laughs. "Good shot," he says.

The seed of something is coming to me. I lean with one hand on the railing. "If it's true that Jude's done some kind of turnabout, he's the key," I say.

Ronan shrugs. "He's just as much a puppet as I am."

"If he is a puppet, he's a puppet with power. They trust him to run the army, don't they?" I pause and turn to Ronan. The solution is coming . . . it's coming.

And I have it.

I grab Ronan's hands and pull him to his feet. "You said . . ." I take a breath. I'm scared that if I don't say it, the idea will evaporate. "You said Jude Caffrey was recruiting. What if . . ." Could it work? Would Quinn's dad do it? "What if he *only* recruited auxiliaries sympathetic to the Resistance? They'd be given training and guns and be privy to inside information. It could work, Ronan. Couldn't it?"

He thinks for a moment, squeezing my hands and gazing at me. Then he smiles. "Holy hell . . . I think it could."

I am about to throw my arms around him and tell him that Quinn's coming, that all we have do is wait, when a noise I recognize too well makes the hair on my arms prickle. The station vibrates and the sky thunders like a vicious storm is passing overhead. "You sent for zips." I drop his hands and back away.

Ronan shakes his head frantically. "I swear I didn't." He doesn't seem to know what to do.

"Take your clothes off," I say, raising my voice. A look of understanding washes over him as he watches me undress and does the same. I untie my laces. "We need to be cold so the thermo-sensors don't find us."

"Yes, yes. But don't cut your feet," he warns. I leave the laces untied and pull my trousers off over my boots. He's already seen me in my underwear, but I still feel exposed. I swallow down the embarrassment and focus on staying alive.

I dash onto the balcony and lather myself in handfuls of slush still frozen in its corners and so does Ronan. I can't help noticing how athletic his body looks. And dark. Next to him, my skin looks bleached and scrawny. He rubs snow over himself and shivers.

The zip appears, weaving between buildings on its approach. It's much smaller than the one I saw when I was with Alina and Maude, and flying low. "It's coming from the west," Ronan shouts over the noise of the blades. "The pod is east." Which means it's coming from the wrong direction.

"Then who?" I shout. Could it be Quinn and Alina? She stole a tank—maybe she'd steal a zip, too. But how would she pilot it?

We hurry inside and foolishly, I cover my head with my hands. The roaring of the propeller blades dwindles, then intensifies again as the zip circles overhead. "They know we're here," I shout above the noise.

"This way!" We don't have time to get back into our clothes, so we stuff them into Ronan's backpack and sprint down the stairs. The noise is deafening. The zip is landing on the road. The whirling blades send debris flying in every direction. "Quick!" Ronan urges. I follow him through the station, jumping over human bones, and onto a road strewn with poles, their old electrical wiring still attached. Ronan heads left toward a clock tower with its hands missing.

He runs ahead and before long there's a distance between us. I stop as the sound of the zip finally abates and everything is still. Ronan gestures for me to follow him, but my heart is pounding, and I can't shout to tell him, so I scuff onward and when I reach him, he takes my hand and drags me along. "What's the matter?" he whispers.

"I wasn't a Premium." He looks confused and then he touches his earlobe. Still keeping hold of my hand, he leads me down an alleyway.

"Breathe slowly," he says. I stop and take in deep lungsful

of air. While he clambers back into his trousers, shirt, and coat, I focus on keeping my heart from bursting through my ribs.

"Here!" a voice nearby calls out. Ronan takes my hand again and we hide behind a stinking old wheelie bin. He opens his coat and wraps me up in it. I feel his chest next to my back and sink in deeper for warmth. He rests the hand holding his gun on my stomach.

"Okay?" he whispers. My teeth are chattering. I am too cold to nod.

Ronan squeezes me tighter as someone prowls the alleyway. Garbage crunches and squelches under the weight of a boot. The barrel of a gun comes into view. And a face.

Quinn.

"Bea?" He stares at me, wrapped up with Ronan.

There are more footsteps and a voice in the alleyway. "See anything?"

Quinn looks away. "Nothing. I'll keep looking. They can't be far." The footsteps recede.

I struggle out of Ronan's embrace and throw my arms around Quinn. He stays still and stiff. "Quinn," I whisper, bending down, picking up Ronan's sweater and pulling it over my head. My legs are bare. Quinn looks away and so does Ronan. I feel tears at the corners of my eyes, which I wipe away with the back of my hand.

"Ronan Knavery?" Quinn says. "And where's Jazz?"

"Your father picked her up," Ronan says. "She's safe."

"My father?"

"He wants you back. He's going to protect you," Ronan says.

Quinn squints. He's as suspicious of Ronan as I was. "Let's go, Bea," he says, taking my hand.

"Where are you going?" Ronan asks.

"None of your business." Quinn begins to pull me away, but I stay rooted.

"I think your dad is really looking for you, Quinn." I press my hand against his cheek, so he'll look at me.

And it works. "You believe him?" he asks. But it isn't about whether or not I believe Ronan, it's about Quinn having a chance to reconcile with his father. If someone told me I could see my dad again, I'd listen to what he had to say.

"We have a plan to get rid of the Ministry, if we can convince your dad to help."

"He'll listen to you, I'm sure," Ronan says.

"*Me?* He hates me. Just go home, Ronan." Quinn's tone is belittling. But Ronan doesn't deserve it. He's only been kind, and Jazz and I would be dead if he hadn't shown up.

"Come back to the pod, and we'll change things together," Ronan says, pounding his palm with his fist. "Why struggle out here?"

Quinn laughs. "The only thing that'll change the pod is if every one of those ministers croaks," he says.

"So let's see to it that they do," Ronan says.

This gets Quinn's attention. He prods Ronan in the chest. "Like you'd give up your fancy house and art studio for the likes of Bea."

"He isn't lying," I say, though how can I be one hundred percent sure? I only know what he's told me.

"Where *are* they?" someone shouts from the road. Quinn blinks and looks at me.

"Auxiliaries wouldn't trust Jude Caffrey or Cain Knavery's son. I need you both," Ronan says.

"Vanya's going to tear out your liver and have it for dinner," the voice shouts.

Quinn holds my face in his hands. Oh, I missed him. "Is there any chance of this working?" he asks.

I nod. "Your dad took Jazz. I think he's changing, Quinn. If there's any chance at all, shouldn't we take it?"

"Vanya's nuts. We're dead if we go back there without Jazz. She's Vanya's daughter," Quinn says, more to himself than to Ronan and me. Suddenly he takes Ronan by the coat collar. Ronan doesn't flinch. "This better not be a trap," he says, and steps behind the wheelie bin so he's out of view of the street. "Now we have to get out of here," he says.

"This way," Ronan says without another second's

discussion, and runs to the end of the alleyway. We follow, but as we reach him, he turns around, his eyes wide.

"It's blocked," he says, reloading his gun. "Only way out is past whoever you came with."

"Quinn, let's get moving. Where are you?" the disembodied voice calls.

Ronan puts a finger to his lips and holds his gun ready.

"QUINN!"

Quinn looks at Ronan's gun. "Unless his shot is spot on, this could go very badly," he whispers to me. I open my mouth, about to tell him that Ronan is a perfect shot, when Quinn releases my hand. "Go to the pod with Ronan and I'll follow. If this is going to work, we should gather everyone to help. I'll get the others and join you."

I feel lightheaded. "I need you," I tell Quinn, hoping he knows how true this is. It was true even when we were only friends.

"Alina and Silas have to be part of this. It's their fight," he says. "Besides, they're the ones with the connections and skills."

"But . . ."

"Hide." He pushes me toward the wall, where I hunker down behind a pile of garbage. "You, too," he tells Ronan, who shakes his head and keeps his gun pointed. "Protect Bea," he says. Ronan hesitates for a couple of moments, then dives next to me. I must be breathing loudly because he puts his hand over the blowoff valve in my mask.

Quinn fastens the top button of his coat and readjusts the strap of his rifle. "Stay hidden," he says.

"Anything?" the voice booms.

"Nope," Quinn says.

"Then let's get out of here. The drifters must have taken them. Vanya isn't going to like this. I wouldn't want to be you when we get back." The man behind the voice snorts.

Quinn stands motionless, and once the man has retreated, looks at me. My hands are still covered in Jazz's blood. My frame is thinner than it ever was. I haven't washed in a long time. I look exactly like someone who needs to be protected. "I love you, Bea," he says, and before I can protest or tell him I love him, too, he takes off down the alleyway and is gone.

27
ALINA

Vanya wouldn't hear of me going along with Quinn in the zip, so we have to sit tight. Maude and Bruce have been put to work in the greenhouse. The rest of us are in a cardio room doing interval training with a girl and guy we don't know.

Terry, who sat with us in the dining hall last night, comes into the room carrying a handful of papers. "Just the newbies," he says. We stop the treadmills, and he hands us each a list printed on heavy gray paper. I rub it between my fingers.

"Is this stone?" Song asks, turning the schedule over in his hands.

Terry nods. "Yep. We finally managed to make up a batch."

"Limestone and resin," Song says. "At The Grove we never tried. Too busy with the trees."

"What is this, anyway?" Dorian asks, reading.

"Schedules for tomorrow. You'll get your permanent ones soon."

I eye the schedule. Morning activities are pretty standard: cardio, meditation, breaks for food. But the entire evening is consumed by something called a Pairing Ceremony.

Dorian waves the paper at Terry. "Pairings?"

"You'll be told your vocation, get paired, and move into the main house. Most of you, anyway. Some people just get given a vocation and the pairing comes later."

Silas, who's breathing heavily after hiking hills for almost an hour, repeats Dorian's question. "Paired?"

Terry fidgets with the schedules still in his hands. "Didn't Vanya explain?" Silas shakes his head. "You'll be given your permanent partners," Terry says.

"Like work buddies," Song says. "I saw people going about in pairs and I wondered."

"Sort of." Terry smiles and makes to leave.

Silas holds him back. "So I could be partnered with Alina?"

"Well, you're cousins, so no," Terry says. He shifts from one foot to the other. "You have to be genetically compatible. You know?" Silas scowls. Dorian and Song, who are standing side by side, frown. But after the tests they've done on us, we aren't completely shocked: Not only will Vanya choose what each of us spends the rest of our lives doing, but she'll also select our mates. It's almost enough to make me pine for the pod. Almost. "Breeding's encouraged and most pairs have children who might actually survive . . . *this*." Terry waves his hand around the room, but he means the world beyond it—Earth. "Comes naturally, I suppose."

"*Naturally?*" Silas says through gritted teeth.

"So where are the children?" I try to keep my voice steady, remembering the girl in the attic, the fear in her eyes, the sweat on her forearms, and the doctor cool and detached as she counted her own contractions. Will motherhood be my fate, if we stay here?

"We keep them in a nursery and train them from birth," Terry says.

"You take away the girls' babies?" I ask, stepping closer to Terry. He doesn't make the rules here, but I have an urge to hurt him anyway.

"I have no intention of breeding. *Ever*," Silas says. Having loved Inger and lost him, I'm not surprised by Silas's outrage.

"But you want to join us. This is what we do," Terry says simply.

Silas sits on the end of his treadmill with his head in his hands. We huddle around him. We're too stunned to ask any more questions, and it's clear Terry has no power, so we ignore him sneaking out. "It's a baby mill," Silas says. "No wonder she's not interested in Maude or Bruce." He glances at the couple training in the room. They're gushing with sweat and probably haven't much energy to pay any attention to us, but Silas waves us to the other end of the room just in case. "We have to get away from here."

"And where would we go?" Dorian asks.

Silas glowers at him. "Does it matter?"

"Maybe we'll all get paired with someone normal," Dorian says. Is he serious? Does he know what he's saying?

"Yeah, cool. Maybe you'll get some hot concubine," Silas says. "Think about it from Alina's perspective." But I wish they wouldn't—I don't want the decision to be about me being a girl. It has to be the best thing for all of us.

"Leaving has to be our last resort. There's no air out there. We'll be dead in a week," Dorian says.

"After this ridiculous ceremony, we'll be forced to . . ." Silas nudges a water bottle on the floor with his foot. I put my arms around him to stop him trembling. He pushes me away. "Inger's dead and I'm supposed to get over it and get it on with some girl?" Silas and Dorian are standing eye-to-eye, ready to wrangle. Song pushes them apart and stands between them.

"We can't do anything until we know what the deal is with Quinn, Bea, and Jazz," I say.

"Then we wait," Dorian says.

Silas rolls his eyes. "If we wait, we might not get another chance to talk about it. Sorry, but which bit of this sickening thing don't you understand?"

Dorian's eyes widen, and he lifts his fists as though about to hit Silas, when the door opens again.

It's Abel. "Don't leave," he says, looking at me and shaking Silas's hand. "Terry said you were in here and that you were pretty upset about what he told you."

"We thought you were dead. As well as other things," Silas says.

"You know each other?" Dorian asks. His hands are still fists.

"Remember when I got to The Grove I told you that Abel had been killed? This is him," I say. I can't look at Abel for more than a second.

"But you're not Resistance," Dorian tells Abel.

Abel ignores him. "You'll be shot before you make it past the fountain. Besides, where would you go? If you don't suffocate, you'll starve. And Vanya doesn't make life easy when you return, which you will." I'm troubled by the idea of pairings, but I can't help wondering how I'd feel if I knew I'd get Abel. Would that change things?

"That's exactly what I've been telling them," Dorian says, as though Abel's his best friend. He folds his arms across his chest. The rest of us look to Silas. If he and Dorian don't find a way to agree, the group will come apart, and that can't happen; we've already lost too many people.

"Whatever we do, we do it together," I say.

"Then we're staying," Dorian says.

"We're *leaving*," Silas corrects.

"Give it a week," Abel suggests. "If you decide I was wrong, I'll help you escape."

"What's in it for you?" Silas asks.

Abel pauses and looks at me. "What the Resistance was doing was worthwhile. Together we might persuade Vanya that there's something to replanting trees." I study him. Is he patronizing us?

If he is, Song doesn't seem to notice. "But Vanya as good as told us she left The Grove because she didn't see a point to planting," he says.

"We have to show her she's wrong," Abel says.

Silas lets out a long, heavy sigh and throws his head back. "Three days," Silas says. "But we still need to talk, Abel."

The building shudders, and we are silent. "The zip's back," I say.

28
QUINN

The seat next to me is empty when Bea should be sitting in it, her leg pressing against mine. My body clenches as I think of her head resting against Ronan Knavery's chest, and the zip lands with a clunk.

We pull off our earphones and jump out of the aircraft.

Maks takes me to an outbuilding and kicks open the door. "Tell Vanya we're back," he tells the pilot, who walks off. I'm yanked along a passageway into a space divided into four prison cells. A girl of about fifteen or sixteen with olive skin is in one and next to her is a guy the same age. She looks up, afraid. "We didn't steal anything," she says.

"Why would we?" the boy adds.

"Please let us out of here." She presses her face between the bars.

"Pipe down," Maks says, and the girl immediately eases herself away from the bars and into a corner. He turns to me and points at an empty cell. "In there," he says.

"What have I done wrong?"

He raises one eyebrow. He's so big, it would take nothing for him to squash me, so I just do what he says.

He hasn't even closed the door when Vanya blazes in, heading straight for my cell. "Where is she?" she asks, prodding my chest with her finger.

"They were probably kidnapped. We found three dead drifters in the station. Looks like there'd been a struggle not long ago," I say. Vanya pinches the tube connecting my air-tank to the facemask, completely cutting off my air supply. I pull off my facemask and try taking a breath. It's no good. It's like swallowing boiling water. I cough and splutter. Vanya lets go of my tubing. I hold the facemask back over my mouth and nose and suck in as much air as I can manage.

"I'm *extremely* disappointed," she says.

"He isn't lying. There were three bodies in the old railway station and blood everywhere," Maks interjects. "Freshly dead, I'd say."

Vanya rubs her head and paces. "Let me ask this: Is it possible Jazz was never with you? Is it possible you knew she was my daughter and decided it would be a clever way of forcing me to look for your friend?"

"Jazz was the one who knew the others were heading here and could lead us."

"My daughter was leading you here," Vanya says, her eyes losing some of their hardness. Maks approaches her and gently rubs her back. She steps away from him. "If what you've told me is true, Jazz is as good as dead and you've proven yourself to be useless."

"He'd fit in okay," Maks mutters.

"Would he?" Vanya says, heading for the exit and disappearing.

Maks shuts the door to the cell and attaches a heavy padlock.

"Why are you locking me in?" I ask again. And for how long? I need to tell the others the plan to get back to the pod and overthrow the Ministry.

Maks laughs. "Makes no difference whether you sleep in here or the main house: You've been a prisoner since you arrived."

29
ALINA

It kicks off in the cabin after dinner. "You want to throttle me? Go ahead!" Dorian shouts. He rips off his jacket and rolls up the sleeves of his shirt.

Song is standing between them yet again, so they don't rip each other to pieces. "Calm down," he says.

Maude and Bruce are lying on their bunks with their hands behind their heads. "Let's have a good ol' fashioned boxing match. *Ding-ding—Round One!*" Maude says.

Bruce laughs but gets up and stands between Dorian and Silas, too. "Not sure what's going on, boys, but you can't be having it as hard as us," he says. He shows us his blistered hands. "So what is the point of all this squabbling?" Bruce asks.

Silas goes to the window and opens the blinds. It's already

dark. "This place makes my skin crawl."

"Silas has forgotten that real revolution means sacrifice," Dorian says.

"And Dorian has forgotten that we don't sacrifice our friends," Silas snaps back. He tries pulling open the window, and when it doesn't budge, he goes to the door and jimmies the handle. "Can you get me out?" he asks Song.

Song crouches down and examines the lock.

"Where you going?" I ask, joining Silas at the door.

"The zip came back, but Quinn wasn't at dinner. Neither were Bea or Jazz," he says. "I'm going to look for them. I want to know what's going on."

"You're determined to get us in trouble," Dorian says.

"Well, I'm sorry if I'm the only one who gives a crap about them," Silas says.

"Hey!" I push him. If anyone's worried about Quinn and Bea, it's me; I know them better than anyone, and I'm the one who got them wrapped up in this mess to begin with. "I'm coming with you," I say.

"Lemme help," Maude says, springing up from the bed. She roots around in her hair and hands Song a pin. He straightens it out and sticks into the lock. We all watch and wait, and after a few minutes the lock clicks.

But Song isn't the one who's opened it. Wren, the girl we met at dinner with the icy eyes and headscarf, stands in the doorway. She's carrying a heavy load of red fabric over her arm.

"I come bearing gifts," she says, stepping into the cabin and throwing the folds of fabric onto my bunk. We gather around. She lifts up one and shakes open a long, red robe with snaps down the front. "For the ceremony. One size fits all." She offers one to each of us. Maude and Bruce watch carefully. We haven't told them about the Pairing Ceremony.

"Am I finally being made a dame? If so, I'd like to request a transfer to the royal chambers and a servant to do my gardening for me," Maude says. "Also, I need a foot rub."

Wren looks down at Maude's knotted feet, frowns, and passes her a robe. "For you," she says.

Maude beams and slips the robe straight over her head. Silas and I share a glance. If they've been invited, then it can't just be about breeding. Silas's face relaxes a fraction, and he holds his robe out at arm's length to look at it.

"Did Maks and Quinn find anyone?" I ask Wren.

"Don't think so," she says. "All dead apparently. Murdered or something."

"Even the girl? Even Bea?" Maude asks. Wren shrugs unsympathetically. I bite down hard and clench my jaw. Bea murdered? After everything she endured?

I don't believe it.

"And where's Quinn now?" Silas asks.

"He's been taken to the lockup."

"Lockup?" Silas pushes.

"Yep," Wren says, and with no further explanation goes to the door. "I finally got a robe today, too. Can't wait to meet my other." She beams, showing her yellow teeth, pulls the door closed behind her, and locks it.

"Ugly-looking bitch," Maude croaks, clutching for a joke. "*I'm* ancient. At least I got an excuse." She returns to her bunk and flops down.

"We should talk about it, Maude," I say.

"About what? I ain't got nothing to say," she whispers.

Bruce sits next to Maude and kisses the side of her head. "Maddie?"

"Jazz was a pain in the butt, but she was just a kid," Dorian says, sounding more like his old self. He folds up his robe. "How many more of us need to die?" He's speaking to himself, but we all nod.

"And now Quinn's been imprisoned," Silas says.

"Because Jazz couldn't be found, and Vanya needs some-one to blame," I say.

"We have to speak to him. We have to find out what hap-pened," Silas says.

Song returns to the door. He tries again to pick the lock

with the hairpin. When he can't, he slumps on the floor. "It's useless," he says.

Maude is on her back. She points upward. "Go through the roof," she says, and we all look up to see what she's pointing at: the skylight.

30
BEA

Ronan and I are in a room on the second floor of an old hotel not far from the station. The floorboards creak, and the walls are ready to fall in on themselves. Ronan uses a finger and thumb to make an opening in the crooked blinds. "What can be taking him so long?" he wonders.

He sits next to me on the bed and sinks into it. We aren't using a flashlight in case an opportunistic drifter sees the light, but even in the gloom, I can make out the wrinkles in Ronan's brow.

It's freezing again and I can't stop trembling or thinking about Quinn. I curl up to keep warm. "How will they escape from Sequoia, if it's so terrible there?" I say. "And what makes Quinn think they can just stroll back into the pod to help?"

I wish I'd tried harder to persuade him to stay. I just watched him leave. And he never mentioned Maude. Does that mean she never made it to Sequoia?

Ronan rubs his eyes. "I don't know, Bea. But what I do know is that Jude asked for Quinn, and what I'm giving him is a sick kid and his son's outlawed girlfriend. Let's concentrate on winning him over, and then worry about Quinn, okay?"

He's right: If I'm going to be any use to Ronan, and if my parents' deaths are to mean anything, I have to focus on what we're about to do. "We just tell the truth: Quinn was here and then he left. Jude Caffrey knows what Quinn and I mean to each other, and he'll know I wouldn't return to the pod if Quinn wasn't following."

"You seem very confident," Ronan says. He stands up and peers through the blinds again.

"I'm not," I say. I'm terrified of returning to the place where my parents were killed and attempting to collude with a man responsible for countless deaths at The Grove.

But if I want to stop others from spending their whole lives under the Ministry's iron thumb, I only have one choice—I have to throw my shoulders back and fight.

31
ALIΠA

Song gives me a leg up, but when I push on the hatch it doesn't budge. "There's a latch," Song says.

I pull it to the left and the piston lets out a gentle puff. Then I haul myself up onto the roof and sit low in case a patrolling guard spots me. Down in the cabin, Song and Bruce are helping Silas. His two hands appear at either side of the opening and then he's pulling himself up through it. He sits on the opposite side of the hatch. "It might not be true. About Bea," he whispers into the night.

My stomach heaves. "I think it is."

"Well, let's wait until we talk to Quinn," he says. "We can't know that anything these people say is true."

I don't want to dwell on it. What's the point? What does thinking ever change? I crawl to the edge of the roof and turn onto my belly. I dangle a moment before letting go and land awkwardly. No floodlight is activated, and I crouch in the stillness. Silas lands next to me with a thud seconds later.

We stay hunched and sneak behind the cabins. As clouds cover the moon, we're bathed in complete darkness, and I feel Silas hold on to the tail of my jacket to make sure he doesn't lose me. When we reach the last cabin, and our eyes have fully adjusted, we stop. The annex is to our right, in front of the main house, the other outbuildings to our left. Between the outbuildings and us is an expanse of open land, and if it's protected by motion sensors, we'll be discovered.

The clouds shift, and the moon dispenses a little light. Silas looks quickly from left to right. "That must be the lockup. Narrow windows," he says, pointing to a squat building in the distance. He's about to speak again when we hear low voices. We flatten ourselves against the wall as Vanya and Maks come into view. I breathe as slowly and quietly as I can.

"I'm sorry about your daughter," Maks says.

"She was dead to me a long time ago," Vanya responds.

"Well, maybe she isn't. I don't trust any of them," he says. "They're too clever."

Vanya smiles. "So what? How many brainy traitors have we buried?"

They are tittering when the area erupts in light. I pull my face around the corner and instinctively take Silas's hand. He puts a finger to the blowoff valve of my facemask. Like he has to warn me to be quiet.

"What are those idiots doing?" Vanya says. "Go and shut down the floodlights." Maks gallops away.

"It's Vanya," a new voice says.

"What are you playing at? What if someone sees you?" Vanya hisses, and the floodlights dim to nothing. I poke my face around the corner. Silas stands over me and does the same. In Maks's place is a pair of men carrying a long object wrapped in plastic. They put down their load and stand panting.

"The buggy broke down," one of the men tells Vanya. "Had to carry it ourselves."

"Just get this garbage out back where it belongs. And if I ever see you two trying something like this again, it'll be you rolled up in plastic." Vanya kicks the load violently and strides away, the men watching her go.

"Hormonal or what," one whispers. The other snickers. As they reach down for their bundle, Silas pulls on my elbow. "We have to follow them," he says.

"What for?"

"Do you want to guess what's in that plastic or shall I?" he asks.

"What about Quinn?" We need to make sure he's okay, and find out what's happened to Bea.

"What if that *is* Quinn?" Silas asks. I stare at the bundle. If Silas is right, then it doesn't matter what Abel says; we can't stay one more day.

"You don't think that," I say.

"He wasn't at dinner."

"Let's check it out."

We follow the men at a distance, stooping low and sticking as close to the outbuildings as we can. They chat, back and forth, and groan under the weight of the load. "Should've waited 'til tomorrow," the one says.

"Best get it over with." Eventually we reach the back wall marking Sequoia's border. Like the front, the top is garnished with broken glass. With a sigh, the two men drop the bundle and stand huffing and puffing. "Need air," one says, coughing.

"Too right. Soon as we're done with this, I'm gonna set up camp next to an oxybox." He roots in his pocket and pulls out a heavy, jangling set of keys, which he inspects in the moonlight. "Got it," he says, and shuffles to the wall with a tiny steel door built into it. He rattles the key in the lock, and the door opens.

The two men let out long breaths as they bend down to retrieve the bundle, and once they have it, they scoot through the door, one walking backward, the other directing from the opposite end.

We spring at the door as quickly as we can, glance around it to make sure the men have moved on, and creep out of Sequoia.

I close my eyes and take a deep breath. "Quick," Silas whispers.

The men are already way ahead, plodding along the uneven ground and sidestepping heaps of junk abandoned on this side of the wall, where no one has to see it. The moon disappears again, which is fortunate, because there are no buildings to hide behind, only the odd boulder or rusting car, and if the men were to turn, they'd surely see us.

They stop for the final time, and we drop behind an upended, rotting wooden table. Silas nudges me. I lift myself up beside him. There is another figure next to the two men now: a scrawny man with a long beard and wearing a face-mask. "The hole doesn't look big enough," one of the men complains.

"Gimme a look," the bearded man grumbles, and knocks the bundle with the handle of a shovel. The men let it drop to the ground and unwrap it.

I lift myself higher to see, sprawled on the ground before us, lifeless and stiff, the body of a man. His head is swollen and his eyes are bulging. I slide back down behind the table and cover the blowoff valve in my mask with my hand.

Silas's eyes reflect a sliver of light. "Not Quinn," he whispers, which makes me feel a little better, but not much.

"He's too wide," the bearded man says. The shovel hits the ground as he digs a bigger hole. "I've another spade over there," he says.

"You do your job, Crab, we'll do ours."

There's a pause and one of the men speaks again. "Hungry?" he asks the other. We hear something being unwrapped and slobbery chewing. I gag. How can they bury someone and eat at the same time?

And that's when I notice the ground: it isn't naturally uneven—it's become that way from the bodies buried here. And though some mounds have already been concealed by rocks and debris, and are almost flat, others are still plump, the earth barely sunken in next to the body.

I poke Silas. "Graves *everywhere*," I whisper.

"Who the hell are they burying?" he says. We stare at each other, not knowing what else to say.

"There you are," Crab says. We peek over the edge of the table and watch Crab throw his shovel onto the ground.

The two men who carried the body throw aside what remains of their food and stand. "You take that end," one tells the other.

"Why should I touch the head?" his workmate barks.

"He won't bite."

"You take the head then," he says, and the other man is forced to swap ends.

"One, two, three," he says, grimacing, and they lift the man by his arms and legs, swing the body, and launch him into the hole where he lands with a crack.

Crab twirls the end of his beard around his finger. "Shall I fill it in?" he asks, nodding at the grave.

"Well, we don't want it stinking."

"Doesn't seem much point if you're gonna have another delivery for me any day." Crab picks up his shovel and sticks it into the heap of loose earth.

"Not your place to keep track of these things, Crab," one of the men says. Crab snorts and covers the dead man with earth. The two deliverymen head back.

"We should've run from Sequoia ages ago," Silas whispers.

"The back gate gives us an escape route. We didn't know about it until now."

Silas rubs his head with both hands. The two men are out of sight. If we want to catch them and make it through the door before them, we have to run.

We pick our way through the junk, veering to the right to bypass the men. It's so dark it's difficult to see where we're going, and we're sprinting so fast, I stumble several times and my boots clank against old metal pipes. Finally the wall appears, and we slam against it, almost knocking ourselves out. I use my hands to feel for the open door. Silas points at it about fifty feet away, but we're too late. The men saunter out of the scrub and seconds later slip though the door, slamming it behind them. We run and I try the handle. "Locked. We'll have to climb over the wall," I say.

"I'm not sure it's possible," Silas says, and I'm about to argue when there's a bang and he crumples to the ground.

I scream and jump just in time to dodge the gravedigger who is aiming his shovel directly for my head.

"Drifters!" Crab yells, grappling for my facemask. I kick him in the chest with both feet and knock him to the ground, giving me a few seconds to grab his facemask. I pull it so hard the tubing comes away from the airtank, and he lashes out. But he isn't as adept at breathing as the others, and after a few seconds he stops fighting, hacking instead, as the sinewy atmosphere attacks his lungs.

"Give me my mask, you dirty br-brat," he sputters.

I dash to Silas, refit his facemask, and shake him violently. "Wake up." I lift his head to see if he's been injured, but I can't see much in the dark, and suddenly there's a rustle behind me and my own facemask is pulled off. I jump up and turn, and as I do, Crab, who looked done for only moments before, puts his hands around my throat. His eyes bulge as he squeezes.

Neither of us has enough air, and together we crumple to the ground.

His hands are clamped so firmly there's no way he's letting go. It feels like he might snap my neck. I dig my nails into his hands and scratch his face, fighting, fighting for life. And then a shadow appears above us.

Silas.

Crab releases me and tries to scurry away but Silas has the shovel. Crab covers his eyes with his hands, as though this will protect him, and Silas smacks the shovel against Crab's head. Crab doesn't utter another sound and drops to the ground. I shudder and stare at Silas.

Silas throws me his facemask, then retrieves mine and puts it over his own mouth and nose. "He's dead," I say.

Silas lifts Crab's head. "Yes," he says. A dark, thick liquid oozes from his head onto the earth. A stabbing of regret trickles into me, but I sweep it away: it was him or us. Right?

"No one can find him," Silas says. He pulls me to my feet.

"What does it matter?" My throat is still stinging.

"They'll suspect us. I don't want to be next."

I bend down and lift Crab's legs. Silas takes his arms. Blood drips from the gravedigger's fractured skull.

Quickly, we carry Crab to the hole he dug himself and throw him on top of the other body. "I'll get the shovel," Silas says. I stare down at Crab, lying cheek to cheek with the other dead man, their limbs bent all out of shape.

Silas begins filling the hole as soon as he returns, and when his muscles ache, I take over. We work like this until we're done. "We're murderers," I say, wiping my sweaty hands on my trousers.

On our way back we use stones and loose earth to cover the track of Crab's blood. "Let's stash the airtank. We may need it later," Silas says, leaving me by the wall for a few minutes while he finds a good hiding spot.

We still have the problem of how we're going to get into Sequoia. There don't seem to be any cameras at this rear exit, but there's the glass on the wall; it won't go unnoticed if we turn up to breakfast gashed to pieces from climbing over it.

"Alina," Silas mutters. He's on his knees. "A way in. Or out," he says. I squat next to him and look.

Someone has furrowed a narrow tunnel underneath the wall.

"Can you fit?" I ask.

Silas answers by crawling into the tunnel headfirst. He has to wriggle from side to side to get through, but he does it, and soon after I am through, too, covered from head to toe in dirt. "Hopefully the flood lights are still off," Silas says.

Tonight we have achieved nothing more than killing a man, and as we head for the cabin, one word repeats itself in my head: *Murderer. Murderer.*

That is what I have become.

32
QUINN

I'm awoken by arguing. "Quit nudging me!" the boy groans from his cell.

"But you won't stop snoring," the girl says.

"I can't help it."

I turn over on the hard slab of concrete. They're standing face-to-face and grappling with each other through the bars. The girl sees me watching and stops.

"What did *you* do?" she asks. I stand up and dust myself off.

"Nothing," I say. "But seems like that's enough here." The girl squeals with laughter. She hits the boy as she continues to titter. It's not a genuine laugh: she's hysterical. "Is there a way out?" I ask. There's a sliver of a window by the roof, but that's about it.

"I wouldn't try to escape, if I were you," the boy says. He pulls up his shirt to show me his chest, which is covered in bruises.

"Maks?" I ask.

He nods and puts his hands between the bars to pull up the back of the girl's shirt. Her skin is crisscrossed with red welts. "He beat me and whipped her," he says. "Because we stole an airtank. That was it."

I dry heave. I miss Bea, but thank goodness I didn't bring her here.

Keys rattle in the lock and Maks pushes open the door. The boy and girl scuttle to the backs of their cells and watch as he approaches me. "Exciting news. Vanya's forgiven you, which means you have a busy day of exams ahead."

"Exams?"

"Just get a move on," Maks says, pulling open the cell door and grabbing me by the back of the neck. I don't struggle, because I could be in for it if I do. Besides, I have a better chance of finding Alina and getting out of here and back to the pod if I'm not locked in a prison cell.

The boy and girl watch me go. They look afraid.

And I should probably look afraid, too.

33
ALINA

I wake in a sweat, sure someone has his hands around my throat. Silas is sitting on my bunk. "It was a dream," he says.

I push my hair out of my face. "What time is it?" I ask. Everyone else is up and dressed.

"Six in the evening. We're getting ready for this stupid Pairing Ceremony," he says.

"I've been asleep all day?"

"I told Vanya you had an iffy stomach," he says.

I think of Crab's foaming mouth as he tried to kill me and I am breathless again. "Did you tell them?" I whisper. I can't remember anything that happened after we snuck back into Sequoia. Silas had to half carry me to the cabin.

Silas slides closer. "They know we saw a body being buried. We'll tell them what we did, if we have to. Keep it together, Alina. You've killed before." I shake my head to contradict him. "At The Grove. You think none of your bullets hit those soldiers?"

But it was easier then—the troops were far away; I couldn't see their faces, and I didn't have to bury them.

Silas turns to the others. "Seeing the body last night leaves us in no doubt. . . . We need to get out of here. Our main concern is oxygen. Song?"

Song bites his lips. "I can find a way to store oxygen and pump it into an airtight space, but we need trees to produce it or the formula for manufactured air . . . plus the chemicals."

"Well, that's impossible," Silas says. We're all silent. Our options are meager. "I have the map that Inger was putting together, which has the locations of solar respirators on it. We can survive on those and wait for Song to design something better." He looks at each of us in turn. I want to have a better idea, but I don't.

"We was fine on solar respirators before you lot showed up," Maude lies. If it was fine, she wouldn't have tried to kill me for my airtank the first time she saw me.

Dorian puts his hands on his hips. "We buried people at The Grove, you know. I don't know why this dead body should change anything."

"This wasn't a one-off, Dorian. There were dozens of graves," I say.

Dorian pulls his red robe over his head and faces us, defiant. "I don't agree with pairings any more than you, but I'm not spending the rest of my life drifting and barely clinging to life."

We all watch Silas and wait, willing him to find a solution to Dorian's fears. Fears that are ours, too. But he has no answer for this. "We have to leave Sequoia now," is all he says.

"We won't make it a mile before they're on top of us," I say. I don't mean to contradict Silas, who is glaring at me, but we have to bide our time, run when they least expect it. Besides, if we run now, they'll know we were the ones who killed Crab. "We found a way out. It's a narrow tunnel under the wall at the back, about fifty feet from a steel door. Anything heavy goes down, we leave that way and wait for one another on the other side. There are only a few places back there to hide," I say.

Song goes to the door, takes the rest of the robes from the hook, and hands them out. The sleeves are too long, eating up our hands.

Silas goes to the wall and punches it. Dorian pulls up his hood and it covers his entire forehead, right down to his eyes. "Red ain't my color," Maude says. She tries to struggle out of the robe, but Bruce stops her.

"It's just for an hour or so, Maddie."

Somewhere beyond the cabin a shrill whistle sounds.

"Pairings," I say.

Before being led into the orangery where the pairings will be performed, we're held in a waiting room with narrow benches running the length of it. Silas is on my one side, Dorian on my other. Apart from those of us from The Grove, around ten people are with us. Abel sits opposite me. When he smiles, I smile back. He's always been able to make me do this, even when things were dire.

I scan the bench and the faces of the other boys. They don't look particularly menacing; I'd be willing to fend off any one of them.

A door opens and another candidate is pushed into the room. "Quinn!" I say, and go to him. "We were worried," I whisper.

"I've just had a three-hour test followed by the most humiliating physical exam of my life," Quinn says.

"Where are Bea and Jazz?"

He edges closer. In the past I might have moved away, but he isn't flirting. "They're alive," he says, and suddenly joy and hope fizz through me. If Bea's alive, and Jazz too, there's no excuse for any of us to give up. "Bea was with Ronan Knavery. They're planning a new rebellion in the pod. They have my father on our side this time and think they can take control of the army. But we need you."

"Cain Knavery's son?" I ask. He nods. It's a lot to take in, and I have a hundred questions, but I haven't time to ask any more because a bell rings, and Maks enters from the opposite end of the room wearing a skintight red shirt.

"Excited?" he asks. He rubs his hands together. I don't like the gesture, or his leering expression. After what I saw in the stairwell, I pity poor Jo and her life with him. "Let's do this," he says. My gut tightens and I pull back the lower half of my facemask, so I can bite my nails.

"So the first civil war in the pod didn't achieve anything?" I ask, taking Quinn by the arm.

"Well, it was enough to make my father and Ronan turn against the Ministry. Will you come back with me?" he asks.

"Yes," I tell him. "Of course, I will."

The orangery is an enormous conservatory attached to the east wing of the main house. Along three sides are rows of Sequoians gawking at us, and on the remaining fourth side is a stage decorated with a red banner that reads *For Air, We Pair*. It doesn't even make sense: the only way to re-oxygenate the planet is to grow trees.

Vanya is standing under the banner wearing a red robe, although hers has no hood and plunges at the neckline where it's held in place with a metal pin. Maks steers us to some empty chairs, then steps up onto the stage and stands next to Vanya.

We sit.

"A Pairing Ceremony is our most valued celebration," Vanya says. "Through pairings, we preserve the human race from extinction. Along with pairings, these candidates will learn their vocations. They will become troopers, responsible for the group's physical needs; academics, responsible for the group's mental needs; or benefactors, responsible for the group's spiritual needs." I look around the room. I haven't met anyone here who seems particularly spiritually enlightened, and she must have forgotten that humans and overpopulation was the reason for The Switch in the first place. Cut down the trees to feed the people—what a good plan that turned out to be.

"I marvel at what we have achieved," Vanya continues. "We've made mistakes and sacrifices along the way, but we are stronger for it, and unlike other groups who have fallen, we prevail." Vanya looks down at our group and I nearly give her the finger. It isn't our fault The Grove perished. "Many of the candidates are refugees. Sequoia is the last stronghold against the Ministry and we defend our right, not only to breathe, but to *breed* a new people invincible to the elements." The audience cheers. I look along at Silas, but he's focused on the floor, his cheeks burning, his hands curled into fists. I wouldn't put it past him to start something right now, but we can't win if we try to battle these people. There are too many of them. When we leave, we should simply sneak away.

Vanya calls forward a set of candidates. "Song Jackson, Dorian Chasm, Juno McIntire, Martha Spencer, Quinn Caffrey, and Clarice Bird, please come onto the stage," Vanya says. Dorian is the only person to stand. "All of you," Vanya says.

"Here goes nothing," Quinn says, and files onto the stage with the others. Most of them seem petrified, or at least nervous, but not Dorian. Since when did he decide that this was what he wanted?

"I present to you . . . our academics," Vanya announces. There are cheers, presumably from other academics. "Please cover your heads," Vanya directs. The hoods completely shroud the top halves of their faces. "The pairings have been scientifically chosen to ensure each person in Sequoia has a mate who is a true fit." Vanya consults a list. "Please hold out your hands." Vanya takes Song and another person's hand and guides them to the front of the stage. "Presenting Song Jackson and Martha Spencer," she says. They are made to kneel, then Vanya places a hand on each of their heads and closes her eyes. "Future generations will mark these days. May your union assist humanity. And may you strive for the greater good."

"For the greater good," the room chants. Vanya bows as though she's performed a magic trick and pushes back the hoods on their robes. Song and Martha look at each other for the first time. Is he trembling? Vanya forces them to hold hands, and Song stumbles as they stand. Martha holds him up. After what happened to Holly, I'm surprised he's been so composed about the process until now.

Vanya chooses another pair: Quinn and the girl called Clarice. Quinn's the only one on stage wearing a mask, and I can sense the audience staring at him. He and Clarice kneel before Vanya who gives her speech and unites them.

Dorian is next, and once he has been paired, he leads his partner, Juno, to the side where he immediately lets go of her hand. Now he's seen her, a round-faced, plain-looking girl with mild acne, he doesn't look as keen on conforming. He leans as far away from Juno as he can.

Maks directs them to a set of seats at the back of the stage. There's nothing funny about the pairings and nothing funny about Sequoia either, but seeing Dorian disappointed, his illusions shattered, makes me smile.

Vanya announces that there will be another group of academics. She calls out names I don't recognize, and more robed candidates mount the stage. I blot out her voice and gaze through the glass ceiling at the black sky dotted with blinking stars. It looks just like the night I slept in the trees at The Grove—before the whole world came crashing to the ground. The peace I felt in those moments was like nothing else, curling up in the thick silence of space.

It isn't long until my name is called. "Alina Moon, Silas Moon, Wren Darson, Sugar Collins, and Abel Boone, please come up." And I am facing a hundred Sequoians shifting impatiently in their seats. Those who are paying attention are peering at Silas and me peculiarly, because, like Quinn, we're wearing facemasks. But they can go screw themselves—they know nothing about who we are or what we've sacrificed to be here.

Apart from Silas, who *can't* be my other, the only other male is Abel. It shouldn't make me happy—none of this is right—but I'm glad for the facemask and hood, so no one will see my relief.

"Let me present the troopers," Vanya says, and then Silas's name is announced along with Wren's. I can't imagine what he must be thinking or feeling. Losing Inger is bad enough, but now this. Now *her*.

And Vanya speaks again. "Presenting Abel Boone and Sugar Collins," she says. My chest tightens. I pull back the hood a few inches and watch Abel and Sugar hold hands and awkwardly step aside. Senseless jealousy ripples through me. There is a murmuring in the audience because I am the last candidate. Does this mean I won't be paired? It feels like a blessing not to be, and yet. . . . My stomach knots.

Vanya forces me to kneel and places a hand on my head as she did with the others. All I can see from under my hood are the feet of the audience. Vanya clears her throat and this is enough to silence the murmuring crowd. "A person gets paired once. This has always been our rule. But what if a pairing goes wrong? What if, when we check the test results, we discover an error? Jo Rose fled Sequoia and returned to us a few days ago. Why did she flee? She knew she was wrongly stationed, and as a result we have retested her and discovered that she never should have been made a trooper nor paired. Jo has been reevaluated and will become a bene-factor, and like all benefactors, she will be our conscience. She will spend her days in a meditative state and attract good energy to Sequoia. This is a role only a select few are cut out for, and it is a role many find difficult to understand. Jo is desperately needed." The audience is silent, soaking in the news. "Jo's other will be re-paired today."

No . . .

I bite on my tongue, and the floor creaks as he kneels. The blood pumping through my ears thrums. Silas and I should have escaped last night when we had the chance, or this morning like he suggested.

We'd seen enough.

My hood is removed and Maks is smiling at me using only one side of his mouth. He offers me his hand. I have no choice but to take it and join the others at the side of the stage.

Maks puts an arm around my waist and tries to pull me close. "Don't!" I say, but he leaves his hand resting on my hip. So I pinch it—hard.

All he does is laughs and moves his hand to the back of my neck, where he pulls on the straps of my facemask. "Careful," he whispers.

Vanya is speaking again, inviting Maude and Bruce onto the stage. They are pronounced benefactors. "That's about right. Always been generous, me," Maude says, which gets a laugh.

The ceremony comes to an end and we're escorted out. The audience is on its feet applauding, but I can't help noticing that some of the faces look irredeemably sad.

Someone stands on the hem of my robe, and when I turn, Abel is shuffling after me holding Sugar's hand. He has the same terrified stare he had when we were stealing from the biosphere. "I'm sorry for asking you to stay. I had no idea you'd get him," he whispers. Thankfully, Maks is several paces ahead and can't hear.

"It's too late for apologies," I say, though this isn't really his fault.

Abel lets go of Sugar, who squints when he presses his mouth close to my ear. "Maude and Bruce are in trouble. And so is Jo," he says.

"What?" I stop walking.

"They could die. We have to—" He stops as Maks pushes back through the crowd to get to me.

"Alina," Maks growls. "Come on."

"Abel?" I say, but he can't tell me any more because Maks has my arm and is dragging me away.

34
BEA

The sound of an engine puttering to a halt in the street below wakes me. And then Jude Caffrey's voice. "RONAN!"

Ronan tears out of the room as I crawl off the bed. By the time I get to the window, he's already with Jude Caffrey, standing next to the buggy. Jude puts his arm over Ronan's shoulder, and for a moment I imagine it's Quinn. My nose tingles: Ronan, Quinn, and I have all lost our fathers.

It's dawn and the buildings draw thick belts of golden light across the street. I step away from the window. I'm really doing this—I'm teaming up with Jude Caffrey.

Footsteps knock on the stairs and Ronan appears. "Ready?" A shaft of light illuminates the top half of his face. His eyes are bloodshot, dark circles beneath them. He must have been up all night.

"Did you tell him?" I ask. He comes to the corner where I'm scooping my things into a backpack and takes my hand. I snatch it away. "Does he know about me?"

"He knows."

"He'll help? He'll protect me and recruit Resistance members to the army?"

"Yes," he says, and beams. I throw my arms around him, unable to contain my own joy. "Oh, Ronan, do you think we can really oust the Ministry?"

"We're about to try," he says.

He pulls several packets of nutrition and protein bars and two spare airtanks from his backpack and throws them on the floor. I frown. "You said some drifters were harmless. They need them more than I do," he says. He tugs on the backpack's drawstrings and throws it over his shoulder. We stand facing each other. After today, we probably won't get many more moments alone, but I can't think what to say.

Jude calls up from the road, and Ronan looks at the window, then at me, and finally at the door. He fiddles with the straps on his facemask. "Come on," he says.

Outside, Jude Caffrey looks me up and down and sighs. "Bea Whitcraft . . . I didn't expect to see you again."

"You mean you didn't *want* to," I respond.

"No. No, I probably didn't," he says. "But here we are." Jude stuffs his hands into his pockets and rocks back and forth. He looks at my disheveled appearance and then at Ronan. "Sorry I couldn't get here yesterday. Things are hectic in the pod."

Ronan shrugs. "You're here now. I wondered whether you'd come at all."

Jude allows himself a small smile. "You sure you want to come back?" he asks me, and I nod. "If the ministers get a hold of you, you're in deep shit," Jude says. "We're *all* in very deep shit."

"They won't find her," Ronan says, leading me to the buggy. "Take the front seat," he says.

And sit next to Jude for an hour? I shake my head. "I'll be fine in the back," I say, and climb in.

Soon the buggy is bumping along the road. None of us talk for a long time. And then Jude turns around and looks at me. "Quinn is alive, isn't he?" he asks. "You wouldn't make it up."

I've never heard him speak like this—with feeling for his son.

"He's alive," I say. "And he's coming."

35
RONAN

The pod has plenty of exit-only doors so rebels can be ejected. Jude guides Bea to one of them, where she waits in the dark.

Jude and I enter through the official border gates.

A steward is scrolling through a pad. When he sees me, he stops. "Welcome back, Mr. Knavery. I'm sure you did your best," he says. He looks at his colleague and smirks.

I'm so tired, I react immediately, resting my index finger on the hollow of the steward's chest. He steps back and I follow him, keeping my finger where it is. "Be careful."

His nose twitches. "I only meant—"

I interrupt. "I know what you meant." He looks at his colleague. I could easily sidestep him. I decide not to. "Move," I say, and he does.

Jude is close behind. We clamber into the waiting buggy. "What does that girl do to people?" he asks.

"What do you mean?"

"Bea Whitcraft turns boys into men."

Every few blocks there's a checkpoint, but the stewards only have to catch a glimpse of Jude, and wave us through. "Security hasn't been relaxed then," I say.

He snorts. "Nightly raids on auxiliary homes began two days ago. More speed cameras, and there's a call to ban auxiliaries from Zone One altogether."

We pull up in front of the Justice Building. Jude climbs out of the buggy, and I follow him up the steps into the foyer. A gaggle of ministers squint when they see me. I'm the first of the Special Forces to return.

"Have you heard from any of the others?" I ask Jude. "Has Rick knifed anyone yet?"

"He radioed in and told me that he's about to rappel down a well because he's convinced he can hear people." He laughs. "I get a feeling the others will be back soon. Robyn knows she's out there for nothing."

"She's as disillusioned as I am," I say.

"You're not to involve her in what we're doing. The more Premiums who know, the more chance we have of being betrayed."

We scan our pads and walk down a hallway lined with doors. The light bulbs flicker. A moan comes from somewhere, and I stop. Jude keeps walking. "We've made over thirty arrests since you've been away. Suspected RATS mostly. That's a hunger pang you're hearing," he says.

"Why are you starving them?"

Jude stops. "The ministers believe they'll talk when they're hungry. Your sister comes down daily to goad them with smoothies and cakes."

"My sister?"

"She's working as Lance Vine's assistant. Seems to be enjoying it."

I can hardly believe it. Niamh has taken a job?

Jude pushes open a door marked *CAUTION— AIRTANKS REQUIRED*. He steps outside and a rush of cold air fills the hallway. He returns with Bea. "In here," he says, jangling a heavy set of old-fashioned keys and pushing us into an empty cell with condensation running down the walls. "I just want to go on record as saying that pod ministers come and go, but the Ministry has always ruled. They won't give up power without a fight."

"And that's exactly what they're going to get," I say. I make it sound easy, though it will be harder than anything I've ever done. "Have you advertised for soldiers?"

"We've had hardly any applications. The lure of living

with the other civic workers in Zone Two doesn't attract anyone anymore. Not now they suspect what's going on." He scrapes his hair back with his fingers.

"In a few days, you'll have hundreds of applicants. Maybe thousands. Bea and I are going to find what's left of the Resistance and explain the plan. They'll get people to sign up."

Jude chews on his thumbnail. "I'm endangering my family," he says.

"But you're already involved." I raise my voice without meaning to and Jude puts a finger to his lips. He can't back out now—we need him. "You're harboring a wanted terrorist."

He looks at Bea and hangs his head, defeated. "I know," he says.

"Where's Jazz?" Bea whispers.

Jude rubs his temples. "She's recovering in the infirmary."

"And her leg?" she asks.

"She almost lost it, but she's okay."

"Did they question her?" I ask.

"She said she was a drifter's daughter and her parents died at The Grove fighting the Resistance. She claims to hate the Resistance for killing her parents. She's quite the actress."

Bea laughs and we both look at her, surprised by the sound. "She's a performer," she explains. "Can I see her?"

"I don't think so," Jude says. He opens a metal locker in the corner of the cell. He pulls out a steward's uniform and hands it to Bea. "You'll have to wear this," he says.

"We also need to find a way to keep the Resistance who are on the Ministry's hit list out of jail," I say.

"Old Watson will know where they are," Bea says.

"Who's Old Watson?" Jude asks. Bea presses her lips together and inspects the steward's uniform. She isn't ready to trust him.

He rolls his eyes. "Where are we hiding you, anyway?" he asks.

"We're taking her to my house," I say.

36
ALINA

The room I'm to share with Maks contains a double bed, a couple of nightstands, and a dresser. He closes the door, locks it, then runs his eyes up and down the length of my body. Whatever I'm expected to do isn't going to happen, so I turn my back on him, take off my robe, and stuff it into the trash can. "Anything else you'd like to take off?" The floor creaks, and when I wheel around, he's so close, his breath is warm against my forehead. "You don't have to be frightened," he says. He pushes my hair away from my face, and I shudder. I don't want him near me. I push him back and try to look tougher than I feel.

I do a quick scan of the room in case there's anything I could use as a weapon, and hone in on a clock with a stone base. If he tries anything, he'll get it to the back of his head.

"Stay on that side of the room," I say, pointing. He rubs his mouth, and before I can get anywhere near the clock, he grabs the back of my head and pulls my face close to his.

"You think I'm going to pop your cherry without permission?" he says. With his free hand, he untucks his shirt from his pants.

Is it that obvious I'm a virgin? I stay very still. "I don't want *you*," I say. Regardless of how scared I am, I mustn't let him see it.

"Oh, come on. I've noticed the way you look at me."

I hold his stare. "Where's Jo?" I ask.

He licks his top teeth and sucks on them. "You heard Vanya. She's a benefactor now."

"Her *and* your baby?"

He releases me, goes to the window, and throws it open, breathing in the night air like I never have. "You think you've got us figured out. Well, you don't. If anything, you've got us all wrong." When he looks back at me his eyes are watery, but I don't buy it. I saw him manhandling Jo. And Silas and I saw his lackeys burying a body. It's impossible we've got them wrong.

"I'm sleeping on the floor," I say.

"Fine," he says. "Jo did that for a year. Eventually she jumped into bed with me, and it had nothing to do with the cold." He pulls his shirt over his head and reveals his chest.

Maybe he thinks I'll be won over by his body. I look away and lie down on the floor.

We should never have come here.

And the only thing to do now is to get back to the pod and make it the home it might have always been.

37
RONAN

Niamh isn't at home, and I manage to smuggle Bea through the garden unseen. When Wendy opens the annex door she smiles and waves us inside, and within minutes of getting to know Bea, she offers up her own bed. She was the only person I could turn to.

I try to convince Bea to rest for a few hours, but once she's eaten and showered, she's back in the steward uniform and ready to find the Resistance. "I'll sleep when I don't have to do it with one eye open," she says. She might not have trained with the Special Forces, but she's as fired up to fight as I ever was.

Bea presses the buzzer on Old Watson's door. "You stay hidden or he won't let us in," she says. She takes off the steward's jacket and hat and stands back from the peephole so he'll get a good view of her.

"Watson," Bea says, as he opens the door wide and grabs her hands.

"What in Mother Earth's name are you doing here? And what's with the bloody uniform?" Old Watson says. He's about to pull her inside, when he spots me. He lets go of Bea's hands and tries to close the door, but Bea has her foot wedged in it.

"He's on our side," she says.

We follow Old Watson as he retreats into his dingy flat and sits on a lumpy couch. I peer into the room's dark recesses and gasp. He has rows and rows of what look like real plants growing in his living room. "What are those?" I ask, stunned he's managed to achieve something like this right under the Ministry's nose.

"They grew from clippings from the biosphere," Bea says matter-of-factly. And she never thought to mention it? I go to the plants, pull a leaf from one of them, and rub it between my fingers. It's waxy and green on one side, rough and gray on the other.

Bea sits next to Old Watson and gives him an awkward, sideways hug. I clear a stash of cups and glasses from a side table and sit on it. "Do you know where the Resistance is hiding?" Bea asks.

Old Watson scratches his head. "No idea what you're talking about," he says, and looks at me.

"The Grove's gone," I say. "The only option for people now is to fight back."

Old Watson's chin trembles. "What about . . . Silas and Alina?" he stutters.

Bea takes his hand. "They made it out. And Quinn's bringing them here. Together we're going to free everyone, Watson." She sounds certain, but before he even hears the plan, Old Watson drops his head in his hands and groans.

"You haven't been here since the riots, Bea. It's pointless trying to win."

"We have Ronan now, and Jude Caffrey," Bea tells him.

"Jude Caffrey? Why would you trust him after what he did to Quinn?" Bea swallows hard. There's no need to remind her about Quinn or what Jude Caffrey's capable of. "And why would you trust Cain Knavery's son?" he says like I'm not in the room.

"Caffrey's going to recruit auxiliaries as soldiers," I tell him. "The Ministry's going to arm people who will turn around and destroy it."

Old Watson stares at me and then at Bea as he digests this plan. "You serious?" he asks. Bea nods.

Old Watson breathes through his nose loudly and hobbles to the balcony doors, where he opens a pair of threadbare curtains and looks down into Zone Three. "If Lance Vine finds out you're plotting against him, you'll wake up with your guts wrapped around your throat."

"Are you willing to take a chance like that, Ronan?" Bea asks.

"I am," I say.

Old Watson snatches up a tattered cardigan hanging on the back of a dining chair. "I'm getting too long in the tooth for this," he says.

The existing Resistance members are scattered through the pod to prevent them all being captured in one lucky raid, but Old Watson knows where Harriet and Gideon are hiding. He guides us through the alleyways of Zone Three to a particularly dilapidated block of auxiliary flats. The winch is broken and we have to climb twelve flights.

Old Watson wheezes and raps on a door three times, then rings the bell twice. It's immediately opened by a tall woman with her hair slicked back into a bun. Right away she spots me and pulls a handgun from a belt at her waist.

"He's with me, Harriet," Bea says, stepping in front of me.

"Bea?" Harriet says, lowering her gun and taking in Bea's uniform.

"It's a disguise," Bea says. "Can we come in?"

Harriet leads us to the kitchen, where we sit and explain. Harriet and Gideon listen patiently. They wait for us to go through everything at our own pace, and when we're through, Gideon goes to the sink and fills a pot with water from the boiling tap. He throws in a few teaspoons of dark brown powder, stirs, and plunks it on the table along with a few chipped mugs. Old Watson pours himself a helping and sips. Like his place, the flat is packed with plants and cuttings steeped in water. All other available space has been used to store sleeping bags and pillows.

Gideon sits down and leans back in his chair. "Jude Caffrey is a scumbag who finished off his own son."

"Quinn's alive," Bea says, and lowers her gaze.

Harriet folds her arms across her chest. "Well, we can't apply," she explains, "we're wanted fugitives."

"But you can persuade others to apply. It shouldn't be hard to find auxiliaries willing to rebel," I say, speaking up for the first time. Bea and I have discussed the plan, but maybe we're being delusional. Bea nods encouragingly. "The riot didn't make a dent because it was impromptu. This way, the Resistance will begin to get training, and more importantly, weapons. We'll have bigger numbers and better organization."

"With all the nightly raids, we'll be lucky to last a few more days without getting caught," Gideon says. "We're only alive because we're always on the move. As soon as the meters show an empty apartment's using oxygen, they come for us."

"So what are you saying?" Harriet asks her husband.

"The border's closed, as is the biosphere. They've shut us down," he responds.

"Not yet, they haven't. Just stay on the move and if we can get hold of any airtanks we'll get them to you," Bea says. "You continue to grow, and we'll all recruit and keep training to breathe with low oxygen."

Old Watson yawns and drains his mug. "So whatever way you look at it, it's either a war, or capture and death," he says.

"That's right," Bea says. "Now let's get on it."

I ensconce Bea in Wendy's annex and head into the house. The toilet flushes and Lance Vine comes into the kitchen zipping up his fly. "Ronan," he says. He wipes his hands on the front of his pants, which are an inch too short for his spindly legs.

"I didn't expect to see you here, Pod Minister," I say. He's the *last* person I expected to see. I focus hard on his face, so I don't spontaneously look out at Wendy's annex.

"Really." Vine pauses, giving me time to respond, but I stand stolid. "Niamh's been helping me type up a new bill.

I've been admiring your lovely home, actually. Real marble?" He touches the kitchen counter and whistles. "Don't
think any of the ministers live in such splendor. But then,
Cain was always a bit of a hedonist." He opens a cupboard
and peers at the array of glasses and tableware. He smiles.
"So no signs of the RATS, then?" I shake my head. "Time
to get the zips fired up, I'd say."

"I wouldn't know," I say—Jude will have to deal with
Lance Vine. "What's the bill you're working on?" I take out
my pad and scroll through the messages, so he won't think
I'm too interested.

"We're siphoning oxygen from empty apartments or ten-
ants who don't pay their taxes. It's only fair." He watches me.

"People will die," I say.

"RATS are squatting and using air for free."

"You're back!" Niamh is standing beaming under the
doorframe, but she doesn't go so far as to rush at me for a hug.

"Your brother seems unsure about the new bill," Vine
tells her.

Niamh tuts. "He acts tough, but Ronan's a softie."

"Is that so?" Vine asks.

"Only where the innocent are concerned," I say, hard-
ening my gaze. He doesn't frighten me half as much as my
father could.

"Well, RATS are far from innocent," Niamh says

pointedly, trying to prove to Vine that we're safely on his side.

"How can you know that for sure?" Vine asks. Niamh hesitates, frowns, and is about to respond when Vine smiles playfully. "Just kidding," he says, and throws his jacket on. "It's late. I'll let you both get to bed." And without another word, he heads out the back door.

Niamh sits on the stool next to me and lets her head flop onto the countertop. "He thinks I'm stupid," she says. She groans and closes her eyes. "I bet he'll sack me."

I make her sit up and look at me. "What are you doing working with the Ministry anyway?"

She stares at me like she's trying to remember who I am. "The RATS killed Daddy."

"Vine isn't going to bring him back," I say gently.

"Lance Vine was Daddy's friend." She goes to the window. "I want to be useful."

And I understand that. I want to be useful, too. But why must we be on different sides? Why can't she see what's happening?

"You should go to bed," I say.

"I'm glad you're home," Niamh says. She fills her water glass and strolls out of the kitchen.

I'm fooling myself if I think I can convince Niamh that our father was responsible for his own death.

And I can't be her conscience; it would be pointless to try.

PART III
THE ESCAPE

38
QUINN

Bea's running, being chased by armed stewards, and my father's at the head of the hunt, carrying one of those old-fashioned muskets. Eventually Bea falls and I'm there, too, rooted to the road and peering down at her. "Anything's better than this," she says, but before I can save her, Ronan is dragging her away. All I can do is retreat slowly into the shadows like a coward. She looks up at Ronan and smiles. Then she kisses him.

I wake with a start, feeling penned in.

Clarice has her arm draped over me. She's snoring. I peel her away and sit up, untangling the airtank's tubing, which has somehow managed to wrap itself around my neck in the night. I wish I'd stop having these nightmares.

I get out of bed, bringing the airtank with me. I'm still

in my pants, but pull on the sweater I left on the nightstand.

Clarice stirs and turns over to face me. "This is a bit awkward," she says through a yawn, which is the biggest bloody understatement ever. "But don't worry. We'll get used to each other." She seems harmless, but I feel too guilty to go as far as to like her; it should be Bea lying next to me, and I would have put my arm around her waist and my face into her neck during the night. As it was, I lay dangled over the edge of the bed in case I accidently touched Clarice, keeping one eye open for as long as I could in case Vanya or Maks stormed in.

"How long have you lived here?" I ask.

"Four years. I used to live in the pod. Glad to be out of there. Especially now with what's going on."

"Yeah," I say. I go to the door, where two pieces of gray paperlike sheets have been pushed under it during the night. They're identical apart from our names. I throw Clarice hers and read mine.

```
SCHEDULE FOR QUINN B. CAFFREY
STATS—Immunity: Level 7   Fert: Level A   IQ: 152
Ox Con: Excellent   Blood Type: A+
PARTNER—CLARICE BIRD
```

```
6:30 am Meditation - Room #12
9:30 am Academics' breakfast - Annex
10:00 am Cardio - Room #20
1:30 pm Academics' lunch - Annex
```

```
2:30 pm Yoga - Room #7
5:30 pm Study - The Main House library
7:30 pm Dinner - Sitting 1 - Annex
8:30 pm Shots - Room #4e
9:00 pm Meditation - Room #12
10:00 pm Lights out
```

NO CHANGES SHOULD BE MADE TO THIS SCHEDULE WITHOUT DIRECT APPROVAL FROM VANYA. ANY PERSON UNABLE TO COMPLETE DUTIES SHOULD REPORT TO A SENTRY NO LATER THAN 30 MINS PRIOR TO A SCHEDULED START TIME. SICKNESS SHOULD BE REPORTED TO NURSE JONES, NURSE LAYAVITCH, OR DOCTOR MARCELA.

ENDEAVOR TO REMAIN IN YOUR PAIR **AT ALL TIMES.**

"What time is it?" Clarice asks.

"Almost six," I say, looking at the clock above the bed and wondering whether Bea's made it back into the pod yet.

"This is the only free time we'll get all day," Clarice says. She sighs and gets out of bed wearing only a short shirt. I make myself busy looking elsewhere.

"And it's hardly free," I remind her. I scan the list of daily activities. Could I skip the study period without being noticed? I can't spend another night in that bed. And Alina definitely can't spend another night with Maks. We've all got to get out of here as soon as possible, if we want to help Ronan and Bea with their plan to take back the pod.

"Sometimes, when people are disappointed with a pairing, they leave. Is that what you're going to do?" Clarice asks, watching me. She piles her hair on top of her head and holds it in place with what look like chopsticks.

"'Course not," I lie, and smile, lacing up my boots good and tight.

"Phew," she says, "because anyone who tries to escape usually ends up dead, and I really don't want you to die. Not before we breed, anyway."

3 9
ALINA

Maks is with me every minute, making it impossible to plan an escape. And the only part of my day that isn't hellish is trooper training. Running, punching, throwing, and dodging are things I'm keen to practice, and even Maks seems impressed when I shoot at cans and bottles suspended from wires, hitting every one. "Not bad," he says. Maybe he believes I'm training to help Sequoia, but I'm just making sure I remember how to defend myself when we get back to the pod.

Whenever I see Silas, Wren is a few feet away, gazing at him longingly, and when I try to speak to him, Maks physically drags me away. And Sugar is attached to Abel. He tries to get my attention at lunch, but Maks watches as I spoon each morsel into my mouth and gives Abel several baleful looks. Whatever Abel knows about what's happening to Maude and Bruce, Maks doesn't want me to find out. Which makes me even more worried.

After working on our marksmanship in the morning, we're given backpacks weighed down with rocks and forced to hike. Even the veterans are given airtanks. "Use them sparingly," Maks warns, and leads a hundred troopers out of Sequoia and along a dirt track to a mountain dotted with rocks, dead grasses, and parched animal bones.

We hike for hours in the pouring rain. Never slowing. Our clothes and shoes are soaked through. I turn up my oxygen, but even then, it's too much: the new recruits, me included, fall behind. I'm alone at the back, Maks up front, when Abel hangs back. Sugar slows, too, but not enough to be right on top of us. Abel tugs on my sleeve and says something, but with the noise of my breath in my ears, the rain, and the thudding of boots, I can't hear him. He holds on to me to slow me down. The group races ahead. We are side by side, and he lifts up his facemask. "Maude, Bruce, and Jo," he says.

"What's been done to them?" I'm guessing that the body Silas and I saw Crab bury belonged to a benefactor. Do they all end up out the back in unmarked graves? But why?

Abel lets his facemask spring back against his face and raises his voice. "I'll take you to see for yourself tonight. We have to act quickly. Every hour that goes by is an hour too long."

I trip on a rock and let out a yelp. Abel catches me and Maks, who is almost a hundred feet ahead, spins around and stops. He allows the pack of hikers to pass him and waits until we've caught up. He hikes next to us.

"Her gauge was stuck. She couldn't get any air," Abel says, sidling up to Sugar again.

"Stay. With. Me," Maks says, and yanks my arm. Pain shoots along it. I wriggle out of Maks's hold, and he lifts his hand as though about to strike me, then thinks better of it. "That's enough for today," he announces to the group. He wheels around and gallops down the mountain.

"Tonight . . . Wait for me in the hallway after you've had your shots," Abel manages to mutter.

Silas finds a seat next to me in the dining hall. "Where's Maks?" he asks. I tilt my head toward the stage where Maks is sitting next to Vanya but eyeing me. "Stalker," Silas says. He spoons a portion of cockroaches onto his plate. "So how are we going to get out of this place?"

"Quinn told me there's about to be a revolt in the pod. We have to go back and help." I take a slice of protein bread and push it into my mouth. It's dry and sticks to the back of my throat.

"Is he sure?"

"He seems to be. But there's something's else. . . . Maude and Bruce are in danger. Abel's going to take me to them tonight."

Wren, who's opposite Silas, leans in. "Huh?" she says, crumbs flying onto Silas's plate.

"Give me peace," Silas snaps, and Wren sulks back, turning her body slightly away. Silas slides closer to me. "Abel was the one who told us to *stay*." He thumps the table and our cutlery jumps.

"Maybe he didn't think any of us would become benefactors."

"You aren't to go with him. I don't want you to end up out back in a fresh grave," Silas says.

"Once we have Maude and Bruce we can go back and overthrow the Ministry. Isn't that what we've always wanted?" It's certainly what I've wanted.

Silas looks around. Quinn and Dorian are seated across the dining room with the other academics, but Maude and Bruce are missing. "Fine, go with Abel," he says. "And as for going back to the pod . . ." he begins, but a hush swims through the room.

Vanya has risen. "I only have one announcement this evening." She pauses and those still eating put down their knives and forks. "Our groundskeeper, Peter Crab, who is responsible not only for the land within Sequoia, but also for maintaining a semblance of order beyond the walls, is missing. If any of you see him, or have an inkling where he could have wandered off to, please inform Maks immediately." Maks is scanning the room. Silas and I don't look at each other.

Not even a glance. We know without saying a word that our time is running out.

I leave the lab feeling a bit twitchy from the EPOs. I haven't swallowed the tablets, at least, and spit them out, hiding them underneath the runner in the hallway while I wait for Abel. He emerges from another room with Sugar, who is rubbing her upper arm. Her coarse blond hair falls over her face.

"I'm skipping meditation tonight, Sugar," Abel says. "I'm not feeling well."

"Really?" she says coldly. I don't want to be jealous of her, but I can't help it. She doesn't even seem to like Abel, yet she gets to spend all day with him. And all night.

"Hurt my neck. Must have been the hike," Abel says.

"Okay," Sugar says. She looks at me suspiciously. "Feel better," she says, and stalks down the hallway and out of sight, all the time rubbing her arm.

"What about Maks? Where did you say you'd be?" Abel asks.

"He has something to do for Vanya. He said he'd see me back in the room tonight. I'd say we have an hour."

"Right," Abel says. Without wasting another second, we scurry along the hallway and down a set of steps. When we get to a landing, he fumbles with a huge painting on the wall until it clicks, and he reveals a hidden hallway. "Follow me," he says. We slip through and Abel pulls the painting behind us. I wait for my eyes to adjust to the darkness, but they don't. The light has been completely shut out. I reach for him and he takes my hand. *This doesn't mean anything*, I remind myself. I won't be taken in again.

"Careful," he says, and we start down the stairwell. My free hand slides along the brick wall, and I feel for the edge of each step with my feet.

"It was hard when you disappeared. They said you were dead. It was on the news," I say. It's easier to talk to Abel now we're in the dark. I can be more honest—less afraid to be myself.

"I'm sorry," he says, which is all I need to hear. But he continues. "My job was to learn as much about the Resistance as possible. Vanya heard you had developed new breeding programs, but the only breeding you lot were doing was with plants."

That mission to steal clippings from the biosphere was the first important thing I'd done for The Resistance, but it meant nothing to Abel. He was just along for the ride. And because of his cold feet, we were almost caught. And because of *that* I had to flee the pod and involve Bea and Quinn in something they knew nothing about. I could keep going, tracing everything that's destroyed us and brought our group here from that moment.

"So you never gave a damn about the trees."

"I believed in what we were doing," he says. "Growing trees was giving people hope. After that day in the biosphere, I so badly wanted to tell you who I was, but before I could, I was picked up." He squeezes my hand.

"What did the Ministry do to you?"

"Beat the crap out of me. They were still waiting for me to spill it when the riot started up, and some minister chucked me out and expected me to choke. By the time I found The Grove, it was a mountain of sludge." He pauses. "We're at the bottom. Come on." We scurry along a tight passageway. The floor feels greasy, but Abel doesn't slow down.

"And Jo?" I may as well ask everything now, while I have the chance.

"I found her at The Grove. She was trying to escape Sequoia and that's why she's a benefactor now."

But that isn't really what I want to know. He lets go of my hand. A meager, gray glow fills the passageway and a gust of icy air rushes at me. "This way," Abel says, and guides me outside and toward scattered splashes of light. The main house is at our backs, and Abel continually checks behind us. As we get closer, I realize that the spots of light are windows—narrow to the point of absurdity.

Soon we're hunkering beneath a row of windows. "Take a look," Abel whispers. My stomach tumbles. Whatever is through this window can't be unseen. I press an eye to the light.

Inside is a bright hospital ward with metal beds down each side and people dressed in flimsy undershirts strapped to them. They all have tubes threaded through their mouths and noses, and IVs stuck in their hands. Everything is connected to hissing machines by their beds. A loud beeping fills the room, and a nurse jumps up from her desk and dashes to someone's bedside, where she tinkers with knobs on one of the machines. The beeping stops, and a deep moan replaces it. The nurse looks down at the person impassively and goes back to her desk.

I slide down next to Abel. "I don't understand," I say.

"That's the testing lab. Their oxygen's being rationed and their organs are being monitored. Vanya wants to understand suffocation and what chemical conditions might prevent it."

I look again to see if I can spot Maude or Bruce, but everyone is uniformly skinny, and I can't make out any faces. "How long are they kept like this?" I wait a long time for an answer, and then it comes without Abel having to say anything. I stare at him unbelieving. "They experiment on people until they die?" It's what I suspected, but knowing it's true is different. It's too horrible. "But what reason does Vanya give for why they don't mix with the others and are never seen again?"

"You heard her in the orangery going on about benefactors dedicating their lives to meditation and how this energy mustn't be contaminated."

"People buy that?"

"Some do. Some choose not to think about it." And why not? It's no more far-fetched than the idea that trees will only grow in the biosphere. People believe what they're told.

"There's more," he says, and crawls to another window.

This room is filled with cribs and playpens. A nurse sleeps in a rocking chair holding an infant. The children are crying, wheezing, or asleep. None of them are connected to tubes, but most are covered in Band-Aids and bruises. There's a shriek and a toddler sits up in her crib, her eyes full of tears. The nurse opens one eye. "Hush," she says.

"They're pumping the air in at fifteen percent," Abel whispers, "and they keep lowering it until a child looks like he might suffocate. Then they hook him up to an oxybox. They're training them."

I look into the room again. "Where are the mothers?"

I ask. Does one of these babies belong to the girl we saw in the attic?

"Vanya believes the kids are hers. The mothers stay in the main house. The older ones are upstairs. If they survive, they'll be brought over when they're twelve. Vanya's only been doing this eight years. She thinks she's creating a better breed of human."

"She's mad."

A shadow blocks the light coming from the window. "We should shut these blinds," a splintery voice says. The light dims, as the window is screened over. I squash myself against the wall.

"You brought Jo back here and you let *us* stay when you knew all this," I hiss.

"Jo needed to give birth somewhere. And I didn't know the extent of things until Jo told me a couple of days ago."

"She knew?"

"Maks took great pleasure in filling her in when she got back," he says uneasily.

"So now what?" I ask. The windows are impossibly narrow and we can't simply saunter through the front door.

"Maks has keys," he says. "If we could get them. . . ." He trails off.

"Are you joking?" He isn't the kind of person to leave keys lying around.

"There's no other way, Alina," he says. He sounds tough, but he would—it's not his neck on the line.

"Well, if we do this, we aren't leaving any benefactors behind. And definitely not the kids."

Abel gapes at me. "What? No. We can't take all of them. We'll be caught."

I pause and listen to the cry of a baby. The cry gets louder and louder until it finally subsides and the night is silent again. "Did you think we'd help you rescue Jo and no one else?" Abel shakes his head. He looks guilty. And afraid. As he should. "Have you always been in love with her?" I ask.

He sighs. "It isn't like that. Jo's my best friend. I've known her a long time," he says. "You and me, we never had a chance to get to know each other. If we did . . ."

I want to tell Abel to go to hell. If he thinks he's going to get me to help him by promising something like that, he's right—he *doesn't* know me very well. "Let's get back before someone notices we're missing," I say. "I'll tell everyone tomorrow what we have to do."

We head through the door leading into the main house, and Abel clutches my arm. His touch still makes my legs wilt, and I hate myself for being so weak. "Why do you have to act so hard-nosed all the time? You don't make it easy to love you."

I almost laugh, but rage tears through me, and I shove

him so hard, he staggers backward. He has no idea what I've been through since he was caught and because of his lies. I look at him squarely. "I'm running out of energy," I say. "I'm going to focus on this one last thing and then I'm retiring from saving the world. Maybe we'll talk about how unlovable I am then. Okay?"

40
BEA

Ronan's attic studio is covered in paintings and drawings and a rainbow of color is splattered across the floor and walls. A large board with bands of gray and red smeared across it in thick, irregular lines is sitting on an easel. It looks wet, but it's dry to the touch.

"What does it mean?" I ask, approaching the easel.

"If I knew that, I wouldn't need my therapist," he says, and grins.

"I like it," I tell him. Something about the fury of the strokes speaks to me. Maybe I could paint. In the future. If I have one.

"Every color I use, I find in the sky," he says. He points at the wide skylight in the roof. The only thing visible through it is the pod's glass surface and the sun. The space is completely private. A refuge. If I were Ronan, I'd never leave it. But now that we know the Ministry is planning to cut off the oxygen in all empty apartments, he's giving it up to hide Harriet, Gideon, and any other Resistance members on the Ministry's hit list—there's been no way for him to secretly get hold of enough airtanks to keep the wanted Resistance members alive in airless apartments.

"You're a good person," I tell him, in case he doesn't already know it.

"Sometimes," he says.

He collects the cans of paint, plaster, and glue, piles them in the corner, and hangs the paintings resting against the walls on crooked nails to get them off the floor. He stops when we hear a light tap on the door and puts his ear against it. When Ronan unlocks the door, Wendy bundles into the studio carrying a stack of sheets and blankets. "This is all I have spare," she says, throwing the bedding on the floor. "I'll look in your room, too. We have to get a move on though. Niamh will be back soon. And what about food? How am I going to justify the expense?"

"I can sort that out," Ronan says. Considering what he's doing, he's very calm. It's not even my house, and my heart is racing.

"And what if they need the bathroom?" Wendy asks. She grimaces and I find myself doing the same. Ronan remains unruffled.

He picks up a drop cloth from the floor and hangs one side to a hook in the ceiling, the other to a screw sticking out from the wall. "It'll be no more than a bucket with a lid, and I can't guarantee I'll be able to empty it every hour with Niamh prowling around, but it's the best we can do," he says.

"How many are there?" Wendy asks. She prods the bedding with her toe. They both look at me.

"Around fifteen," I say.

"Once Niamh's gone to bed, we'll bring them up. But I still think it's an awful risk hiding them here," Wendy says. Keeping me in her annex overnight has been stressful enough, but the idea of hiding hordes of Resistance members in the house, right above Niamh and any visiting ministers, has Wendy on edge.

Ronan picks up a blanket and shakes it out. "No one will think of looking here," he says. "Would you?"

Wendy shakes her head. Still, keeping everyone fed, clean, and quiet won't be easy.

"Did you bring up my stuff?" I ask Wendy.

She blinks and looks at Ronan. "There's no need for you to sleep here with everyone else, love," she says. "After what you've been through, a little privacy is what you need." Ronan coughs and Wendy stops talking. She pulls her lips into her mouth. He must have told her what happened with the drifters.

"It wouldn't be fair if I got special treatment," I mumble. I wish he hadn't said anything. Quinn never would have. He knows how to keep a secret.

"I'll see if I can dig out more sheets," Wendy says, opening the door and tiptoeing away. Ronan locks the door behind her. "You don't have to be a martyr, you know."

What? Is that how he thinks I behave? "I act like a martyr?"

"Bea . . . I don't mean it like that. Please stay in the annex with Wendy." He tilts his head and looks inconsolably sad.

I turn away from him and step closer to one of his paintings: a series of blue circles along with smaller, seemingly arbitrary turquoise splotches. "You don't paint real things. And there's a violence to them. Why?"

"People see what they want," he says. "And you see violence."

I ignore him and reach out to touch the painting. The color looks like it might drip down the board and onto the floor, but it's hard and rubbery. "Do you think we can recruit enough people to make a difference?"

He squats next to me. "We have to try, don't we?" he says.

"No, Ronan. We have to win."

"And we will," he says.

• • •

Ronan powers up a radio and a thick beat thunders through the studio. Everyone looks at him. "I play music when I paint," he tells us.

"Well, you were right. Two hours ago the air in the apartment got siphoned off," Harriet says. She unrolls her sleeping bag next to Gideon's, then puts her hands on her hips and studies the other Resistance members unpacking their meager belongings. A group of girls is beneath the skylight setting up. When they see me, they smile. Some men and boys are at the far end of the studio whispering and arranging.

I've already chosen a spot by the door, and Wendy has given me an extra blanket in case I get cold.

"What now? We're useless in here," Gideon says.

"You're alive," I tell him. Plenty of people aren't.

Ronan runs his hand through his hair. "Tonight Old Watson and I will round up more applicants for the army. When we have enough people and they're all armed, we fight."

"Could be a long wait," Gideon says.

"And we can wait," Harriet says. "Bea's right. Not being dead or imprisoned is enough for now."

"And what if his sister comes up here?" Gideon asks, speaking to everyone except Ronan. I keep quiet when what I should do is remind him that Ronan has just saved his life—he could be a little more grateful.

"It's thumbprint activated, and mine is the only one registered," Ronan says.

"A thumb pad. *That's* safe," Gideon says sarcastically.

I can't listen anymore. "Ronan is doing his best. If you want to go out and live in the alleyways until you get picked up, do it. This is no one's ideal situation," I tell him.

Harriet frowns at her husband. "Gideon's grateful. We all are," she says.

Ronan rubs his hands together. "I'll be up once a day, if I can. I'll bring food." He switches off the music. Everyone in the studio looks at him. "You should tiptoe and avoid raised voices," he says.

I join Ronan by the main door. Suddenly I don't want him to go. I hold on to the tail of his shirt. "You're in charge," he says. He looks at my hand, which is still clutching him, and touches it with the tips of his fingers. If I asked Ronan to take me with him, he would. But I have to keep order up here.

I release him. "Goodnight," I say, and he slips out the door.

I go to my sleeping spot and lie down facing the wall. I close my eyes and see Quinn. For a while I thought I might never see him again, even clearly in my mind. But that was only because I was scared of losing him forever.

I don't think I'm scared anymore.

41
QUINN

Every time the dining hall doors open I hope it'll be Alina, and after I've given up on her, she marches in. She gives me this stony look and takes a seat with the other troopers. A server lays a red dessert at the other end of my table, and the academics ladle out hefty portions for themselves, ignoring our end. "I'll get us some," Clarice says.

"Not for me," I say, and push my bowl of green food away. I rest my chin in my hands, waiting for dinner to end. I can feel Clarice watching me, but I don't bother making conversation.

After a painfully long time, the bell rings and we're allowed to leave. I make for the doors, and Alina, when there's a tug on my arm. "Are you trying to lose me?" Clarice asks teasingly.

"Of course not. Come on," I say. The last thing I need is her running to Vanya to tell her I've been inattentive.

I pull on my facemask as we get outside, where Alina's waiting. "Hey," she says. She ignores Clarice.

"Can I catch you up, Clarice?" I ask.

"Sure," she says. She smiles and goes ahead.

"She seems friendly," Alina says.

I roll my eyes. "I wish she wouldn't be." Now that I've stopped acting like an idiot when Alina's around, we're easy with each other.

"We leave tonight," she whispers.

"Good," I say. We haven't had any time to prepare, but if Alina thinks it's time, I believe her.

She pulls me into the shadow of the main house. "We have to get Maude, Bruce, and some others before we go. We'll meet on the second floor of the east stairwell at midnight. Be there, and make sure Dorian and Song are there, too. I don't know if I can tell them. Maks has me on a leash." She stalks off without any further discussion.

I chase after her. "And the pod?" I ask. I shake her without meaning to, and she pushes me away.

"Relax. We're going to go fight alongside Bea and my aunt and uncle, but we'll keep it between you, me, and Silas. No one else needs to worry about that yet."

"I think we should head straight for the pod. No detours."

Clarice suddenly appears. "Seriously? Are you going with the troopers?" she asks.

Alina glares at me, like Clarice's superhuman hearing is my fault. And I'm about to make up some lie when I remember the conversation back in our room. Clarice mentioned being glad she wasn't in the pod, and I thought she meant because of the riots. Did I misunderstand? "Only a few people have been told we're going back," I say slowly.

"Oh." Clarice looks over her shoulder. "Did Maks tell you when you're leaving?" Alina gives me another look, but this time it's because Clarice must know something we don't, and she wants me to get her to talk.

"Tonight," I say. I push Clarice's hair away from her face and grin. This is how I used to flirt with girls. It didn't always work and, unsurprisingly, it doesn't work with Clarice. She steps back.

"But none of the other academics are going," she says. I shrug and Clarice kicks a stone against the main house. "Why should I lose my partner? It isn't fair. Maks said it would only be the troopers going and that's why they've been training so hard. Is it because you know the pod? Is it because you have inside information or something?" She stops speaking as someone comes up behind us. She waits until he passes.

"My dad's the army's general," I say hesitantly.

"And you agree with what Maks has planned?" she says. "I want a new place to live, like anyone here. But cutting the tubing on the recycling stations? Isn't there another way to destroy the Ministry?"

Alina and I freeze. Can it be true? Would Vanya and Maks really murder so many innocent people? I start to panic, and have to increase the volume of oxygen coming into my facemask. I'm thinking of Bea and my brothers and mother. Of my father, who saved me in the end. And I'm even thinking of Riley and Ferris, who are royal pains in the butt, but were my friends in another lifetime. Even *they* don't deserve to suffocate.

"How did *you* find out about the mission?" I ask Clarice.

"Jo," she says nonplussed. "Maks told her, I think."

"Shit," Alina says. "Shit, shit, shit, shit, *shit*. When I see Abel . . ." She screws her hands into fists.

"Abel knows?" I ask.

"Of course he knows. He's very selective with his information."

A group of troopers passes us on the path. "Alina, you coming?" one of them asks.

"Sure," she says, and walks backward toward them mouthing one word to me: *midnight.*

42
ALINA

Maks won't sleep. He's in the bed, and I'm on the floor. Every time I open my eyes he's ogling me. And when he sees I'm not asleep, he smiles. Sometimes he winks, but usually it's just the cool smile, like he knows what I'm planning. "You can climb in here with me, you know," he says at one point, and pulls back the covers, unveiling his thick, tattooed torso and a faint musty smell.

"No thanks," I say, and close my eyes.

It's close to midnight and everyone will be waiting. Still, I try to relax, and after what feels like hours, his breathing changes. I sit up and crawl over to the bed to get a better look at him. Although one of his eyes is half open, he's totally out.

His pants are hanging on the back of the door. I slide my

hand into one pocket and then the other to feel around for the keys. They aren't there. I rummage in one of the back pockets where cold metal finally licks my fingers. As carefully as I can, I pluck the clump of keys from his pocket. Maks gibbers in his sleep. I could do anything I wanted to him now. He isn't so tough snoring with his mouth open. But I haven't time to waste. I have to get out of here.

I pick a key from the bunch at random and try it in the lock. It doesn't fit. The next one slides into the lock but won't budge. And on and on until, after trying nine or ten keys, one of them slides into the lock and turns, and with a low groan, the door opens. I tiptoe into the hallway, using the key to lock Maks in the room, and run.

They are waiting: Silas, Song, Abel, and Quinn. And they're all carrying several airtanks and small bags. "Where have you *been?*" Silas whispers.

"Maks wouldn't go to sleep."

"The keys?" Abel asks. I pass them to him and he curls his fingers around them like I've handed him a hunk of gold.

"Where's Dorian?" I ask.

"He must have decided to stay," Silas says, unperturbed.

"He wouldn't do that. I'll go find him."

"We haven't time." Silas grabs my arm. "And he's obviously made his choice."

"He told us himself he doesn't want to live as a drifter," Song says.

"We can't go without him," I add. We came together and that's how we should leave. Besides, we won't be drifters if we can oust the Ministry.

Voices echo from one of the floors above. "Keep it down," Abel says. He slides the painting to one side. "Are you coming?" The voices from above are getting louder and are accompanied by footsteps. If we stand around prattling, we'll be caught and then no one will be able to leave.

"I'm coming back for him," I say. And I mean it. I'm not saving Maude and Bruce only to leave Dorian behind. He's been with the Resistance since the beginning, and I've known him too long. He hasn't changed overnight. I know he hasn't.

"Come on," Silas says.

Abel ushers us behind the painting. The door clunks shut and we descend slowly, careful not to slip and tumble on top of one another.

"I'll lead the way. I've been observing The Sanctuary for a few days now, so I've a good idea of the lay of things," Abel says.

"And the plan?" Silas asks.

"We get in, unbuckle as many benefactors and kids as we

can, and get the hell out of there," Quinn says. Thankfully he doesn't mention the pod or Bea.

One thing at a time.

Abel unlocks The Sanctuary door, and as we're about to creep inside, a voice calls out. Damn. We have no weapons; wrestling with a nurse or several nurses isn't part of the plan.

"Everyone get back," Silas whispers. We jump away from the door. A shadow hovers over the light.

"Vanya?" The voice is tight and cautious, and as the light is being sliced away, Silas leaps out of the night and on top of the nurse. We pile in after him. The nurse thrashes on the tiled floor in her white overalls, screeching like a tram coming into a station. I pull a T-shirt from my bag and stuff it into her mouth. Abel holds her arms, and Quinn and Song stop her kicking.

Silas stands up and pokes her in the side with the toe of his shoe. "Tie her up," he says. She continues to writhe. He roots in his bag and pulls out a T-shirt of his own that he rips into pieces. I quickly tie the ends of the fabric together and use them to bind the nurse's hands and feet.

"Some of us should go and release the benefactors while you take care of her," Abel says. "The nurses only check in when the oxygen levels change, so we have about twenty minutes."

Silas thinks for a moment. "Where's the air?" he asks. We can't go anywhere if we don't have a decent supply.

"There's a room down the hall where they give the benefactors tanks and make them climb and run. Look in the closet. Here," Abel says. He throws the keys to Silas and Silas pulls a handgun from the nurse's belt and throws it to Abel.

And we're off, Song, Abel, and I, hurtling along the hallway and leaving Silas and Quinn to deal with the nurse.

The room we enter is unlit apart from a thin moonbeam. Abel pulls out a flashlight, which he shines around the room. It's the same ward I saw yesterday, beds along each side and people tied to them. The machines by the beds hiss and beep.

"Over there," Abel says, aiming the light at the far corner of the room. "Jo!" He goes to her, shakes her awake, and unfastens her wrists and ankles. He pulls the tubes from her mouth and nose, then looks down at the IV in her hand.

"I can take it out," I say, pushing him aside. I've never done anything like this, but I know what Abel's hesitations have led to before. I put pressure on the needle and slide it from her hand. She squeaks. She points to her mouth and gasps and Abel puts his own facemask over her mouth to help her breathe.

"You came," she says, pushing the mask away. She hasn't

had the baby yet; they're experimenting on her while she's pregnant.

I'm about to unbuckle the benefactor in the bed next to Jo's when Maude pipes up. "You took your sweet time. I've probably got bedsores on me bum. Untie me. Hurry up!"

She isn't wearing shoes and throws off a surgical robe revealing her emaciated, naked body. "Where are your clothes?" I ask. She points to a bin in the corner of the room brimming with rags. I help her up, pull out the tubes and IVs, and she hobbles over to the bin and scrambles into an outfit that looks far too big for her. Within a minute, two more benefactors are next to her doing the same thing.

I go from bed to bed, unbuckling scrawny ankles and wrists and pulling out tubes. "Quicker!" Abel says.

Silas barges in holding a bawling toddler, its mouth a perfect ring of noise. Abel groans. "Shut. Her. Up." If the situation weren't so serious, his nerves would be comical.

"*You* shut it," Maude snarls and slaps Abel. Abel puts his hand to his face like it's too hot to touch.

"There aren't that many of them," Silas says.

"Did you find the tanks?" I ask.

"Quinn's sorting that out," he says.

Abel scratches his eyebrows as the baby continues to bawl. The cry wheels around the room like a security alarm. Silas tries to cover the baby's mouth.

Jo is sitting on the end of a bed near the door rubbing her belly. She reaches out her arms and Silas hands her the baby he's holding. Looking at them, I'm struck by the hopelessness of the situation. How will we care for infants? How will Jo crawl under the wall and away with her large belly, and who's going to deliver her baby when the time comes? None of us are doctors. We aren't even proper adults. She looks at Abel and rocks the baby. We aren't on the run yet, and I feel defeated.

"Show me the nursery," Maude says to Silas, and that's when I remember she was training to be a nurse. After everything I've felt about Maude, could she be our one hope? "The rest of you, keep releasing these ones," she says, and they leave.

We release the remaining benefactors as fast as we can. Most sit up and get dressed, but a few refuse to stir, the whites of their eyes glowing. And we haven't time to convince them to leave.

"Help us," Silas says, darting back into the room carrying a child in each arm. Bruce seizes a sleeping girl from Silas. The rest of us tear toward the nursery and carry off a child apiece. Abel meets us in the hallway with a gaggle of children ranging from about four to eight. Their eyes are wide. "We're saving you, okay?" I say, using a gentle voice. They nod, but they still look frightened.

Within minutes we're with the duty nurse, who is attempting to wriggle away. Some of the benefactors kick her, then choose an airtank from the floor where Quinn has piled them. Bruce has put down the toddler he was carrying and has a stack of sheets in his arms instead. He throws them next to the airtanks. He folds his and shows us how to make a sling. "Take one to carry the little 'uns," he says.

Maude is the only one of us not carrying a child. She chose to stock up on diapers, feeding formula, spoons, and bowls instead. She jangles when she runs, and a peculiar flood of true affection for the old woman washes through me.

I push open the main doors with my hip, carrying a toddler in my sling at the front. And out of the shadows, Dorian appears.

Without a word, Silas takes a swing at Dorian. Apart from the thud of Dorian hitting the ground, it's silent—all the children and benefactors look on in wonderment.

"Silas, what's wrong with you?" Song hisses.

"Where have you been?" Silas demands.

Dorian struggles to his feet and uses Quinn as a crutch.

"I heard a ruckus outside my room. Maks is rounding up troopers, but I don't think they know you came here."

"You didn't meet us like we planned," I say.

"Juno wouldn't go to sleep," he says. I'm not sure I believe him. But he's here now.

"Can we make it out in time?" Song asks no one in particular.

I look at the benefactors we've released. They're wearing facemasks, and look frighteningly similar to an army of zombies. "They'll expect us to use the front gate and go north like everyone does," Abel says. "They won't suspect the back wall."

And we're off again.

I wait until last, following the benefactors along the wall that separates Sequoia from the world. The baby in my arms giggles, tipping her head back and looking up at the stars. Thankfully none of the babies are crying.

We reach the back wall and edge along that, too. The benefactor in front of me stops, and I bump into her. But no sooner have we stopped than we're moving forward again slowly as our group slides through the hole one by one. And then it's just Silas and me staring at the tunnel burrowed beneath the wall. He takes the child from me, putting her on her tummy in the dip and letting whoever is on the other side pull her through. "Is this crazy?" I ask Silas. His expression is hard and before he has a chance to answer, floodlights illuminate Sequoia and an alarm blasts out. The ground vibrates under the force of marching troopers. Silas pushes me to my knees, and I slink under the wall and out.

"Hurry!" I say, breathing in freedom. And as I sidestep the junk and crawl down a shallow ravine to fetch Crab's airtank, I can't help watching the frail figures of benefactors and children smearing the wasteland and wondering how long until our oxygen expires—or we get caught.

PART IV
THE RETURN

43
RONAN

The gymnasium is packed with the new recruits. They're scrawny and sunken-eyed, but there are at least fifty of them, and although their bodies look weak, they are doggedly determined. "Another set! Go!" Jude bellows through a megaphone, and they're off—climbing ropes, leaping onto vaulting horses, swinging on the rings, or jogging around the track.

Jude sees me and makes his way over. "Not bad, huh?" he says. He looks proud. He should be. I can hardly believe it.

"You managed this in a few days?" I say, as an auxiliary runs past us. Runs!

"*They* managed it," he says. "See her?" He points at a girl on a balancing beam with braids twisted into buns at the sides of her head.

"What about her?" I ask.

"First time with a rifle she shot the bull's-eye dead on. I thought it was a fluke. She repeated it three more times."

I laugh. "She must have joined the Resistance a while ago but managed to stay off the radar." Jude nods. "Any sign of Quinn and his friends yet?"

"I'm afraid not," he says. A boy sprints past us and Jude claps. "Good job!"

"When will they be ready to go?" It has to be soon. I can't keep the Resistance in my studio much longer. It's only a matter of time before Niamh starts to suspect something.

He sighs. "It usually takes six months for the basics. I'm condensing it into four weeks."

"That's still too long."

"What's the rush?"

I haven't said anything about hiding the Resistance in my studio. Jude would only have freaked out about the risk I was taking, and I didn't want him to get cold feet and wash his hands of us. But it's time for him to see how urgent this is. And he should shoulder more of the burden.

"Can you break for half an hour? I want to show you something."

He checks the clock on the wall. "I have another unit coming at eight. And another at ten. I finish at midnight."

"Fifteen minutes," I say. Jude consults his pad.

"Ten," he says. "Another set after this and then rotate!" he tells the soldiers. They don't groan or huff or any of the things I used to do. They smile, happy to be driven hard.

I tap on the studio door a couple of times, then let myself in. Bea is standing with her arms wrapped around herself. Jude gazes at her and then at the people strewn on the floor, the table with boxes of protein bars and jugs of water arranged on it, and the pile of airtanks in the corner. "What *is* this?" His jaw tenses. "You haven't . . . I thought they were living in the alleys."

"We're running out of space," I tell him. Old Watson brought me another five fugitives yesterday. The studio is crammed to capacity, and there'll be more.

"With Niamh downstairs? You're asking to get caught, and when you are, we're all in for it." A few people are meditating on their sleeping bags.

"Harriet's training us as best she can," Bea says. "We do sit-ups and push-ups, yoga and meditation. It's only been a few days and already I'm so much stronger. If only we could lower the levels of oxygen in here."

Jude presses his lips together like he's preventing himself from saying something cruel. "The buggy's waiting. I have to get back." He charges down the stairs.

"Have you asked him yet?" Bea asks. I shake my head and she shoos me out the door.

By the time I reach the bottom, Jude's out of sight. I catch him as he reaches the buggy. "This is the last straw. We'll be hanged. I should never have agreed to any of it," he says, climbing into the back of the buggy.

I stick my head through the window. "You have to train them quicker."

"I'm doing the best I can." He rubs his temples.

"Can you hide a few in your house?" I whisper, keeping an eye on the driver.

Jude laughs, banging his fist against his leg. "You can't be serious." He pauses. "You *are*. You're serious." He laughs again so hard he coughs. When he's recovered, his expression becomes hard as granite. "The girl doesn't love you. If that's why you're doing this. If you think you'll win her over, you're going to be disappointed. I've known her since she was a child and she's always been devoted to Quinn. And he's been devoted to her. I don't like it, but that's the way it is." He stares at me: a challenge. And I have to think about it. Is all this about Bea and some latent feelings I have for her? It's true she makes me want to be a better person and fight for a better world. I think of her earnest round face framed by black hair. She's pretty and smart and brave and kind, but Jude's right—she doesn't look at me with eager eyes. Maybe that's why I've never let myself be drawn to her. I know it would be hopeless, and hopeless is not the love I want.

"Something should have been done about the Ministry a long time ago. Bea woke me up."

Jude wipes his eyes. "I have a double garage. But with the buggy in there, it wouldn't leave a lot of room," he says.

"Can I give you ten people?"

"You can give me eight. But we do it at night. I don't want Cynthia finding out. She's close to her due date."

"Tomorrow," I say.

Jude leans forward and taps the glass between the backseat and the driver. "Get me out of here," he says.

44
ALINA

Abel knows the area better than anyone, so he has been heading up the group, finding the safest route down slopes and over streams for the last three days. The rest of us stay in small groups, and we do a regular headcount, so no one gets left by the wayside.

When we left Sequoia, we scuttled along lanes and through fields for what felt like hours. And we never slowed. Not when the benefactors got weak or when those of us who are inefficient breathers had to increase the density of oxygen in our airtanks. Only when the children began to cry did we stop to feed them.

We're huddled among a cluster of moss-covered boulders by the edge of a half-frozen lake. Mostly we're quiet; if we hear anything, we're ready to move again at a moment's notice. It's night, so we have barely enough light to see what we're doing. When the sun is up, we'll move on.

"What was that?" I whisper. I can't rest and jump at the slightest crackling. When the Ministry was after me, I was afraid, but it was a faceless enemy. I can't think of anything more horrible than being caught by Maks.

Maude stops stirring the powdered formula and water. She clicks her tongue. "I don't hear nothing. Just these poor babies' tummies grumbling. Mine, too. We got any more grub for the adults?" She lifts the milky spoon out of the bowl, licks it, and grimaces. I go back to rocking Lily, the child I've been carrying. She wriggles and reaches out to Maude. Maude pulls Lily onto her knee and forces a spoon into her mouth. "Shh, pet," she soothes.

My stomach is knotted in hunger, and I only have one protein bar left. I break off a small piece of it and pass it to Maude, who chews and swallows it in a few seconds. I hand the rest of it to Jo. She looks down at the offering and wells up. She has plenty of reasons to cry, but I pretend I don't notice and join Silas, who's poring over a map. He's put himself in charge of the route, and no one's arguing, not even Dorian, whose clamor for control has come to a swift end. "We've almost no food," I tell him. We didn't have much in the first place, but now we're dangerously low.

Silas points to a spot on the map. "Another day at most,"

he says. "I'm ninety-nine percent sure that's where we'll find solar respirators. We can leave everyone there and head for the pod."

"Great, Silas, but you said that yesterday." He continues to study the map. "Silas?" I say, and prod him. He looks up. His eyes are deep in their sockets and he has a glazed expression, like he can't really see me properly. I've always looked up to him; he's older than me and tougher, but sometimes I forget Silas is just as breakable as any of us. "Have you slept since we left Sequoia?" I ask.

He turns to Song, who's sitting against one of the boulders, a toddler asleep in his arms. A girl of around eight, who's been helping Maude carry supplies, is asleep with her head on his shoulder. "Do you think there might be a way to transfer the air from the solar respirators to airtanks?" he says.

"It's possible," Song says wearily. Being on the run is hard enough, but doing it and carrying kids is backbreaking. Song checks the gauge on the toddler's airtank and puts a hand to his chest to make sure he's breathing.

Bruce has taken over stirring their formula, and Maude is busy feeding the babies. I go to him. "Bruce . . . How did you survive when you were drifting? What did you eat?"

He clanks the spoon against the bowl. "Well, it's too cold for berries, but if we can make it back to the city, we can find us some houses that ain't been ransacked. Plenty of supplies in houses," he says. He pulls me toward him. "But listen . . . Maude and me were talking about it. We've had a good go of things. If it gets bad, and I mean stinking terrible bad, I'm happy for you to chew on my old bones." He smiles, and when I try to pull away, he clings to my arm. "I'm serious, Alina." With his other hand, he makes the motion of slicing his own throat.

I put my hand to my mouth, and try not to heave. Bruce pats me and laughs, but how is what he's saying or how I feel or any of this mess funny? "Get off me." I push him. "And if you ever say anything like that again, I'll break your nose."

I stomp off.

I want to be alone.

The children have been fed and most are sleeping along with the benefactors. The rest of us are huddled in a circle to stay warm. Quinn sidles up to me. I surprise myself by being pleased to have him close. He puts the opening of his blowoff valve to my ear. "We have to tell them what Vanya's planning," he says. I nod. He's waited a couple of days to bring it up, but with the city in sight, he's worrying about Bea. And if Clarice was right, we should all be worried—the pod will soon be a graveyard. "If we want to save *anyone*, we have to split up. The children are slowing us down," he says. He isn't being callous; if he were, he would have left a long time ago. And he's right: Vanya has a zip and could be at the pod already. Then what use will a revolt be?

I drag myself off the ground. "We have to ask the group," I say.

"I'm heading for the pod in the morning, Alina. I hope I'll have company, but I'll go alone if I have to."

"You'll have company," I tell him. "Listen up," I say loudly, and briefly tell everyone what we know about the brewing coup in the pod and Vanya's demented plan to cut off its air supply.

"You kept this from me?" Silas exclaims angrily. But at least he knew half the truth. Song, Dorian, Maude, and Bruce have been kept in the dark about everything. I just figured they all had enough on their plates. Anyway, it's too late for Silas to be upset.

"You can have a go at her another time. Tonight, let's talk about what we're going to do," Quinn says, sounding nothing like the person I met only weeks ago. He's grown a backbone. And a purpose.

Dorian snickers. "Oh sure, let's think . . . How can we save ourselves and a load of children, join up with rebelling Resistance members, and *then* stop Vanya's armed troops from irreparably damaging the pod and killing everyone in it?" I pick up a pebble and hurl it at him. The last thing we need is his sarcasm. Lives are at stake. "Who threw that?" he says, putting his hand to his forehead.

"I wish *I* had. Keep your trap shut for once, you dozy twit," Maude says. "Me and Bruce know how to take care of the little 'uns and survive out here. And we got a map to help us find air. You go and save the world. Save Bea," she says.

Song raises his hand. "We have no food, our air is low, and we have one gun between us. I'm not sure we're in a position to be saving anyone."

"All we have to do is warn them. Let's try not to forget that there are thousands of lives at stake," I say.

"And most of those people are auxiliaries. They're *your* people," Quinn adds.

"How can we warn the Ministry without getting killed?" Abel asks quietly, pretending this is the first he's heard of Vanya's plan. If I had time, I'd call him out on it because if Jo knew about it, so did he. But it isn't worth wasting my breath.

"I'll speak to my father," Quinn says. "He's on our side."

"What if he isn't? You saw what he did to The Grove. What if Bea's wrong about him and Ronan Knavery?" Dorian asks.

"So maybe I'll be arrested. But by then my father will know, and he has nothing to lose by being prepared."

"I'll go with Quinn," I say. A baby lying in Maude's arms

squeals. She puts her knuckle in its mouth and it settles.

"I'll go, too," Silas says. "The rest of you help Maude and Bruce find the respirators and keep the others alive. You'll have to carry two kids apiece."

"Not a problem," Song says.

"Then it's settled," Silas says. "Now let's get some sleep. We'll leave at first light."

I drift toward the group of benefactors, looking for Lily, when Abel stops me. "The Ministry won't welcome you. And what if Maks catches you before you get to the border?" I look deep into Abel's eyes, wondering what it was I ever saw in him. He's dangerously close to being a coward.

"Maks will make you pay," Jo says. She has been quiet for most of the trip, but if there's one thing she can speak to, it's Maks's vindictiveness.

"Not if I make him pay first," I say. It's bravado; I'm terrified. Taking a risk is all very well, but not when the odds are stacked so high against us. The rate things are going, we'll all be dead in weeks.

And I can't help feeling that I'm going to have a notable part to play in everyone's destruction.

45
RONAN

After spending my second day helping Jude drill the soldiers at the gymnasium, I'm exhausted. I want to have some dinner and go and see Bea, but when I get home, Niamh is pacing the kitchen. Wendy, who is cooking dinner on the stove, shoots me a look I can't translate as Niamh storms toward me. "Everything okay?" I ask.

"No, it is *not*." Niamh has my pad in her hands, which she thrusts at me.

"Were you trying to contact me? I forgot it." I look down. She's managed to get into it. But what did she see? I haven't been sending any incriminating messages or pinging anyone I shouldn't. I've been very careful. "How did you open it?"

"Your password has been the same for years, Ronan.

Picasso. Anyway, that's not the point. The point is, why do you have a picture of Bea Whitcraft on your pad?"

I freeze. She's right. At the station I took a photo of Bea, and she told me to delete it. Why didn't I?

Wendy is stirring the pot furiously. "Anyone hungry?" she asks.

"Well?" Niamh says, prodding me.

I step back and open the photo application on the pad, then scroll through trying to look as nonchalant as possible. "That's weird. Probably from school or something."

Niamh snatches the pad from me and pulls up the picture. Bea's fretful face is vaguely distinguishable—an orange sunset and ramshackle buildings behind her. "I checked the date and location. You took it when you were in The Outlands. Don't bother lying. You met Bea?" I stare at Bea's picture, not saying anything. If I look suitably ashamed, will she let it go? "So you *did* meet her," Niamh says. "And instead of killing her, you took pictures. What the hell's going on?"

"I met her, yes. But she's no threat. She's living like a drifter, and she'll die out there. I couldn't kill her in cold blood, Niamh. I just couldn't. Could you?"

I mean it to be a rhetorical question because I don't think Niamh has it in her to kill anyone, but she jabs Bea's picture with her finger. "Anyone who contributed to the riots and Daddy's death deserves to die. I'd knife her if I got the chance," she says. Her face is steel.

"Dinner?" Wendy asks. She is trembling, and I should be, too.

I have to move Bea and the others, and I have to do it soon because if Niamh gets a sniff of who she's living beneath, we're all done for.

46
BEA

We've been cooped up in Ronan's attic for a week, and it's already taking its toll on the group. None of us have showered, and the occasional buckets of water Wendy sneaks in for washing quickly turn brown. The smell is acrid. Conversations are turning into debates, debates into arguments, and Harriet and Gideon are constantly forced to mediate over sleeping spaces. I keep to myself and focus on training.

Today Ronan is late, and when he arrives he's in a hurry. "Everything okay?" I ask.

"Niamh's only gone down to the store to get a shake. I can't stay," he says. He won't look at me. Is there something he isn't saying?

"One of the girls is sick. She's been on the bucket all day long," I say.

"Gideon told me. I'm going to try to bring up some loperamide later."

"Thanks. I was worried about her." I turn to make sure no one's listening. "Can I take a shower?" I ask.

He looks at me uneasily. "Downstairs?"

"I need to get out of here," I admit.

"I don't think it's a good idea."

I wring my hands. "Please." I sound desperate, and I can't help it.

He looks down the stairs and taps his index finger against his chin. "I have an en suite bathroom," he says.

"Perfect."

His bedroom is larger than the entire apartment I used to share with my parents. He has a monstrous wall-mounted screen at one end facing a set of sofas and easy chairs, and a huge bed at the other end. The adjoining bathroom contains not only a mammoth shower, but also a Jacuzzi tub and double sink. I'm irritated by the extravagance. It doesn't fit Ronan's character. But this is his life.

"Towels are in the cupboard," he says.

I take a quick, hot shower, and when I emerge, Ronan is sitting on his bed rooting through his nightstand. He waves me over. "I have something for you," he says. I sit next to him and he hands me a printed picture of me with my parents. I trace my finger across their faces. My mother's sweet, haggard smile, and my father's unshaven chin. Their frayed shirts and too-tight clothes. I press the picture against my chest.

"Where did you get it?" I wipe the corners of my eyes with my knuckles.

"I went to your old place," he says.

"You never stop surprising me," I say. He is not only a better person than I thought he could be, but he's my friend, too.

"I looked for one of Quinn, but I couldn't find any and didn't want to rummage through your stuff," he says.

I close my eyes, so I can imagine Quinn as Ronan launches himself at me. He throws me onto the bed and covers my body with his own. He presses his face against mine. My instinct is to struggle, but when I hear a voice, I know he's protecting me.

"Ronan, we need to—" It's Niamh. "Ronan?" She laughs. "I didn't know you had it in you."

"Have you heard of knocking? Get out!" he yells. I bury my face in his pillow. There's a scuffle and a couple of hard bangs. "She's gone." I sit up and he turns the lock on the door, which he should have done when we came into the room in the first place. I deliberately wipe my mouth with the cuff of my sweater. Was there no other way to stop Niamh seeing me?

"Sorry," he says.

"You didn't bother locking it?"

Ronan sits on the bed and turns me so I'm looking straight at him. "I'm said I'm sorry. And I'm not them. That's not what this was."

"I know," I say. But every fiber of my body has stiffened anyway.

"You can't leave until she's asleep," he says. I nod and he smiles. He hands me the screen's remote control and stands. "Watch something trashy. I'll get us some drinks." He heads for the door. "Lock it behind me."

I look at the door closing then retrieve the photo from the nightstand. The girl in the picture is smiling, believing anything is possible. She looks like me, but that girl is dead. And maybe it's just as well; this world needs a new girl. Someone who doesn't blame anyone else for her lot.

I don't wait. I go to the door and peek outside. The chandelier in the hallway dashes the light in all directions. I hold my breath and listen for Niamh, but the house is still, so I tiptoe my way to the staircase. The first step creaks and I pause, putting as much weight as I can on the bannisters. Nothing moves. I take another step, and another, creeping my way to the top. When I reach the door, I knock gently. No one responds. I try again. Maybe everyone is asleep.

I hold my fist a few inches from the door and knock more

loudly. Ronan appears at the bottom of the stairs holding a bottle. "What are you *doing?*" he whispers. I wave him away, irritated that he's followed me, and knock a last time. And as I do, the door to the attic opens and a grinning man appears. I stare down at Ronan. Did he plan this? Is that why he wanted to keep me in his room?

It's too late to find out. A sweaty hand drags me inside and knocks me to the floor.

Everyone is standing at the far end of the attic with their hands in the air, and a row of stewards have their guns aimed at the Resistance like a firing squad. Some of the younger teenagers are sniveling. I am towed by my heels to the opposite corner of the room. Harriet looks down at me and catches my eye. She is trying to convey something, but I don't know what it is. The tall, thin man laughs. I recognize him from Ronan's description: Lance Vine, the new pod minister. Then Niamh steps out from behind him. She is carrying a small handgun and points it at me, closing one eye as though ready to shoot. "Bea Whitcraft?" she says. She looks mildly pleased and then, as her mind makes the connection between what she's just witnessed in Ronan's bedroom and me standing here now, her eyes bulge.

Vine rubs his hands together as though he's about to be served a large meal. "This is getting better and better," he says.

Niamh stares at me for a long time, then, remembering herself, shakes her head a little and goes to a heap of blankets. She picks one up between two fingers and, keeping it at arm's length, studies it. "This is one of Wendy's, I think," she says. She doesn't sound convinced.

Vine scratches his chin. "Isn't it just your brother whose thumbprint will read for this room?" Niamh has her back to everyone. She bites her bottom lip. It would take an idiot not to guess Ronan's involvement. And Niamh is not an idiot. But it takes her a moment to find a defense for her brother.

"Wendy has access to the whole house, Pod Minister," she says, which has to be a lie.

The stewards use the barrels of their guns to nudge the Resistance members toward the staircase, where they stand in a line, but they leave me where I am. I pull myself onto my feet and rest against the studio wall.

The door opens and Ronan marches in. The stewards aim their guns at him. "What the . . ." he says angrily. He waves at the stewards, who keep their guns trained at him. "Lower your weapons and someone tell me what's going on." The Pod Minister's expression is inscrutable. Niamh looks doleful. Neither of them seems to know how to react to Ronan, so I know for sure he had nothing to do with this raid. Not that I really believed he'd betray us. No.

"Wendy's been up and down those stairs twenty times

this week. And then, while you were out this morning, I heard someone sneeze," Niamh says, her voice a quiver, trying to repair the fact that she's informed on her own brother. "That's what I was coming to your room to tell you," she says, glancing at me.

I am standing apart from the other Resistance members and Ronan turns to me suddenly. Roughly, he turns my face to the light. "Bea Whitcraft?" he says.

Niamh watches Ronan and me, and covers her mouth with her hand. "What should we do with her?" she asks Ronan through her fingers. "She was wandering around the house. She could've killed us in our beds."

"Tried for treason. Her parents provoked the revolt," Ronan says calmly, keeping his eyes on me. I hope he knows what he's doing.

"When she's found guilty she'll be put to death," the Pod Minister says. He is quiet and testing. Ronan doesn't flinch. And neither do any of the Resistance. If I didn't know Ronan better, I'd believe he was washing his hands of me.

Vine's mouth twitches. "It doesn't look good that it's your studio, Ronan. But if you're prepared to let this ugly little sub die, the Ministry will have some reason to believe you aren't part of this." He sweeps his arm out wide, taking in the room.

"Arrest me, if you think I'm involved. I'll happily answer

your questions," Ronan says. His expression is cool.

Niamh looks at the stewards. "Go to the annex and arrest our servant." The stewards look at the Pod Minister, who nods. Niamh speaks again. "And get these RATS out of my house!" She is shrieking, suddenly on the verge of hysteria.

A steward binds my wrists in plastic twine and uses the cold barrel of her rifle against my neck to drive me down the stairs behind the other Resistance members. Without warning, Niamh is beside me, grabbing my arm and spinning me around.

"You and yours are going to pay for what happened to my father," she snarls, and pushes me down the last few steps so that I fall forward onto my face. When I lick my lips, there's blood. I roll over and she looks down at me under the lights of the chandelier with nothing but contempt.

A few weeks ago, I'd have whimpered if Niamh touched me. Instead, I pick myself up and stand nose to nose with her. Harriet tries to pull me away, but I won't be moved, not today. "You don't scare me, Niamh," I say.

"Well, you should be *terrified*," she says.

I shrug. "If you have to hurt me, that's your choice."

But how I react is mine. And I won't cower to anyone anymore.

47
RONAN

I'm pacing a Zone Three alleyway waiting for Jude, who's late. I check my pad for the third time. Only a meager light steals its way between the apartment blocks. It's as dingy as ever. I can't believe Bea spent her whole life here.

"The senate meeting ran over," Jude says, appearing at the end of the alleyway. He strides toward me and we shake hands. "Were you followed?"

"Two stewards. I lost them in Zone Two," I say. "Is Bea okay? What about Wendy?" I've been awake all night worrying, and even though Niamh knows what's happening, I can't ask her. She hasn't spoken to me since they found Bea and the Resistance in my studio. I'm just lucky she hasn't informed on me.

"Lance Vine proposed a private trial and public

execution for Wendy and everyone found in the studio. No one opposed."

"So we'll stop it," I say.

Jude takes off his hat and scratches his head. "I have a family, Ronan. I didn't come here to plot a rescue with you, I came to tell you that . . . I'm out. I've given the Resistance members I was keeping in my house airtanks and access to an empty apartment in Zone Two." He is unapologetic.

How can a man charged with protecting the pod and leading the army give up so easily? I stare at him, wavering between anger and disappointment. "But the soldiers you're training?"

"I'm discharging them tomorrow for ineptitude."

"How can you be such a coward?" I say. I thought he'd changed.

But he isn't hurt by my words. He puts his hat back on and straightens it. "When you're a father, maybe you'll understand."

"Well, I'm not giving up," I say.

He turns to leave when a siren whistles through Zone Three and winds its way down the alleyway. Jude punches the wall. "NO!" he shouts.

"What's happening?" I ask. Instinctively, I take the gun I have hidden in the band of my pants and release the safety catch.

Jude pulls me along the alleyway. "It's the border alarm," he says. "The pod is under attack."

Jude pings all the soldiers, Resistance and non-Resistance, and gathers them in the gymnasium. With their uniforms on, I can hardly tell them apart. The walls vibrate with uneasy chatter.

Jude puts his lips to the megaphone. "The pod is under attack. We don't know from whom, but we have to pull together."

Robyn has returned from The Outlands and is standing beside me. "Another joke of a war. I'm sick of it." She's lost weight and has dark rings beneath her eyes.

"I think this is the real thing," I tell her. I wish it weren't. I wish we could have used these recruits to change things in the pod instead of sending them out to fight a war that was never theirs.

"Many of you are inexperienced and scared. I would be, too, but you have to be strong. We are *all* going to keep it together and . . . live." He pauses. "Are you ready?" He is shouting, trying to rally the troops like he did at The Grove. The gymnasium crackles with silence.

They aren't close to ready. Not that it matters. We're going out to fight. Ministry and Resistance together.

Now.

48
QUINN

The pod is still only this tiny speck in the distance when we hear blasts across the city. The horizon's clouding over with silver-gray dust. My gut wrenches. If we're too late, I'll never forgive myself. Never.

"We have to move faster," I say, and Alina picks up the pace, jumping over unstrung guitars and a ton of other trash.

I wish I could run faster. Silas and Alina keep stopping so I can catch up, which isn't all that helpful because as soon as I do, they move on again and I never get to rest. Not that I want to. I have to get to the pod. I have to tell my father what's happening and find Bea.

As we get closer, the pod becomes clearer, and so do the recycling stations connected to it. "They're still working," I call out. Four steam clouds spiral into the sky from the tops of the stations.

Alina stops. "What?" She pushes her hair out of her face with both hands. Her ears are red from the cold, but she's also sweating from the run.

I'm too out of breath to repeat myself. I point and she nods, taking off after Silas. But no sooner has she caught him up than they both stop and stare. The air is vibrating. It can't be. But it is.

A zip appears in the sky, guns ready. After all we've struggled against, don't we deserve a bit of luck? But that isn't how life works, and there's no time to be a baby about the unfairness of it. We have to move faster.

Less than half an hour later, we've made it to within a few hundred feet of the pod's glass walls, where we hide behind a buggy that has its hood open and engine smoking. We haven't been spotted because the stewards normally stationed around the pod in concentric circles are protecting the border in four rigid lines. Several gurgling tanks are idling next to them and a handful of stewards are tinkering with the innards of the zips. But no one's bothering to guard the recycling stations.

"Are we too late?" Alina asks.

"I'm not sure," Silas says, and the zip we saw earlier

appears over the rim of the pod. Without warning it fires at the lines of stewards.

"It's Maks," Alina shouts over the propelling zip blades.

The tanks on the ground raise their guns and fire back. The stewards scatter. Loads of them have already fallen to the ground and one of the tanks is in pieces. The zip spins around and comes back, and this time it ignores the army on the ground and fires at one of the recycling stations. A hole appears at the bottom of the station, but the tubing remains intact. A figure appears from a tank not more than fifty feet away and, lifting the visor of his helmet, holds a megaphone to his face. He barks at the stewards. "Back in line!" The voice is my father's. But why is he keeping the army at the border? Can't he see what's happening? The border isn't under threat. The Ministry zips should be in the air. Their tanks should be attacking Vanya's zip, so it doesn't damage any of the recycling stations.

"That's my dad," I shout. "We have to tell him what they're planning." The zip disappears and everything goes quiet.

"We won't get a better chance," Silas says. He pulls a white shirt from his backpack. "Let's go!" he says. He stands up and, in full view, hurtles toward my father waving the T-shirt above his head. The soldiers who have broken ranks raise their guns. They don't shoot, but they run toward us.

I wave my arms manically and dash toward my father, who lifts his rifle and points the muzzle at me. "Father!" I shout. "Dad!"

But before I get to him, I'm jumped by two stewards and tackled to the ground. My face hits the dirt. I look up. Alina's facemask is pulled from her and Silas is kicked to the ground and a foot jammed between his shoulder blades. Alina doesn't struggle. Has she learned to breathe? But I see no more because a pair of feet in scuffed black boots blocks my view.

"Quinn?"

"Yes," I croak.

"Release him," my father tells the stewards. I scramble to my feet and dust myself off as the soldiers dart this way and that, howling at each other and loading their guns. It's obvious they weren't ready for this attack.

"They're after the recycling stations," I tell my father. "They plan to cut off the air supply."

"Damn," he growls as the zip returns, blowing the ground to pieces. I throw myself down and cover my head with my hands. The zip sinks and retreats like they're playing a game. But they aren't. They're just trying to hit the right target.

My father's lying next to me. He pulls himself to his feet and helps me up. "You need to get the zips in the air," I tell him.

"They've been sabotaged," he replies. He presses the

megaphone against the blowoff valve in his facemask. "Unit Bravo, relocate to Recycling Station North. Juliet and Romeo South. Zulu East. Tango West. Delta, stay at the border. Double time, MARCH!" He looks at Alina and Silas still pinned to the ground. "They're Resistance," he tells the stewards, who look stunned and apologetically help Silas up and hand back Alina's airtank. They must be two of the new recruits armed to help fight against the Ministry, not for it.

"Make us useful," Alina says.

"This way," my father says, and we leg it to the border. We slip through the revolving doors and into the tunnel. Someone rushes us from behind and reaches for my father.

"Jude?" It's Ronan. When he sees me he claps me on the back. "You made it," he says.

"They want to destroy the recycling stations," my father tells Ronan, who pushes up the sleeves on his shirt.

"What can we do?" I ask.

"If there's air rationing, auxiliary houses and the prison will get cut off first," my father says. He reaches into his pocket and pulls out a bunch of keys. "The Resistance has been imprisoned and that includes Bea. Security will be lax. And Jazz is at the infirmary. You know where that is?" I nod.

"Is there any way to fit everyone with a tank as a precaution?" Alina asks.

"And we need cuttings," Silas adds. He can't look at my

father, and I don't blame him. I can hardly look at him myself after what he's done.

"We keep tanks at the Research Labs." My father rubs his forehead. "Is it just a zip they have?"

Alina shrugs. "We didn't stay long enough to find out. But their troops are strong."

The ground shakes again. A soldier rushes toward us. "General, some of the units are breaking up. We're awaiting orders."

"Make sure the south station is covered. It's the control tower," my father tells her. He looks at us. "D-day," he says.

"Shall I come with you?" Ronan asks me.

"He can handle it," Alina says. "Can't you?" she looks at me with steely eyes. "Give us guns," she tells my father.

"Gladly," he says, and hands his rifle to Silas, who looks at the gun, then at my father, and nods. My father takes the steward's gun and gives it to Alina.

He holds out his hand to me. I take it and we shake, staring at each other. "However this ends . . ." He pauses. Silas walks away. Alina follows. "You're a brave person, Quinn," he says. It's not an apology, but it's as much as he can give.

"Don't be so dramatic," I say, kind of joking. I pull my hand away and run into Zone One.

49
BEA

It must be at least a day since they threw me into this windowless, airtight cell. I've had nothing to eat or drink and my arms and legs are tied to a chair. I wet myself a couple of hours ago. The smell is odious, and I keep shifting in the chair to ease the discomfort of sitting in damp underwear and pants. I won't snivel and give them the satisfaction of thinking they've broken me.

But I cough and my throat is so dry it comes out like a sandy wheeze. I've also managed to dribble down my own face. I try to yank my hands free but just tear another layer of skin from my red-raw wrists. I stop struggling at the sound of scraping as a guard opens the cell door.

He holds it open for Niamh Knavery, who stalks in and looks at me as though I'm something someone's puked up.

"It reeks in here," she says. "Did you piss yourself?" I'd sit straighter in the chair if my limbs didn't burn, to show her I'm not embarrassed. *They're* responsible for the smell in here, not me.

After a brief pause, Lance Vine appears. He covers his nose with his arm. How ironic that he finds *me* disgusting. "Give us five minutes," he tells the guard, who nods, the keys tied to his belt jangling as he retreats down the hallway.

"I haven't done anything," I say.

"Don't give me that," Niamh says, bristling with contempt.

"Your father killed my parents. I have every reason to hate *you*," I tell her, though then I'd hate Ronan, too, which I don't. Neither of them is to blame for who Cain Knavery was.

Vine stands next to Niamh and rubs his nose between his thumb and index finger. "If you ask me, there isn't any point in delaying things. I've heard from Jude Caffrey that it's getting worse. Time to act." He steps in front of Niamh and grabs my face, his sweaty hand over my mouth. "We thought we hacked most of you down when we destroyed The Grove. So who's attacking us?"

"Is there another riot in the pod?" I ask. And is Quinn a part of it? Could he be here? Hope trickles its way back into my body. "If you're so tough, why aren't you out there battling the bad guys yourself?"

He smacks me hard across the face. The chair teeters on its back legs and crashes to the floor. I land on my hands tied to the back of the chair and clench my jaw to stop myself from whimpering. I roll to the side and try moving my wrists.

Niamh presses her lips together. "Was Wendy behind all this?"

"Or was it Ronan?" Vine adds.

Niamh shudders. "And Wendy's helped these new terrorists attack us, I suppose," she says, not giving me time to answer his question. "Let's just shut off the air to the cell and let her choke," she says. Vine stands over me and shrugs. He couldn't care less what happens to me.

A noise in the hallway makes me tense and another steward bumbles in. He looks at me and gulps. "They're waiting to start the chamber meeting, sir," he says.

Vine turns to Niamh. "Tell them I'll be there shortly."

"Yes, Pod Minister," she says. She pokes me with her foot.

"I'm no different from you, Niamh," I say. I don't beg or plead with her to help me, I simply give her a chance to do the right thing.

"No, Bea," she says. "We're innately different, and that's part of the problem: you and your RATS think we aren't." She leaves the cell, slamming the door shut on her way out.

Vine crouches down and strokes my face with the back of his hand. I try to bite him. He pulls his hand away and laughs. I'm like prey, and it feels far too familiar. I scream as loudly as I can, to startle him if nothing else, and only stop when an alarm blares from the speakers in the wall and a red light on the ceiling flashes and spins. "It can't be," he says.

"What can't it be?"

He looks down at me. "You know very well, it's the air siren. The Resistance must have damaged the tubing. You'll pay for your involvement in this."

"The tubing?"

"They should have remembered that the first places air is siphoned from is the Penal Block and auxiliary apartments." He heads for the door.

"You're leaving me here?" I ask. I'm not scared of dying—I've been faced with the prospect so many times I know it's inevitable, and suffocating is the most inevitable thing of all—but I don't want to die alone. Someone should witness my last moment. I deserve that, at least, don't I?

Vine sneers and presses a bell on the intercom. He waits several moments, then pulls on the door handle, but it doesn't budge. He clears his throat and tries the intercom again. "I'm ready to leave now," he says into the mouthpiece, furrowing his brow.

I cough because the air in the cell has already thinned.

"What if no one comes?" I ask, goading. "If there's trouble, wouldn't everyone be recruited to fight? Wouldn't the stewards run scared if they thought the air was being siphoned?"

He puts his hand to his chest then thumps the cell door with his fists. "Let me out!" he bawls. He clutches his chest and thumps that too. I focus on stretching out my exhalations. My breath sounds like the ocean. Vine kneels on the floor next to me and puts his ear to my mouth. "What kind of trick is that?" he asks. His breathing is rapid.

"No trick," I say. "I have all the air I need."

"Get me out of here!" He blanches, going back to the door where he cranes his neck and opens his mouth wide to catch all the air he can. "It burns," he croaks and starts hacking.

He tries his finger against the button one last time before sliding to the floor panting and then kicking the door and yowling incomprehensibly. And soon he is on his knees hyperventilating, and with very little warning, passes out. I watch his chest rise and fall. He'll live a while longer. But only a while.

And I stay as still as I can on the floor preserving my oxygen. The air is very thin, but it's enough to live on. For me at least.

For now.

50
ALINA

Whole regiments are surrounding the three recycling stations that have their tubing intact and snipers are positioned in their towers. "We can shoot," I tell Jude Caffrey. He dips his head, as if to say, *of course you can*, and points to Recycling Station North. "Go with Ronan," he says.

We bolt toward the station and hurdle hastily erected sandbags. A soldier on the door recognizes Ronan, lets him through, and we take the winch to the top. My heart thrums so loudly in my ears I can almost hear it over the gunfire. All I can think about are my aunt and uncle, and Bea and Jazz, who'll suffocate if we don't stop Sequoia's troopers from blowing up the pod's tubes. It's what the Ministry always feared, what they told people terrorists might do, and at The Grove we laughed at their fearmongering.

At the top, we dash from the winch and onto a balcony, where we throw ourselves onto our stomachs and inspect the ground below through the scopes of our rifles. Vanya's troopers have appeared from the west and are advancing on the stations. Only their helmets and shields, fashioned from old car doors, protect them. Occasionally one of them falls to the ground, but the dead and injured are trodden over and the troop continues. Ministry soldiers are taking cover behind the sandbags and firing continuous rounds of ammo; the Sequoians are undaunted.

The clunking zip appears to my right as it loops the pod. It fires again at our station and for a few seconds the building buckles. Silas, Ronan, and I gape at one another wondering, for one horrifying moment, if the whole thing will topple to the ground and us with it. But the damage is superficial and the building quickly stops shuddering.

Ronan elbows me. "What are you waiting for?" he says. He has eyes the color of steel and the bearing of someone used to war.

I look through the scope again. To avoid the debris from the station the Ministry soldiers have broken ranks, giving Vanya's troopers time to dart forward and leap over the sandbags. Guns are fired, but all the soldiers are suddenly forced to use knives and the butts of their rifles to protect themselves. One of the Sequoians throws a Ministry soldier to the ground and repeatedly pounds his head against the ground. My stomach heaves. I take aim and fire. The trooper lets the soldier go and clutches his side. He pulls off his helmet. It isn't a he at all. I've shot Wren. She falls, like a heavy lead pipe, into the dirt. Within minutes other troopers have trampled over her and if she was alive after being shot, she isn't now.

"I've killed Wren," I tell Silas.

He squints. "It's her or my parents." I hate the truth of this. I hate all the killing and the weighing of one life against another. When will it be over? I need it to be over. I can't live in a world like this anymore.

"They're too close to the tower. I can't get a good shot," Ronan says, standing up. "And if they break in at the bottom they could use the emergency staircase to get to the control room. We'll never hold them off from here."

We jump up and follow him. Was Ronan one of the soldiers I was shooting at a few weeks ago when the Ministry destroyed The Grove? I am a turncoat, I realize, fighting side by side with an enemy. But today we fight together to protect the pod and the people we love.

And that seems the right thing to do.

51
QUINN

The rationing alarm is whirring like mad through Zone One and probably all across the pod. The streets are empty. All the Premiums must have taken cover at home or in a Ministry building. How long will it be before even these places get the air cut? The death toll doesn't bear thinking about.

In houses along the street, faces are pressed to windows. People are too afraid to come outside.

I check the gauge on my airtank. It's running low, but it'll be enough, I hope.

I sprint along the wide boulevard toward the Justice Building because that's where Bea is.

And she's okay.

She is.

I know it.

52
BEA

Lance Vine has turned blue. And it won't be long before I look like that myself. I close my eyes and block out the thought. I block out every thought and focus on my exhalations. I count them out, only inhaling a little when I get to ten, so I can ration the remnants of oxygen lingering in the cell. The air is so fine, every breath hurts. And I have a searing headache.

I open my eyes and look at the red light flashing on the ceiling, when Niamh bursts into the cell.

"Don't close the door!" I wheeze over the siren blasting through the speakers. She doesn't hear me, and the door closes behind her.

"Oh no." Niamh gapes at Vine sprawled on the floor. She nudges him with her foot. "What have you done?" She puts a hand to her chest. "The air," she says. "I can't . . ." She starts to cough so hard, she's unable to finish her sentence.

She looks like she wants to hurt me, but she also looks afraid. I'm alive and Lance Vine is dead. "The guards have all gone AWOL, but we'll fix them . . . just as soon as everything gets back to normal," she says. She goes to the intercom panel and is about to press her finger to the button when she realizes no one's stationed outside to hear it buzz. She looks at me and gasps, and I sigh, expecting to have to watch Niamh die, too, but as she pulls on the handle, it opens. She cries out. And so do I.

It's Quinn.

"Oh, Bea." He pushes Niamh aside and rushes to me. He holds my face in his hands and looks at the dead man and then at my chafed wrists. "Are you okay? I'm sorry. I'm so sorry." He uses a knife to free me, pulls up his mask, and kisses the palms of my hands. "I knew you were alive. Alive and kicking everyone's asses," he says.

"You're here," I say. I throw my arms around his neck and squeeze him so tight, I'm afraid I might hurt him. He kisses me on the mouth, the forehead, the neck, then puts his mask over my mouth and nose. For a moment I forget how filthy I am. "We need to find Ronan and your dad. They'll help us," I say.

"Leave my brother out of this," Niamh says. She's

holding open the door and a little air from the hallway is filtering into the cell. If she leaves, we'll both be dead. I have to keep her talking.

"Ronan's on our side, Niamh. You *know* that." I get to my feet.

"You poisoned him against us," she says.

"No we didn't. He joined of his own free will, and you could, too." The alarm is still blaring.

Niamh's neck reddens. "And become like *you?*" I don't do any more to convince her. I rush forward, knocking her to the floor, and lie on top of her in the doorway to keep it from swinging shut. She scratches my face, but I don't retaliate. I raise my hand and Quinn lifts me up and into the hallway, dark apart from the red lights.

Niamh scrabbles to her feet. "You're going to be sorry."

"No, I don't think I am," I say.

She looks like she is about to say more, but instead runs away along the hallway, shouting for a guard who will never appear.

"The pod's under attack," Quinn says.

"Then we better hurry up." I grab his keys and open the cell door opposite. Old Watson is slumped in a corner. I didn't even know he'd been caught. "Watson!" I drop to the floor and shake him. He doesn't respond. I put my ear to his face, but I can't hear breathing. Am I responsible for his capture, or was it his plants?

I rip the facemask Quinn gave me away from my own face, press it to Old Watson's, and pull his legs from under him so he's lying flat. I pump his chest, leaning hard on my hands, and Quinn tilts back the old man's head and breathes into him.

Once. Twice.

But nothing happens.

"*Breathe*, dammit," I say, and try compressions again.

Quinn stands up. "It's not working, Bea. We have to get out of here." He doesn't understand: Old Watson saved me when I had no interest in saving myself. I won't leave him here.

"I'm trying again," I say, and lay my hands over his heart. I count out the compressions, one to thirty, and Quinn kneels back down and blows into his mouth, filling him up with air.

And it works! Old Watson gasps. I push the few strands of hair he still has away from his eyes and he opens them. "Don't try to speak," I say, and help him sit.

I throw Quinn's keys back at him. "The other cells."

"You'll be okay?" he asks.

"Yes," I say. "Of course, I will."

5 3
QUINN

Bea, Old Watson, about thirty Resistance members, and I flee the Justice Building. Auxiliaries crowd the streets, frantically darting this way and that, and most of them are carrying a weapon of some sort. I stop a boy about my age as he gallops by. "What's going on?"

"The bastards have cut off the air to Zone Three apartments." He pulls himself loose from me and runs away as best he can. A humanoid voice comes over the loudspeaker. *"Air rationing stage three in operation. Premiums must return to their homes. Air rationing stage three in operation. Premiums must return to their homes."*

We look at one another anxiously and then Gideon, Silas's father, turns to me. "We need airtanks."

"This way," I say.

"Where are we going?" he asks, racing alongside me.

"Research Labs."

We careen along a street, which is quickly clearing as auxiliaries jump over gates and high walls to get to Premium homes. It's complete chaos: windows are smashed and gunshots fired. I slow down. "My brothers," I say.

Gideon shakes his head. "We haven't time."

"I'm getting them," I tell him.

"Fine. We'll meet you at the border in an hour. Give me the keys and we'll find the tanks," Gideon says. I throw the keys at him.

"What about Jazz?" Old Watson asks. He's right next to me, but his voice sounds far away. He's way paler and more hunched than he was when I last saw him. He isn't cut out for all this. Then again, who is?

"The infirmary isn't far. I'll get her," Bea says, stepping forward, her chin high.

I seize her by the shoulders. "We keep bloody leaving each other," I say, which wasn't part of the plan. The plan was to find Bea and never let her go.

She smiles. "Some things are more important than us," she says, and I kiss her. There might be a million things more important than us, but I can't think of anything more important than her. "The border in an hour," she repeats.

• • •

The auxiliaries are pressing in on my street with broken bottles and pipes. I gallop past them and up to my house. My brothers and mother are watching the news on the screen—explosions and rising dust.

Lennon glances at me and waves. Keane does the same. Then, simultaneously realizing I shouldn't be here, they jump up and throw their arms around me. "Quinn, is it you?" Keane asks. He jabs me in the ribs. My mother turns like a mechanical doll, and her mouth drops open.

"I told you he wasn't dead," Lennon says. I kiss the top of his head and hold Keane close. Man, I missed them.

My mother totters toward me using the back of the couch for support. Whoa—she's so big, she looks as if she's going to pop out my new brother any minute. "We're leaving," I tell her.

"Oh, Quinn, my darling." She clutches my arm and looks like she really wants to feel something. But her eyes are empty.

"We have two minutes before auxiliaries come crashing in here," I say. Something booms in the street and my mother jumps. Maybe we have one minute. "Come on."

My mother smiles condescendingly. "We're safe here. Don't worry about *us*." She tries to coax the twins away from me, but they cling even tighter. It isn't right that they'd rather be with me than her. But if they leave, at least I'll be able to save them.

"They're coming with me," I say. "That's nonnegotiable. Are you coming, too?" I ask. I don't want her to die. She's my mother, after all.

"Do you know how much trouble you've caused? Your father hasn't been the same since you—" She presses her thumbs against her eyelids, draws in a quick breath, and holds her belly.

"Mom?" Keane says. I keep a tight hold of him. She's faking it.

"You've destroyed this family." She starts to sob—big, blistery tears. But they're not for me.

"I'm taking food and airtanks," I say.

"Take what you want, but please leave the boys," she whimpers. A rock hits the living room window and she screams. She drops to her knees and puts her hands over her head.

"Go get a few things! Quickly!" I push my brothers toward the stairs. "Mom, we *all* have to go," I say. I can't leave her at the mercy of marauding auxiliaries.

She looks up from the floor. "You've chosen your life, stop dragging us all down with you." Another window smashes and a screwdriver lands on the couch. "What's happening? The world's gone mad."

I lift her up. "The world's changing, that's all. And you have to change with it."

"They're going to destroy my beautiful home," she says.

"You have to pack some stuff," I say, and steer her into the hall and then her bedroom.

I sprint down the hallway and into the basement, where I snatch as many airtanks as I can carry. By the time I'm back, Keane and Lennon are standing at the bottom of the stairs, packs slung over their backs. They're ready to leave everything behind and join me.

"Mom!" I call out.

She appears wearing a heavy coat. She doesn't look angry anymore. She holds her stomach and winces.

"The baby's coming," she says.

54
BEA

I leave the other Resistance members to loot the Breathe headquarters and head for the infirmary on the Zone One–Zone Two border. The oxygen in the streets is dwindling, but it's more than I had in the cell. I walk quickly, passing brawling groups of men and women, until I turn a corner into a quiet street where two boys are grappling over a mini-air-tank lying next to them. I snatch it, cover my mouth and nose with the facemask, and speed off. They holler things after me, but I'm faster than them. Stronger. Running hurts my legs and my breathing gets short, but it feels like a small triumph against the Ministry.

When I get to the infirmary, a broad white building taking up an entire block, the security hut is empty, and the gate is open. I scamper along the lane and into the deserted lobby where the switchboard is madly ringing and blinking and cots and wheelchairs are strewn in every direction.

A doctor with a stethoscope around her neck and blood spots on her white coat stumbles from a room. "We don't have any spare oxygen for visitors," she says, and tries to jam me back through the revolving doors.

"I'm looking for a child," I say.

She lets me go and rushes to the switchboard, where she mutes the ringing. "Auxiliaries have been moved to Premium wards upstairs. We'll lose our jobs over it, but looks like we won't have jobs anyway." The building shudders and the doctor takes a long look me. "I have my own kids. I have to go," she says, and scrambles through the infirmary doors and away.

I take the stairs two at a time to the third floor. The hallway is alive with brittle chatter and crammed with people coughing or hooked up to IVs. I weave my way through the throng and make out Jazz at the end of the hallway, her leg in a heavy cast, her curly red hair heaped like spaghetti on top of her head.

Thank goodness.

"Jazz!" I shout. She hops down the hallway holding her crutches.

"You took your time," she says, and hits me hard in the stomach.

I'm unable to resist kissing her fist. "You ready to get out of here?"

"I was ready yesterday," she says, and continues to hop all the way to the staircase. She clings to the handrail and takes the steps two at a time. "Hurry," she says as a door at the bottom slurps opens.

I grab Jazz, ready to defend her if I have to, when Keane and Lennon appear, followed by Quinn, who's supporting his mother. "We need a doctor," he shouts. His mother's bump has dropped. I don't believe it. Today of all days.

"Stay there," I tell Jazz, and help haul Mrs. Caffrey to the third floor. She screeches and writhes when we lay her on the floor. "Someone help us!" Quinn calls out.

"The doctors have all left," an auxiliary with a bandage taped to his eye says.

Cynthia Caffrey howls and grips her stomach. "I have to push," she says.

Quinn turns to me. The blood has drained from his face. "She has to push," he repeats.

55
QUINN

Every bed in the ward is taken and the people in them avoid meeting our eyes. I'm about to flip out when a pale woman with wispy hair drags herself out of bed so my mother can lie down. "There isn't a nurse in the whole bloody place?" I ask. Alarms start to whir all over the building.

The woman shakes her head. "All the medics who bothered to stick around have gone to deal with a burst appendix," she says. She lifts a set of stirrups attached to the side of the bed and places my mother's feet in them.

My mother clutches the mattress. "Get me Doctor Kessel!" she shouts.

"There are no doctors, Mom," I say.

She tries to stand. "I won't do this here. No. No." And then she screams and squeezes her eyes shut.

Bea rolls up her sleeves and turns to my brothers. "You shouldn't be here. Go and take care of Jazz, the girl who was with me on the stairs." Keane looks like he might cry. "Be brave," she adds, and they both run off.

"We need hot water," I tell the pale woman. I don't know exactly what for, but I've heard it said and hopefully we'll know what to do with it when the time comes.

"Yes, yes. And other things," she says, and rushes away.

Bea pushes my mother's skirt up past her knees and pulls down her underwear. I hold my mother's hand and she looks up at me. "You've changed," she says. I nod; I have, but I'm not sure whether or not my mother means this as a compliment.

"You don't need to stay, either, Quinn," Bea says. A month ago I might have been squeamish and wanted to get as far away from here as possible, but as the alarms ring and more screams and shouts filter up from the streets, it isn't seeing my mother give birth that's worrying me; all I'm thinking about is how we're going to make it out alive, and what's going to happen if we do.

The woman returns with her arms loaded. She joins Bea at the foot of the bed. "I need something for the pain," my mother pleads.

"Too late for that," the woman says. She nudges Bea. "Ready?"

Bea pulls her lips into her mouth. "Yes."

"Where did you get that stuff?" I ask the woman, looking at the gauze and scissors.

The woman waves distractedly toward the hallway. "Closet was smashed open." My mother's face is maroon.

"Go and get what we need," Bea says. She doesn't know that we've gathered up dozens of kids from Sequoia, but she realizes we'll need supplies. "You have time. I don't think babies come shooting out."

I zigzag my way along the hallway until I find the closet. Bottles, linens, and pacifiers have been tossed everywhere. I find a sheet and spread it out on the floor, then scan the shelves. I throw all the formula I can find onto it then Band-Aids, acetaminophen, codeine, blades in sterile packets, cotton wool, alcohol wipes, and one of everything else, just in case. I fold the ends of the sheet into the center, tie them together, and as I step into the hallway, I hear my mother. She is so loud, everyone goes silent and turns toward the ward. I shudder and rush back.

Bea is staring down at a messy purple bundle in her hands. "Well, I guess he was in a hurry to see everyone," she says.

The woman uses a towel to reveal a puckered face.

My brother—with sticky black hair and a flat nose.

He squirms and cries. Bea hands him to my mother. A part of me wants her to be indifferent, to prove what kind of person she is, but she's crying, too, and kissing the top of my brother's head and filled with all the love I imagine she had for me—once. Sixteen years ago I was perfect and pure and anything was possible. I just didn't grow into the person she wanted.

"We can't stay," Bea tells me. "Did you get everything we'll need?"

"And more." I stare at my brother's tiny toes. He has toenails. "We have to take them with us."

My mother looks up. "I'm staying here," she says. Despite all the noise and blood and people, she is smiling. I've never seen her like this—I've never seen her happy.

"Why?" I ask.

"The pod's my home. I won't leave it."

"You want the baby to grow up here?"

A siren sounds somewhere beyond the infirmary and does battle with the alarm on the lower floors. "I doubt Premiums will be very welcome wherever you're going," my mother says.

Bea puts her arm around my waist. "Quinn," she says.

"But . . ." I begin.

"It has to be her choice."

"His name is Troy," my mother says. She breathes him in. He scrunches his toes, and I stretch out my arms to take him from her.

"No," Bea says, and blocks my brother from view. "It's not okay for him to lose his mother." And she should know. I should know, too.

I kiss Troy and my mother turns her cheek toward me, so I can kiss her, too. But I can't. I step away.

An explosion booms through the pod and the ward of the hospital. Bea takes my hand. "We've done all we can," she says.

"I just . . ." Words stopper up my throat.

"She knows you love her," Bea says.

My mother is sniffling. Maybe she loves me, too. I take one last look at Troy, and turn around.

We have to go. There's a war on, and we're needed.

56
RONAN

The bottom of the tower is being pummeled from outside and the door has a sizeable dent in it. The gunfire makes my teeth vibrate. Shots are fired and the thumbprint panel on the wall sizzles and sparks. "They're almost through," Silas says.

"We only kill if we have to," Alina says. Silas looks at her warily.

"We *have* to," I say. I sound sure. I don't feel it.

We reload our rifles and crouch beside the door. It's a pack of them and three of us. In place of fear, impatience streams through me—I want us to have won already.

The locks are bombarded with bullets, the door crashes inward and with it, a band of Sequoians. They charge the spiral staircase, not bothering to check behind them and giving Silas, Alina, and me a chance to unleash a round of ammo. Shots ricochet through the tower and blood flecks my face. I keep firing. Better to shoot than to think.

Many of the rebels fall backward down the stairs, their limp bodies cracking against the floor. It's hard to tell in the dimly lit tower which of them are dead and which injured, but they're all young. They're as young as I am.

Silas and Alina go to the pile of groaning bodies to collect the guns. One boy lying on a low step clings to his rifle, and as I make a grab for it, he tries to kick me with both feet. I dodge him and use my own rifle to jab one of his legs. He howls and releases his gun. I seize it and jump over him to get to two others, but they're quite still, their eyes glinting. I look away; the last thing I want is to see their eyes.

"Ronan!" Alina calls. I join her and Silas at the door. The enemy has overpowered our inexperienced army and charge toward the door to Recycling Station East. Our soldiers are either lying dead or with their hands behind their heads, their faces in the dirt. Now I know Jude was right; you can't train an army in weeks.

What now?

Before I can decide, Silas and Alina are gone, sprinting toward the station. I try to catch them, but they're too quick. They leap over the station's sandbags, use them for cover, and begin firing. I drop next to them and do the same.

Half the rebels trying to get through the door collapse

under our gunfire. The rest turn their car door shields around trying to protect themselves. But the doors aren't bulletproof and within a minute we've taken down all but a few. It's easier than it should be.

Those still alive abandon the tower and make a run for it. I watch them through my scope, but I can't get a good shot, and they escape.

"They're heading for the south station," Silas says. "Caffrey said it was the control tower."

"Damn!" I say. "If that goes down . . ." I don't need to finish. Alina and Silas zoom away again. Anyone would think *they'd* been training with the Special Forces. I follow, but no sooner are we away than a rebel with a thick neck and tattoos down each arm is barring our route. He isn't wearing a helmet nor carrying any kind of shield. And he has an assault rifle trained at us. The others all had simple rifles. We stop running. We haven't got a choice.

"Drop the guns," he growls.

"Maks?" Alina says. Her voice quivers. But the only thing that scares me is the fact that he's stopping us getting to the south station.

"Guns down, hands up," he repeats, and we throw our guns to the ground and put our hands in the air. "On your knees."

"Get on with it," Alina says. I can feel her shaking. I'd grip her hand, but I have a feeling she wouldn't appreciate it. And neither would this thug.

"Where are the others?" Maks asks. I look at Silas, not sure who he means.

"They're safe," he says.

"They won't be when I find them," Maks says.

"I should've killed you in your sleep," Alina says, acting more like herself. She spits into the dirt. Maks laughs.

The zip fires and showers us in small rocks and shards of metal. We shrink from the shrapnel and Maks is thrown to his knees, his gun knocked from his hands. It gives me just enough time to retrieve my own and aim it at him. He puts his hands up and grins. Silas and Alina snatch up their guns, too, but they don't shoot him, so neither do I, though one bullet is all it would take.

"You'd rather fight alongside the Ministry than fellow rebels," he sneers at Silas and Alina.

"Thousands of innocent people live in the pod. You're lunatics," I tell him.

Alina approaches Maks and his chest puffs out. She rams her gun against it. She pauses, and I think she's about to say something, but without warning, she pulls the trigger.

Maks stares at Alina in disbelief and falls forward. His face hits the clay and his green jacket darkens where the blood soaks through.

Alina looks at me. "He would have killed us." She doesn't

have to explain; I should have done it for her.

"The south station," I remind them, and we take off, leaving Maks to bleed into the earth.

We squat behind the sandbags again, scanning the battlefield teeming with bodies and soldiers for a safe way into the station. "Straight through," Silas says. Alina nods in agreement as one of our tanks grinds past.

It fires and hits the zip. Shrapnel showers down and both Sequoians and Ministry soldiers are injured.

Everything stops, giving Silas, Alina, and me a chance to get to the tank. The hatch opens and a figure appears, lifting the visor on his helmet. It's Jude. He shouts, but over the thunder of engines and distant gunfire, it's impossible to tell what he wants.

And then a round of gunfire rattles the air and Jude reels like a spinning top. He falls from the tank. I turn to see Maks on his elbows holding his gun, smiling. Silas and Alina flog him with bullets. This time he stays down.

But Jude is down, too. A soldier is next to him. "Medic!" he shouts, and I run to them. I pull Jude's radio from his inside pocket. "General Caffrey has been shot. Send a stretcher." No one responds. Just static.

Silas and Alina are next to me. Neither of them tries to help, and I don't bother appealing to them. I wrench off my jacket, and place it beneath Jude's head.

"Is he dead?" Alina asks.

"He's got a pulse," the soldier says.

Jude opens his eyes, and I take a relieved breath. "It's too late," he croaks. "They're at the south station. Get the people out of the pod. Get them all out." He pulls at his collar. He's been hit in the only unprotected place—his neck. I rip the arm from my shirt, scrunch it into a ball and press it against the wound. He can't die. We need him.

"There's no time to evacuate so many people," I tell him.

"The south station," Silas says coldly. He isn't looking at Jude. He doesn't know what Jude has become or that he's spent these last few weeks protecting the Resistance.

"Go," I say, and they are gone, as is the soldier who clambers through the tank's hatch and rolls away. Sequoia's zip aims for the tank, barely missing it.

Within a minute the piece of my shirt against Jude's neck is soaked through with blood. My stomach clenches. I try appealing to whoever is on the other end of the radio again. But I may as well be talking to myself.

Jude fingers his facemask. I increase the density of oxygen, for all the good it will do.

"What now?" I ask, hoping he knows how to save himself.

He coughs. "You seem capable, Ronan. You tell me."

57
QUINN

The blasts outside have covered the pod in a film of dust, so it's pretty much impossible to see what's going on. And Zone One is a mess. Alarms are ringing in every Premium building as auxiliaries loot them. There are bodies everywhere. No one's safe, and the Ministry is visibly absent.

You've got to wonder if this is a bit like The Switch—people so hungry for air they'd do anything to hang on a bit longer. And in the end, they all died anyway.

I have Jazz on my back, and Bea is holding Lennon and Keane's hands. We are on our way to the border. A figure rushes at me, and I hold tightly to my tank. I'm about to lash out, when I realize it's Gideon. And he's carrying a massive backpack. "I broke into the biosphere. Got bulbs, seeds, and a few cuttings: everything we need," he says. He eyes Lennon and Keane.

"My brothers," I say. "Where's everyone else?"

"They went on ahead."

We turn into Border Boulevard and stop short. A group of men with airtanks and broken bottles sees us and charges. "Keep back!" Gideon says, waving a kitchen knife. The men come to an abrupt halt a few feet from us.

"We could leave via the trash chutes?" Bea says, backing away from the men.

One of them points at me. "You're the Premium who spoke at the press conference. They said you were dead."

"I'm not."

"You said we could breathe outside," the man continues. The rest of the gang listens. A larger group—kids my age wearing balaclavas—stop and watch.

"It's that guy from the screen," one of them says. "Oi, everyone, it's that Premium guy!" Within seconds we're surrounded.

"So *can* we breathe out there?" the man repeats. Looking at their faces—afraid and guarded—I realize that they don't want to attack us; they want to be shown the way out of their miserable lives.

"It's complicated," I say.

The crowd presses in. "What do we do?" someone

demands. "You're the one who started this." A couple of months ago I didn't believe I could start anything, and even now I'm not sure I can lead.

"Tell them what to do," Jazz murmurs in my ear.

"It takes dedication," I say. "But you can train your body to exist outside. And we can help you do it."

"Stuff that. I'm getting out of here and joining the Resistance. They'll know what to do," someone says.

"We're all that's left," Bea says. "The Ministry killed the others."

"You think we've been growing avocadoes and beets just in case you ever found the guts to leave? Get real. You need air but you need food, too. Nonperishable food. Everything you can find. We'll wait for you at The Cenotaph," Gideon says.

"And be ready for it to get tough out there," I warn them.

"Right," the man says, and the crowd disperses. They'll probably loot for food, but if anyone can afford to have some stuff nicked, it's the Premiums. It's no use worrying about them, when the poor can't even breathe.

Harriet, Old Watson, and the rest of the Resistance are at the border waiting for us. They're loaded down with tanks, food, and weapons. No one's guarding the border. "It's a war out there," Harriet says, as we trudge down the glass tunnel. She opens her backpack and hands out a slew of guns.

"And in a couple months when we're out of air and food?" Bea asks, speaking to me from the side of her mouth so no one else hears.

I point at the bag of clippings and seeds Gideon's carrying. "We'll grow it," I say, pushing on the revolving doors at the end of the tunnel and leading everyone out into the war zone.

A solider is standing by the exit. When he sees me he gawps. "Quinn Caffrey? General Caffrey's son?" He lets the empty stretcher he's holding on his back fall to the ground and pulls up the visor on his helmet, so he can look me in the eye. "Your father's been shot." I am silent. Bea seizes my hand. "I was about to bring the stretcher. Come with me," the soldier says.

Surely I should stay with Bea and help the Resistance escape. But when I look at her, she shakes her head. "Go," she says.

I grab one end of the stretcher and follow the solider into the battlefield. I have to find my dad.

58
ALINA

Silas and I lie on the ground. Dust swirls around us. "Where are they?" I say, eyeing the south station for Sequoian troops.

Silas rubs the mirrored surface on the scope of his rifle and looks through it. "If they know this controls the supply for the other stations, they'll be back," he says. So we make for the tower, expecting to be met by defending Ministry soldiers on the other side of the sandbags. The area's deserted.

The gunfire lulls to almost nothing.

It's weird because Vanya didn't strike me as a quitter. "Something's not right," I say. They must be planning an attack, and if they are, Silas and I won't be able to hold them off alone. And then it dawns on me. "Oh no," I say.

Silas realizes it as I do. "We're cornered," he says. "Let's try to get into the station."

And it's then that Vanya's voice rings out like she's talking through the clouds. "I wouldn't go near the tower, if I were you," she says.

"The west tower," Silas says, and points. Recycling Station West had its tubing cut long ago, and Vanya must have taken control of it. I peer through the scope. She's standing on its balcony, a megaphone to her face.

"It's going to blow," she says.

"Don't bombs need oxygen?" I ask Silas, not that he'd know.

But he does. "They only need fuel and an oxidizer. I'm sure someone in Sequoia would have thought of that."

"She really means to blow everything up?" I wonder aloud. The biosphere is located at the south side of the pod. Could the blast be so bad it destroys that, too? And what would we be left with? A smattering of people, no trees, and no pod? It would be worse than The Switch. I can't let it happen. I dart toward the door, Silas behind me.

Without a valid thumbprint to get inside, we have to shoot at the locks. A bullet whispers past my head and sears through the door.

Vanya's shooting at us.

The door jiggles in the frame but still won't open. I lie on the ground and kick with every ounce of strength left in me. Silas rams it with his body.

"Troopers!" Vanya calls out, and within seconds a band of Sequoians is pounding toward us.

But finally the door moans and falls open. I jump up as Vanya's troopers come at us in one angry herd. Silas pulls me into the tower. "Find the bomb and do what you can. I'll . . ."

He doesn't finish because what can he do against almost thirty of them? He peers around the door frame and starts to shoot.

The winch squalls its way to the top, where the door to the control room is open, but it's empty. I rush onto the balcony where four snipers are lying dead, their blood dripping over the ledge, and next to them is a solar respirator.

I lean over the railing.

The Sequoians are almost at the sandbags. I shoot wildly, unable to take a steady shot. And then I spot them—a gang in plain clothes who are following Vanya's troopers.

I squint and can't help punching the air—it's Uncle Gideon, Aunt Harriet, and the Resistance, shooting and almost in line with the Sequoians.

They need my help, and I'm about to take the winch back to the ground when I glance at the respirator and see what I missed before—a box wrapped in yellow plastic with a panel of digital numbers on it has been taped to the back. Vanya's bomb.

The numbers flash: *two hundred and nineteen, two hundred and eighteen*. Seconds? How many minutes is that? I haven't time to do the math, and I've no idea how to disarm it. I'm not Song.

Two hundred and fourteen, two hundred and thirteen, two hundred and twelve . . .

I could leave the bomb and make a run for it, but if I survive and nothing else does, what's the point? If I can't defuse the bomb, I'll have to take it with me and get it as far from here as possible. It's too big to carry except on my back, but I can't do that with my own airtank tied to my belt. I unbuckle it, pull off my facemask, and put the solar respirator's filthy apparatus over my mouth. It stinks. And it's so heavy, it's like carrying a boulder.

The digital screen and numbers on it are now out of sight, which is probably for the best.

I scrape my way to the winch and take it to the ground. Silas has gone. When I look outside, he is restraining a trooper on the ground. My aunt and uncle aren't far away, warding off troopers with their guns. The Sequoians are strong, but they weren't expecting the Resistance to reinforce the Ministry soldiers.

I sprint around the back of the tower and stumble into the open land.

The air coming from the solar-powered respirator is damp, and the mask scratches my face. I'd be better off without it, so I pull it off and throw it aside. The oxygen in the atmosphere is thin, but it's enough after my training.

A voice cries out. "Put it down, Alina! Put it *down*."

But I can't. Not until I know everyone will be safe. I don't care how heavy this thing is, or how scorched my throat feels.

When I eventually look behind, the pod is lit by the setting sun. I think I'm far enough away to save it, so I shrug off the respirator and, without looking at how much time I have left, jump away from it. I just run. I run as fast as my lungs and legs will carry me.

The voice comes at me again. It's Silas. "Run, Alina! ALINA!" But he doesn't need to worry. "ALINA!" he shouts.

And I smile.

59
QUINN

A blast throws me forward and onto the ground, where I smash my face against stones and scrape the skin from my hands. The air is suddenly gray. I stand up, but the steward doesn't, so I roll him onto his back. He groans. "You all right?"

"My leg," he says. But I can't help him, be with my father, and go back and deal with whatever caused that explosion.

I have to make a choice.

"Stay there," I tell the steward, and run to my father and Ronan, who are sitting in the open by one of the stations. Ronan's hand is against my father's neck.

"Is he alive?" I ask.

"He's slipping in and out of consciousness," Ronan says. The gunfire in the distance stops. Ronan and I look at each other. Can it be over?

"Dad," I say. "Dad?"

He pulls off his facemask and coughs blood all over himself. "Quinn?"

"It's me." I use the sleeve of my jacket to wipe the blood from his face. I try to move his mask back into place, but he rolls his head from side to side to stop me. Ronan lets go of the fabric he's pressing into my father's neck, revealing a sinewy wound.

"He was shot," Ronan says, like I can't figure that out for myself.

My father moans and coughs a jellied blood clot into his hand. This time he doesn't resist when I try to refit the facemask. "The stations have faucets in them for filling tanks," he wheezes. "Even if they manage to . . ."

"Don't talk," I say, seeing how the effort hurts him. "Let's try to get you inside."

"Quinn . . ." Ronan begins, and puts a hand on my arm.

"Help me!" I tell him, and together we lift my father onto the stretcher. On the ground beneath him is a dark puddle, dry at the edges. I've never seen my father bleed, and in some childish way I thought he couldn't.

Blood pools on the stretcher, and it's too hard to carry him because he's struggling so much. We put it back down and I kneel next to him.

"The twins. Your mother," he says.

"They're fine," I say, or at least I hope they will be. "Mom had the baby."

My father squeezes his eyes shut and when he opens them, they're wet. He raises a finger and gestures for me to move closer. I put my ear to the blowoff valve in his mask. "I'm not the best father," he says.

It's true; he's been an awful father at times. But it kind of felt as if he just didn't know how else to be. I pull back and meet my father's eyes. "Ronan told me you sent him to find me. Thank you."

A shot breaks the stillness and Ronan lifts his rifle. "We're sitting ducks," he says. He tries to lift the stretcher. I don't help him. There's no point.

"You said once that in another world we could have been friends." I pause and wait for him to show he's heard me. I have to know he's listening.

"Stop," he whispers.

"And I think you were right." He rips the mask from his face and this time flings it several feet away. Blood trickles from his nose. His eyes are vacant.

Ronan jumps up to get the mask. But my father won't need it.

I place a hand on his chest. He looks at the sky and then at me. "Quinn," he says. His breath is short and soft. "Quinn," he repeats, and closes his eyes.

60
BEA

Sequoians, Resistance, and Ministry stare at the black vapor filling the sky. I'm behind a bombed-out buggy, scrabbling to stop Jazz from joining the fray. Lennon and Keane sit on her to keep her down, and we watch Silas sprint toward the explosion. Gideon and Harriet are close behind. Alina is nowhere to be seen.

"The tower!" Vanya blares into the megaphone, reminding her troopers of their mission. And then she vanishes from the balcony of the station. She wants them to storm it, but there are too few of them to do anything. I peer over the hood of the buggy. Only four Sequoians are still standing, their backs to the tower, their hands in the air. The others are supine, Ministry soldiers and Resistance members pinning them down with their boots. If Vanya thinks she still has a fight on her hands, she's delusional. She's already lost.

"Charge!" Vanya screams, rising out of the dust and storming our way.

Before I can stop her, Jazz has my gun and is aiming it at Vanya. If what Quinn said is true, she's about to shoot her own mother. No matter how crazy and dangerous Vanya is, I can't let Jazz do it. I knock the gun from her hands and it lands next to Lennon. He looks down at it, horrified.

"The pod is *mine*!" Vanya screams. She has no gun, only the megaphone. Two members of the Resistance who lived in Ronan's attic with me march toward her.

"Shoot her," Jazz tells Lennon, reaching for the gun.

"No," I say, and stand on it. Maybe I should tell Jazz why, but I don't. That can wait for another day.

The Resistance members pull Vanya to the ground and stomp on her megaphone. She kicks and claws at them.

Silas, Gideon, and Harriet are specks. And I still can't see Alina. "Stay here," I say.

Jazz holds on to my leg. "Take me with you."

I shake my head. "I'll be back. Keep an eye on Lennon and Keane." She looks at the twins, who are sniffling, and rolls her eyes.

"*Fine*," she says.

I take off as fast as I can, repeating the words *Alina is alive, Alina is alive* in my head over and over. She is the toughest of us, and when the time comes, she'll be the last to go.

As I reach Gideon and Harriet, a strong chemical smell penetrates my mask. The ground is covered in confetti pieces of metal. They are crouching beside Alina. Silas is standing over them. They look up at me as though I'm a ghost.

"Alina?" I say. Her face is blackened, her hair charred at the ends. I wait for her to open her eyes and say something cutting. "Alina."

"The blast . . ." Silas says, and stops. He can't speak for choking.

"But she's okay, isn't she?" I kneel next to her and touch her hand. It's warm. There's a nasty gash above one of her eyebrows.

"She's gone," Silas says.

"No, she isn't. . . . Give her some air." I put my hands over her chest and begin compressions, pushing hard on her heart like I did with Old Watson. It has to work—Alina's always survived.

I lean over to blow into her mouth when Harriet lays her hand on my arm. "Stop," she says. "Please."

And I do. Because Alina no longer looks like herself. She's completely serene.

She's dead.

Gideon takes off his facemask and kisses Alina's forehead,

then uses the heels of his hands to wipe away tears.

It's too much for Silas; he walks away and bellows into the sky.

I brush Alina's face with the back of my fingers. Her skin is soft. The last time I saw her was at The Grove. It was the briefest good-bye. It wasn't enough.

Tears trickle over my facemask into the earth.

I've felt this before, like someone was ripping out my heart, but it doesn't make it any less painful.

I am crying so hard now, I can barely see. I squeeze Alina's hand.

I want to tell her what's happened. I want to tell her who she is and what she's done. For me. For all of us.

But there's only one thing that would matter to Alina.

So I lift my facemask and press my lips to her ear.

"I think we won," I say.

PART V
THE SPRING

61
BEA

A girl arrives on-site with a small pot of cement powder and Maude squeals at her. "Are we building a house for leprechauns? I said we needed a barrel of the stuff, you nincompoop."

"I'll get more." The girl scuttles away.

"Looks great," I say. And it does. It's the tenth dwelling we've built. At this rate we'll have a place for everyone to sleep by summer. Maude rubs her nose along her sleeve.

"Where's lover boy?" she asks.

"Mine or yours?"

"Oh, get out of it, Bruce and me's just pals, that's all." Her skin burns red.

I take a few gulps of air from the facemask hanging around my neck. "We've had more petitions from Premiums asking to join the settlement. Have you time to interview them with me?" I look at the pod in the distance. It sparkles faintly. Now that people can come and go freely, and have seen what we're building, they want to join us.

"I need to refill this," Maude says, tapping her airtank. "I can meet 'em when I go to the recycling station."

Dark clouds murmur. A droplet lands on my arm. "Rain," I say, and smile.

"Oh yeah, the plants'll love it, but what about me 'do ?" She pushes her scraggly hair behind her ears and pulls her hood over her head. She shuffles away toward the small hut we've built for Jo and her baby. Abel takes care of them, and maybe they're a couple, but it doesn't stop him visiting Alina's grave every day. And he's obsessed with planting. It's because of him the nursery is blooming.

"Where's *she* going?" Ronan asks, appearing on the half-finished roof of the building.

"You can't work in the rain. Come down," I tell him.

He waves away the suggestion and tightens the straps on his dungarees. Quinn is coming our way, and as he passes Maude, they exchange a few words before moving on.

He stands behind me, puts his arms around my waist, and nuzzles my neck. "Wanna take a trip into the city for a few days? Just the two of us," he says.

I hold out my hand and allow the rain to pool in it. "We

tried that once before and it didn't work out," I say.

"Just 'cuz something doesn't work out the first time . . ." He trails off.

"Maybe we should invite Ronan, just in case," I say. "Or Maude." I laugh.

"We can handle it. We don't need anyone else," he says.

"Are you talking about me?" Ronan calls from the roof. He never stops working, and he's been teaching me how to paint. When I spend time with him, Quinn is quietly jealous, but I suppose that's okay. And normal.

"Quinn and I might take a trip. We wondered if you wanted to come with us," I say.

He laughs loudly—sarcastically. "Yes, I'd love to join you on your snog-fest."

"I promise we won't make out at all," Quinn says, and kisses the back of my neck.

"Stop slacking off," Ronan says, and returns to work.

Quinn smiles and lets me go. "Do you want to see something?" he asks.

I follow him to the garden where Abel is on his knees in the dirt. "There," Quinn says, pointing. I crouch and touch green shoots that have burst through the soil, clawing for light.

"Pear trees," Abel says, smiling. "And I reckon the strawberries will be ready by summer."

"At this rate, we might live another few years," I say.

"We made it this far. It would be irresponsible to die now!" Abel says.

"I better get to it," Quinn says, passing a trowel from hand to hand. "We have a lot to do."

And he's right. We all have a lot to do. A lot to learn. A lot still to be afraid of. But today, I'm glad of the rain on my hand and my own shallow breath.

The elements finally belong to us all.

And for now, that's good enough.